MW00856176

WOOING THE WITCH QUEEN

WOOING THE WITCH QUEEN

STEPHANIE BURGIS

BRAMBLE

TOR PUBLISHING GROUP

NEW YORK

This is a work of fiction. All of the characters, organizations, and events portrayed in this novel are either products of the author's imagination or are used fictitiously.

WOOING THE WITCH QUEEN

Copyright © 2025 by Stephanie Burgis Samphire

All rights reserved.

Interior art by Shutterstock.com

A Bramble Book
Published by Tom Doherty Associates / Tor Publishing Group
120 Broadway
New York, NY 10271

www.torpublishinggroup.com

Bramble™ is a trademark of Macmillan Publishing Group, LLC.

The Library of Congress Cataloging-in-Publication Data
is available upon request.

ISBN 978-1-250-35959-9 (trade paperback)
ISBN 978-1-250-35960-5 (ebook)

Our books may be purchased in bulk for promotional, educational, or business use. Please contact your local bookseller or the Macmillan Corporate and Premium Sales Department at 1-800-221-7945, extension 5442, or by email at MacmillanSpecialMarkets@macmillan.com.

First Edition: 2025

Printed in the United States of America

0 9 8 7 6 5 4 3 2 1

For Molly Ker Hawn, amazing agent and friend.
I appreciate you so much.

WOOING THE WITCH QUEEN

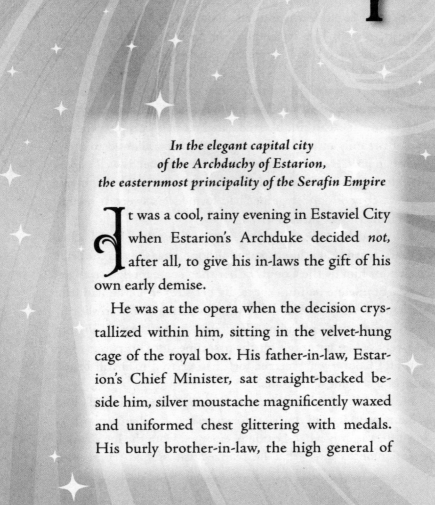

1

*In the elegant capital city
of the Archduchy of Estarion,
the easternmost principality of the Serafin Empire*

It was a cool, rainy evening in Estaviel City when Estarion's Archduke decided *not*, after all, to give his in-laws the gift of his own early demise.

He was at the opera when the decision crystallized within him, sitting in the velvet-hung cage of the royal box. His father-in-law, Estarion's Chief Minister, sat straight-backed beside him, silver moustache magnificently waxed and uniformed chest glittering with medals. His burly brother-in-law, the high general of

Estarion's armies, lounged carelessly on his other side, one leg spread out to block him from going anywhere. On the stage below, a soprano warbled tunefully about lost love, while opera glasses sparkled eagerly across the tiers, all fixed upon the most famous young widower in the audience: Archduke Felix Augustus von Estarion.

The Archduke was, of course, clothed in endless black. It was the only color ever to be found in his wardrobe nowadays, no matter how many times he requested otherwise. It would make the perfect, breathlessly awaited climax to this evening's public performance for him to simply lean forward, overwhelmed by his so-famous grief, and topple from the high royal box onto the stage below.

Felix, the twenty-three-year-old man behind the title, *had* grieved his wife's death thirteen months ago. He had grown up with Emmeline, the kindhearted daughter of his grim regent and one of the only other children he'd ever been allowed to meet. They had protected one another against her father as well as possible throughout their shared childhood, and the quiet moments of peace they'd found together had formed his sweetest memories during those cold years.

Felix had been not only glad but desperately relieved when he'd first learned, on the cusp of adulthood, that *she* was the bride chosen for him by the Count, rather than some foreign stranger. When Emmeline had unexpectedly been taken ill, he had held her hand to the very end—and when her eyes had been shut by the highest of the attending physicians, he had lost all dignity and wept before witnesses for the first time since his parents had died and Count von Hertzendorff had arrived to instill brutal rules of discipline upon him.

He was surprised, at the time, that his father-in-law allowed so many servants and courtiers to witness such a shameful breakdown. It was only when he finally emerged from the fog of grief, several months later, that he realized the simple truth: with

Emmeline's death, Count von Hertzendorff had lost his prime claim to the Archduchy of Estarion—so he was already planning his next move.

At three-and-twenty, Felix was too old to require a regent. In the eyes of the law, he could—theoretically—dismiss his father-in-law from the role of Chief Minister and wrench control of the army from his brother-in-law's violent grasp. He could even choose to wed again and bring a rival family into power.

It all seemed wildly unlikely to Felix himself, who barely knew any of the other members of his high cabinet and had never been allowed a private conversation with any of them . . . but Count Gerhard von Hertzendorff had not become the most powerful man in Estarion by dismissing any potential threats on the horizon. He had been preparing, even at the moment of his daughter's deeply disappointing death, for the worst that he could imagine to happen . . . and Felix had played directly into his hands with his "unmanly" display of emotion.

The Count would never willingly give up the power he had seized fifteen years ago. Having been appointed temporary Regent by his fellow members of Estarion's high cabinet, he had chosen to appoint *himself* Chief Minister on the day of Felix's eighteenth birthday, although he'd had the political sense to send out that proclamation in Felix's name.

By then, Felix hadn't even tried to protest. He had been taught for years, by means of ruthless beatings, strategic isolation, and carefully calculated starvation, that the Count would brook no challenges to his authority . . . and Count von Hertzendorff recognized no mercy when it came to enforcing his will.

The laws of the Empire and the force of public opinion were both strong enough that he couldn't push Felix over the balcony now, in front of hundreds of fascinated onlookers. However, he could make utterly certain that no one would be surprised when news of the Archduke's eventual, tragically self-inflicted death was finally released to the newspapers.

Felix had no doubt that all the details of that upcoming death had already been carefully planned.

He'd learned when he was young that the only way to survive and ensure Emmeline's safety was to bury himself in the dreamy world of books and poetry and leave every higher decision to the Count's authority. But as Felix looked across the sea of glittering opera glasses now, an astonishing realization suddenly formed within him. Those old flames of rebellion, which he'd thought so thoroughly quashed years ago, popped up a few last, burning embers after all.

He had nothing left to lose.

Emmeline was gone. There was no one else he cared for. Count von Hertzendorff had taken the utmost care to manage that state of affairs by keeping a steady flow of new servants in regular rotation.

In other words . . . no one Felix loved could possibly be hurt by his actions anymore.

The shining liberation of that realization lifted him up out of his cushioned seat and all the way to his feet. As the entire audience gasped with shock at his first-ever public breach of protocol, he opened his mouth and drew a deep breath to speak every damning truth at the top of his lungs for *everyone* to hear and every newspaper to report across the continent . . .

Just as his brother-in-law's steel-toed military boot—hidden from the rest of the audience by the low, swag-draped wall of the opera box—swept out to slam into the back of his knee, sending Felix toppling back into his seat with an undignified, yelping crash.

"The Archduke is ill!" the high general bellowed, pressing one large hand firmly against Felix's chest to hold him down. "Close the curtains!"

Uniformed footmen leapt forward to untie the silk ropes that held thick crimson curtains open around their box.

"*No*," Felix gritted, pushing against his brother-in-law's grip, "wait! I—"

The curtains fell closed around them as a roar of sound filled the rest of the theatre, the audience losing all interest in the drama onstage.

There was no chance of being heard outside the royal box anymore.

"What the devil do you think you're playing at?" His brother-in-law, Radomir, shifted his grip to a hard clamp on Felix's closest wrist to keep him safely pinned. "Thinking of taking up a singing career, little brother? I wouldn't try it, with your voice."

"Enough of this nonsense," snapped Felix's father-in-law, glowering over his moustache. "We'll have a physician summoned to the box, then bundle him home before he can cause any more trouble. You and I will stay here so no one goes into hysterics. In the meantime . . ."

Ignoring Felix, as usual whenever politics came up, the Count held up a letter that had been discreetly passed to him by a servant during the opera's first act. "What's all this nonsense about surrender to the Witch of the East? Do you have any idea how many hundreds of gildar we've sent her uncle over the years to keep those cursed mountains under our control? Damn it, Kitvaria's directly on our border. We can't let her little uprising win!"

"Sorry. I called back our final troops this morning . . . at least, the hundred that survived." Radomir shrugged. "I was planning to tell you after tonight's performance: there's no use wasting money on any more attempts at taking back that kingdom for her uncle. It's not worth it, even for the sake of protecting our border. She's set a damned unbreakable spell around the whole thing. No one with an offensive weapon or a military uniform can even pass into her territory anymore! And when you add in all the monsters and misfits who've followed her in there over the past few months, wanting nothing more than to tear apart any civilized invaders . . ."

"Unbelievable." The Count crumpled the letter in his hands. "So we're to admit humiliation and defeat and leave her squatting like a spider on the very edge of Estarion? Thumbing her nose at the Empire without a qualm?"

"Unless the Emperor decides, for once, to send his own people to deal with her instead of wasting ours . . . yes," said his son flatly. "Unless you want her to take over Estarion next—because so far, none of our troops or wizards have managed to cause her the slightest bit of trouble."

The look of simmering fury in the Count's hard grey eyes sent instinctive dread into Felix's heart. He knew only too well what could come of that sort of rage. His scarred back still twinged at the memories of it.

But apparently, there was now one person in the world whom even the Count couldn't intimidate . . .

Which meant that Felix had just discovered exactly where to run.

He only had to find a way in.

2

W hat you don't seem to understand," said the witch of Kadaric Castle, without looking up from the glittering silver powder that she was carefully measuring into a copper tube, "is that this is a highly inconvenient evening for a dark wizard to turn up. *You* know what they're like, Morlokk—all ominous glowering and puffs of smoke and noisy incantations. They're so desperate for attention, the first few days of any visit are always fatal to my work. Now that we're finally finished with all of that tedious fighting, I'm in the middle of a particularly interesting experiment—"

"And yet," said her majordomo, "the fact remains, Your Majesty, that a man in an all-enveloping cloak is currently on the road approaching our castle, clearly in answer to the advertisement that *you* directed me to place when we took over your uncle's library. And if you recall any of the tantrums that other wizards have thrown in the past when they did not receive what *they* termed a proper welcome to our last home . . ."

The witch, Saskia, winced, her fingers stilling mid-measure. "Oh, yes, I do recall. The front hall . . . and the library . . . and the kitchen, too, wasn't it, last time?"

"Our last keep and its inhabitants," pronounced Morlokk, "eventually recovered from every incident we faced. We shall continue to persevere in this castle when required. However, we would all prefer to avoid any more such unnecessary calamities . . . if you think it possible." It was difficult for an ogre to look wry; their craggy faces weren't built for subtlety. But Morlokk had been Saskia's majordomo for years, and he had never yet shied from a challenge.

"I see." Saskia gave one last, wistful look at the closed beaker full of bubbling green liquid that she'd been just about to unstop for the next step of her project. "Well, you'd better show him in as soon as he arrives, then."

". . . Mmm?" One bushy green eyebrow rose meaningfully.

Saskia followed his gaze across her outfit: the comfortably worn old grey gown covered by a sensible apron, itself covered with stains from old experiments, and a cheerful purple handkerchief that held her long, thick hair out of danger's way.

She liked that handkerchief. It had been sewn for her by a wickedly bawdy old goblin chieftain last year. She thought it looked quite well against her pitch-black hair and pale skin.

She sighed, though, as she accepted the inevitability. "You're right, of course. As usual." Shaking her head, she stepped back from the lectern where she kept her notes. "I'll be ready in a quarter of an hour. If you could prepare the entrance chamber?"

"I'll start the skulls boiling now," said Morlokk, and he bowed his way out of the room, letting the heavy wooden door fall shut behind him.

Saskia's shoulders sagged as she trudged towards the door at the opposite side of the room, leaving behind all of her lovely, smelly, *interesting* magic to prepare herself to overawe yet another tedious wizard.

Really, if she'd known how much protocol was involved in being a famously wicked queen, she might never have overthrown her uncle in the first place.

The first sign that Felix was nearing his destination came when a line of skulls suddenly burst into flames directly ahead of him. Green fire belched from open eye sockets and gaping jaws all along the winding road. It led high up the mountain to a massive, shadowy castle in the distance, finally lit now by those wildly leaping flames.

It was an intensely unnerving sight. But in the last four days, Felix had faced so many unnerving new discoveries that he was almost—*almost*—inured to any shock.

He'd been so lucky—suspiciously lucky!—in his escape from the archducal palace that he'd spent the first day of his journey unable to stop peering over the shoulder of the all-enveloping hooded black cloak that he'd scavenged from the depths of his wardrobe as his only, paltry means of disguise. Why hadn't anyone caught him on his stealthy way out? Was this all a trap?

Of course, he hadn't dared show himself in the archducal stables, and without any coins, he couldn't hire a horse for his journey, either. Incredibly, though, Felix had found a mare grazing unattended in a farmer's field, only four hours' walk from Estaviel

City. Guilt had nearly choked him at the theft, but desperation had won the internal battle.

He'd find a way to repay that farmer one day. He *would*. And with luck, that sweet mare would have found her way home by now, too . . . because no matter how desperate he might have become, Felix wasn't cruel enough to risk her life with his in the terrifying, thirty-foot-high wall of rippling magic he'd found waiting for him on the Kitvarian border.

It was that impossible sight that had brought home the reality of his destination. As he'd stared at that eerily rippling line of air before him, stretching across the horizon to both sides, every hair on Felix's arms had stood up with prickling awareness.

Over the years, he'd seen more than one public demonstration of strength performed by Gilded Wizards in the Serafin Empire's service—but even when three or four of those highly trained wizards worked together, not one of their demonstrations neared this level of power. Yet the notorious Witch Queen of Kitvaria had famously created this *on her own*.

How could any mortal hold so much magic in her body? And how could anyone stand against her?

Leaving the mare behind, he'd stepped through her creation with his eyes held fatalistically wide open, prepared to accept whatever came.

What he'd actually found on the other side was three hulking, moss-covered trolls with five-foot clubs lying in wait for any would-be invaders. They, too, had formed an overwhelming sight—the first magical creatures he'd ever seen outside of books, clearly prepared to enact brutal violence upon him, just as every warning pamphlet in the Empire claimed—but the fact that they waved him on after a cursory look at his black cloak had stunned him even more.

He supposed the fact that he wasn't carrying a weapon must have been proven when he'd crossed through the barrier. Still, he'd expected, at the very least, a demand for his intentions before they allowed him to safely pass into their kingdom. Instead, they voluntarily offered up gruff directions to the queen's own castle before he could even ask that question.

It was almost as if they'd been expecting him . . . which would have worried him far more if he hadn't already been floating in a haze of disbelief, sleeplessness, and surreality.

How could all of this have been so easy?

He'd tried to escape so many times when he was young. He'd made such careful, detailed plans every time, only to be thwarted, again and again, until he'd finally learned better. The Count was always waiting, always ready, impossible ever to defeat . . .

So it had been almost eight years since the last time he'd even tried. After that last attempt, he had finally given in, his back in shreds, his voice hoarse with screams, and his chest suffused with a despair so deep, it felt almost like relief. If there was nothing left to hope for, he'd thought, then at least there was nothing left to fear.

How many years ago had the Count finally relaxed his guard?

The bitterness of that question could have brought him to his knees. But the sloping mountain path that led to Kadaric Castle was far too narrow and rocky to risk any stumbles. It was, in fact, an absurdly impractical place to seat the center of any government—even Felix knew that much. But then, the sort of person who greeted her visitors with flaming skulls probably didn't care what anyone else thought of her decisions.

According to the stories he'd heard, Queen Saskia not only delighted in surrounding herself with vicious, inhuman monsters—she was one herself and always had been.

By the time he reached the final pair of skulls, Felix wasn't even surprised to see the great black wooden doors swing open before him without a single servant in sight. The flaring green light from the skulls sent lurid streaks into the darkness of the entry hall beyond.

The only magic ever allowed in any of the twelve archduchies that made up the Serafin Empire was carefully leashed Gilded Wizardry, kept safe for the nonmagical citizens through rigorous, lifelong Imperial training and strictly enforced regulations. Before he'd crossed into Kitvaria, Felix had never seen a nonhuman creature in his life. Until today, he couldn't have imagined the sight before him.

But the only way to guarantee his own survival was to secure the patronage of a ruler more powerful than the Count—and he could only pray that Queen Saskia's enmity with his tormentor would convince her to grant him shelter in this kingdom, so famously full of all manner of magical horrors and misfits.

If she decided to feed him to her monstrous friends instead? Well . . .

Felix lifted his head and squared his shoulders beneath his cloak. At least, for once—no matter what happened next—his father-in-law wouldn't have the satisfaction of deciding his fate.

Felix took his life into his own hands for the first time in far too long and stepped into the gaping hole of the castle entrance.

3

Saskia's crown of bones was poking into her skull, and it *itched*. She would have reached up to rearrange it—or at least to give her head a good scratch—but Morlokk loomed on one side of her massive throne while Mrs. Haglitz crouched on the other, both looking appropriately doom-ridden and forbidding. She couldn't bear the looks of disappointment she would get if she let them down so badly.

So she lifted her chin and curled her upper lip into an appropriately disdainful sneer as she flicked her fingers in the direction of the great doors at the opposite end of the reception hall.

They crashed open in response to her command, and she prepared to look unimpressed.

It wasn't difficult. A tall, slim figure stepped silently into the hall, wearing a cloak so oversized it could have hidden half an army and pacing as slowly and deliberately across the ancient flagstones as if he were waiting for a cheering crowd to hail his wizardly progress.

Honestly, how many more times would she find herself inflicted with men so drunk on their own power that they insisted on constantly interfering with her work? From the bullying magical guards her uncle had first forced upon her through all the tedious assassins he'd sent after her escape . . .

Once she'd finally dealt with his nonsense by taking back his stolen throne, she'd been naive enough to imagine that she'd be free of the plague of interruptions forever after.

Saskia's nostrils flared with intense irritation as the doors slammed shut behind her latest guest. He didn't even give her the petty satisfaction of jumping at the echoing crash.

"Well?" Back in her laboratory, the silversand she had so carefully prepared would be losing more and more of its efficacy with every passing minute. "Out with it!"

The cloaked figure stilled at her demand . . . but surprisingly, he didn't respond with any of the sinister bluster that most of his ilk seemed to prefer. Instead, there was a long moment in which she gathered the unsettling impression that he was studying her far too keenly from within the shadowy folds of his hood. Then he stepped gracefully forward and spoke in a low and perfectly calm voice. "Your Majesty, Queen Saskia. You honor me with your welcome. I appreciate—"

"Yes, yes." Saskia waved one annoyingly beringed hand to speed him up. "And I appreciate that you haven't tried to blow up any pieces of my home to prove your power, like the last one did."

"Ah . . . ?" The cloaked figure's head tilted in what looked dangerously like a warning gesture.

Saskia's two most loyal retainers both stiffened as one, bracing for an explosion of magical offense.

Argh. This was one of those moments when, as Morlokk was always ready to point out, Saskia needed to focus more on diplomacy than potions, wasn't it?

"I'm sure your power is extremely impressive—*far* more impressive than any other dark wizard's," she said swiftly, "but let's cut to the bone, shall we? We both know why you're here, and if I don't return to more impor—that is, to my own work, quickly, I'll have wasted an entire batch of silversand. I'm sure you know how difficult it is to get hold of any of that nowadays, what with the Archduke of Estarion being more of a pigheaded brute than ever!"

"... Ah." There was another long silence. "Your Majesty, I think, perhaps..."

"Must we discuss the terms first?" There were no clocks in this hall to help her gauge the time; she flung a desperate look towards the high windows that she'd had chiseled for her crows and bats, but all she could see through them was a steady, pressing darkness. "I thought the advertisement had covered all of that, but I suppose, if you're not satisfied with the payment offered..."

"It's not the payment." Yet another maddeningly long pause lingered in the room before he finally continued, sounding distinctly choked. "The Archduke... that is, on the matter of the Archduke of Estarion... or his policies..." He cleared his throat. "I can't..."

"Oh, I know." Incoherent rage vied only with despair as the most popular reaction whenever this topic came up within the magical community. She should have known better than to bring it up when her silversand was waiting. Saskia's fingers tightened around the arms of her throne with the effort of infusing sympathy into her voice. "We all wish only the worst to come upon him, of course, but I'll tell you what I've told everyone else, including my own First Minister: I've dealt with more than enough battles for the time being. If anyone wants to send me the Archduke trussed up on a plate, I'll be more than happy to see to his execution, but otherwise, I'll settle for keeping my own people safe and my work *undisturbed*."

Possibly, she shouldn't have added that last note. Judging by Morlokk's barely withheld sigh and the wizard's blank silence in response, it might not have sounded quite as sympathetic as she had intended.

Oh, botheration! She'd waited weeks for this batch of silver-sand to arrive so she could test her theories out. If they did work, she could do far more good for her kingdom than even the most accomplished wizard ever would. She was *finished* with placation!

"All I need you to do is sort out the library for me," she said sharply. "Arrange it all into some reasonable order, set aside anything that looks particularly dangerous or useful, and catalogue the contents. Do you think you could do that?"

"I . . . probably could." He still sounded disturbed, perhaps still embroiled in the emotional turmoil of whichever unfortunate memories she had stirred up with her earlier, careless reference. "But . . . that is, the moment I remove this cloak, you're going to . . ."

"Of course, we'd all be traumatized by your sinister magnificence if we witnessed it unhindered." She sighed. "I understand the danger, believe me. Many—*many*—wizards have explained it to me before, in"—*mind-numbing*—"detail."

Unable to sit still for even a single moment longer, she leapt to her feet and hurried down the stone steps to the flagstones before him, her crimson silk skirts rustling. "Keep the cloak on as much as you like," she told him briskly. "We're quite used to it, I assure you. Or you could wear a nice mask, if you prefer! I think the last wizard left behind a silver moon-mask from one of his rituals—I'll see if Mrs. Haglitz can root it out for you. My uncle kept a collection of masquerade half-masks stashed somewhere in this castle, too. Feel free to use any of them."

"But . . ." From within the depths of the cloak, a black-gloved hand appeared, reaching towards her. "Your Majesty, I really must . . ."

"Morlokk and Mrs. Haglitz will see to everything you need!" she caroled brightly over her shoulder as she strode towards the closest side door. "They'll show you to your bedchamber tonight and direct you to the library tomorrow morning. I'm sure you'll be pleased with your accommodations. My uncle always liked to put up his visitors in style." *Unlike his family.*

"But—!"

Ignoring his final, outraged protest, she lunged through the side door and slammed it shut behind her. The moment that she was safely out of view, she yanked her queenly skirts above her knees and hurtled down the darkened passageway as purposefully as if she were still a girl on the run from her uncle's minions.

She had no more time for interruptions.

Felix stared blankly at the closed door. His head was whirling again—and this time, not just from exhaustion. The moment he'd glimpsed that extraordinary, beautiful, terrible figure in her nightmarish crown of bones, the earth had seemed to shift beneath his feet. For all he knew, it really might have; judging by that magical barrier between their realms, Queen Saskia was more than capable of bending the physical world to her will.

But what—*how?*

"Sinistro." The massive ogre who hulked on one side of the empty throne growled out the unfamiliar word, and Felix's attention snapped immediately to the most terrifying of the two occupants left in this hall.

He had seen depictions of ogres many times before, of course, in textbooks and in the sort of prints that were hawked by vendors around Estaviel City, passed with gleeful horror from hand to hand and finally left to flutter onto the crowded pavements for passersby to trample. In those prints, the ogres were generally shown rampaging through peaceful Estarian villages, adorned only in loincloths and smeared blood and wielding their giant fists and tusks against small children.

The ogre before him now was disconcertingly different and yet no less intimidating. That perfectly fitted, silver-trimmed black uniform and stylish crimson waistcoat, studded with buttons at least as big as Felix's palms, only emphasized the inhuman breadth and bulk of its vast chest and arms, while the gold caps that covered the sharp tips of its tusks brought attention to that barely shielded danger. Its yellow eyes held far more intelligence than he'd expected . . . and they were fixed upon him now with open speculation, while Felix remained in frozen silence.

Damn it!

Wincing at the realization, he sent up thanks to Divine Elva that the hood of his cloak so thoroughly hid his face. The ogre before him might think him eccentric in his silence, but at least it hadn't seen him gaping like a fool. His parents and every one of his tutors in courtly courtesy would have been ashamed if they had seen him gawking at anyone—human or not—in such an uncouth manner.

"I do beg your pardon." Gathering his wits together, he tried to recall exactly what the monster had just said to him. *Sinistro?* He didn't recognize the word, but it had carried the ring of a title. Considering that he was, apparently, meant to carry himself off as an expert librarian-slash-dark-wizard from now on—*Elva preserve me!*—he should probably not ask for explanations. "Ah . . . Morlokk, I presume?" He nodded as politely as he could within the constraints of the hood.

"I am Her Majesty's majordomo," said the ogre, in a deep and growling voice that somehow managed to convey an accent of high culture while still sending cold, instinctive warning down Felix's spine. Like Queen Saskia, the ogre spoke Kitvarian rather than Imperial Serafin, but fortunately, Felix had been drilled in all of the continent's native languages early in his childhood ... and, in a useful reminder, the formation of Morlokk's title also included a clear gender.

From now on, Felix would have to remember to think of the ogre as *him*, not *it*. The Count would have snapped a scorching rebuke if Felix had ever dared refer to any inhuman creature in such a respectful fashion—but Queen Saskia had shocked the continent by declaring all sentient creatures in her domain to be equal citizens. It was a complete overturn of her own nation's previous laws as well as a stark contrast to those in place across the Empire, and Felix would do well to remember that difference if he wanted any chance of fitting into his new role.

"And this is Mrs. Haglitz, Her Majesty's housekeeper." Morlokk gestured with heavy courtesy to the troll woman who huddled on the other side of the throne, wrapped in a black-and-purple embroidered shawl that covered most of her large head and the top half of her body. Only the tip of her long, green nose poked out, but somehow, Felix still gathered the strong sense of a suspicious glower coming from deep within. Hidden bottles and jars clinked noisily from within her coverings as she gave a notably late and grudging half-curtsey.

Felix nodded deeply in return. "I'm pleased to meet you."

"Hmmph." The tip of that green nose twitched sharply with Mrs. Haglitz's sniff. "We'll see. Just don't come rummaging around my pantry without asking, *especially* if you're planning to try out any new spells. And if you think I'll stand for any more of my good curtains and bedcovers being burnt up in some wizard's rage—!"

"Ah ..." Felix blinked twice behind his hood. "I'll do my best to restrain myself."

Morlokk sighed and reached up with one massive, gnarled fist to rub at his rock-studded forehead. "I assure you, Sinistro, Mrs.

Haglitz means no disrespect. We merely . . . understand how easy it is to forget about such mundane and lowly concerns when bearing the, ah, burden of such immense power."

"I see."

They actually imagined *they* might be in danger from *him?* It was so far from the truth that Felix could have laughed hysterically . . . if he didn't understand exactly what would happen when this misunderstanding was inevitably uncovered.

"If anyone wants to send me the Archduke trussed up on a plate, I'll be more than happy to see to his execution."

"Sinistro?" Morlokk repeated. "Shall I show you to your bedchamber?"

The world was tipping woozily around him, and he knew he'd more than likely be killed in the morning . . .

But after four long days of travel, Felix couldn't bring himself to turn down the prospect of at least one proper sleep beforehand.

"Lead on," he said firmly, and did his best to pace in a sinister and wizardly manner from the entry hall.

4

Felix woke to utter darkness. Was it the middle of the night? In his first, unsettling moment of confusion, his mind grasped frantically for possible explanations. Had the Count's assassins finally arrived and woken him by slipping through the door? Or . . . ?

No. Felix's body felt well rested for the first time in days. Better yet, the bedchamber around him was safely silent, with none of the telltale heavy breathing of the brutes the Count usually sent to inflict his calculated punishments. The room was only pitch-black now because a previous dark wizard who had slept here had demanded thick curtains no sunlight could pierce—something which Morlokk had pointed out as a pleasing feature when he had left Felix here last night.

. . . Because Felix was meant to be a dark wizard.

Ah. Memory lanced him. For one shameful moment, he seriously considered pulling his blankets over his head and hiding from the truth of it forever.

Instead, he took a slow, deep breath, ignored the gnawing hunger in his stomach with the ease of long habit, and set his mind to working out this latest challenge.

As his tutors had always been quick to remind him, Felix had been given the priceless gift of a classical education, for all that it had focused—on his regent's orders—on abstract mathematical equations and poetry scansion rather than practical government affairs. So, what exactly *did* he know about wizards?

Firstly, of course, that there were two sorts: the carefully leashed and regulated Gilded Wizards who were allowed within the Empire, and the sinister dark wizards who flourished outside of it in the various small kingdoms around the continent that had, thus far, stubbornly resisted the Empire's civilizing influence.

Within the Empire, any children who showed magical tendencies were carefully identified at an early age, removed from their families, and placed into established schools where they could be safely trained to control their more dangerous natural impulses and funnel their power towards the good of the state.

Outside the Empire . . . well, there, Felix's knowledge ran into a darkness nearly as complete as that which filled this bedchamber now. His tutors had simply agreed that outside the Empire, life was generally lawless and full of peril. There, dark wizards were left to their own devices, allowed to sell their wicked services to any bidder, while monstrous creatures prowled the woods and wilds and the worst magical villains were allowed to mingle in high society.

But as for any useful details about exactly *how* those notorious dark wizards were meant to go about their dastardly work . . .

Sighing, Felix forced himself out of his comfortable bed and strode across the luxuriantly carpeted floor to pull open the thick curtains and face the day ahead.

The view outside stopped his spiraling thoughts completely.

Yesterday, he had trudged his way through the rocky landscape in a fog of weariness and aching muscles, mindlessly following the winding carriage road without raising his gaze from the ground until those flaming skulls had forcibly seized his attention.

Now, his stomach abruptly dropped as he found himself looking out over a vast drop—the other side of the high crag that this stone castle perched upon. Swallowing, he unlatched the leaded window and put his head outside. Cold wind buffeted his face and hair as he stared out at the winding river, far below, that cut through the mountains. Even higher peaks rose in the distance, stabbing towards the wide blue sky. Birds skimmed and circled overhead, letting out hoarse and predatory calls that sent a strange thrill prickling through his skin.

His fingers closed instinctively around his window frame, tightening hard to keep his body grounded.

How could this wild, untamed landscape exist in the same world as the busy, cobblestoned streets of Estaviel City—much less the polished and elegant halls of the archducal palace that had enclosed him all his life?

Felix had never felt so unanchored, adrift from all he'd ever known . . .

But every shockingly cold, fresh breath he drew tasted enticingly like freedom.

"Your riding gryphons are fighting again," Saskia informed her uninvited guests. She pressed her delicate coffee cup against her forehead, hoping that its soothing heat might make up for the racket of screeches and growls that had broken out just beyond the closed library doors.

It didn't work—but the noise didn't seem to bother either of the infamously wicked queens who were currently lounging about on her couches, paging through her uncle's books without an apparent care in the world. *Ugh!* She squeezed her eyes closed against the sight.

If it had been up to Saskia, she would still have been fast asleep in her own bed after a long night of fascinating experimentation. Adding silversand to hellbane *did* work every bit as well as she'd hypothesized! The possibilities opened up by that discovery were exhilarating—but nothing else seemed to be working at all, starting with today's unexpected and unwanted meeting of the Queens of Villainy.

It was Queen Lorelei of Balravia, of course, who had named the three of them when she'd appeared four weeks ago in a whirl of sparkling fae magic, blonde curls, manic pronouncements, glittering scarlet lips, and gleeful demands.

"We're the only three queens still holding the line against the gods-damned Serafin Empire, and even our so-called allies in the other free kingdoms all loathe us for holding power instead of ceding it to a man. We need to stand together to stay strong!"

Saskia was, in fact, quite certain that what *she* needed was magic and *time alone to work on it* in order to maintain her own strength—but, as she had quickly learned, it was difficult to edge in a word of debate when Lorelei was in full flow. At the time, wrung out by a hundred other demands in the wake of seizing her uncle's throne, it had seemed easiest to nod along so she could shoo the continent's most scandalously blood-soaked seductress on her way.

That, however, had been before Saskia realized that she was expected to attend monthly *sociable meetups,* of all horrifying prospects. She had shuddered and tossed aside the invitation that arrived in a puff of rose petals on her desk two weeks ago. However, when she'd failed to arrive today, the other two had used one of Lorelei's shimmering fae portals to travel here instead and make themselves fully at home in her private castle library, which was *not* open to visitors. They'd been safely ensconced there—with delicious refreshments supplied by Saskia's own traitorous servants—by the time she was finally rousted out of bed.

It was no wonder they were hated and feared across the continent. Together, they really were unstoppable.

"I rather like the look of this one," Ailana announced, entirely ignoring the furious gryphon shrieks that rattled the door. Her voice was cool and unaffected, matching the pale blue of her gown and the plain, neat chignon that held her curling dark brown hair high above her light brown neck—a distinct contrast to Lorelei's wild and unrestrained curls, which were currently bedecked with lush poppy petals and busy shedding pollen onto Saskia's favorite seat. Indeed, everything about Ailana's attitude signaled such emotionless detachment that it would have been only too easy to forget she was there.

However, as much as Saskia tried not to pay attention to gossip from the outside world, she knew enough not to underestimate the Queen of Winter. Ailana of Nornne had earned that nickname across the continent when she enclosed an entire invading army in ice, using ancient aelfar magic even more perilous than the winters of her northern domain . . . and the book that Ailana was currently leafing through was one of the most ancient and dangerous tomes of magic in this whole mishmash of an unsorted library.

Lorelei, who lay stomach-down on the facing sofa with her fashionable leather boots kicked off nearby and her long layers of berry-colored chiffon skirts trailing onto the floor, leaned precariously over to see what Ailana was pointing at. "That old cantrip?" She sniffed dismissively. "Not worth the trouble, trust me. It might work to break a fae spell that was already weakened, but gathering nettles with your bare hands *hurts*—and I can think of far better things to be doing at midnight on a full moon." Her lascivious wink left no room for misinterpretation.

Ailana, who had clearly grown inured to Lorelei long ago, only raised one sardonic eyebrow before turning the page without further comment.

"Don't you think you should separate your gryphons?" Saskia winced as the screeching outside grew even more heated. "Or shift them to the stables, at least?"

"Nonsense!" Lorelei tossed aside her own ancient reading material in a careless gesture that sent delicate pages fluttering free from its spine. "They'll settle down as soon as Ailana's steed agrees to give mine proper precedence—and my sweet Bluebell doesn't care for stables. Being around too many horses that he's not allowed to eat makes the poor boy cranky."

"I don't recall my Frost ever losing a battle over precedence," Ailana murmured without looking up from her own book. A small smile twitched at the corner of her lips. "Bluebell might finally see sense this time, though."

Another crash sounded just outside the library doors, and a lance of corresponding pain pierced Saskia's head.

"Enough!" Setting down her empty coffee cup with an impatient clatter against its saucer, she jumped to her feet. "Perhaps *your* kingdoms are so peaceful that you have time for empty chatter, but I have actual work to do. We've all seen each other's faces and remembered that we're allies, just as you wanted. Now, if you'll pardon me . . ."

"We are here to work." Ailana calmly set aside her book. "We were only giving you enough time to wake up properly first. Was the coffee not strong enough?"

Ha. Mrs. Haglitz had taught the cook here to make proper troll coffee. If it had been any stronger, Saskia wouldn't have been able to wrestle it out of its pot in the first place.

"*I* understand," Lorelei said sympathetically as she pushed herself into an upright position on her seat, tucking her legs up beneath her. "It's always dreadful to be woken early to talk about business when I've been up all night playing with some delicious new toy. There's a new opera composer I met just last week . . ."

Saskia stifled a groan.

Ailana's upper lip curled as she reached for the saucer that held her cup of fragrantly cinnamon-laced tea. "Haven't you learned your lesson yet when it comes to musicians?"

Lorelei's blue eyes narrowed dangerously for an instant. Then she blinked her long, sparkling eyelashes and the glint of warning was gone, leaving her expression implausibly guileless. "Oh, I *count* on them to spread my fame now, darling. That's the difference between you and me, remember? *I* don't hide my heart like a coward and pretend I can keep myself safe."

Ailana's teacup rattled as sudden frost raced across the saucer below, encasing the patterned crockery in fine white crystals. Still faintly smiling, she took a long sip and set the saucer back on the table.

Saskia sank back onto her seat with a sigh. At least that saucer didn't *look* cracked. She would have more than enough household complaints to deal with once Mrs. Haglitz discovered whatever destruction those gryphons had wreaked outside.

Still, that sight had been the reminder she'd needed. It wasn't worth risking war with either of these powerful women only to win herself a few more hours' sleep. Saskia refilled her coffee cup, took a deep, sustaining sip of the thick dark brew, and growled, "Fine. What did you want to discuss?"

"Our next moves, of course." Lorelei's voice was suddenly crisp and businesslike as she leaned forward, all eyelash batting abandoned. "You've managed to bring the Serafin Empire to a halt at your border . . . for now. But you know they won't give up that easily."

Saskia's fingers tapped irritably against the side of her cup. "The Archduke's high general ordered all of his troops to retreat almost a week ago." It had been an unspeakable relief to finally leave the tedium of battle behind and return here to focus on her *real* work . . . if only visitors would stop interrupting it.

"Von Hertzendorff may have surrendered this first round to you, but we all know the Archduke won't give up his plans that easily. This kingdom was held as a client state in the palm of Estarion's hand for well over a decade. He and his former regent both sank significant funds into bribes to keep the upper hand over your uncle. He won't be prepared to give up that investment so easily—and neither will Emperor Otto in Fiora."

"That man's a menace," Ailana said with quiet conviction. "Since inheriting the Empire, he's been held back by his most powerful advisors, but in private, he's growing more and more obsessed with proving himself to be the equal of those ancient Serafin emperors who held the entire continent for over a thousand years. No matter how his high priest and gathered generals may work to hold him back, Otto is nearly ready to break free of all restrictions—and he's on the hunt for any excuse to expand. My spies say he's even beginning to consider taking up the cause of Purification to fire up his people and give him justification to crush all of us."

Purification. Saskia's fingers tightened around her cup. "I despise that word."

Even before that hateful new fringe movement had sprung up with a few loud and angry groups scattered around the continent, there had always been bigots who feared and mistrusted anyone who wasn't wholly human. It hadn't been full humans, though, who had dared to defy Saskia's uncle and risk their own lives to shelter her when she'd escaped his clutches as a young girl. And it hadn't only been full humans who'd stood by her side this year and fought under her banner though her uncle had claimed that her powers made her a monster.

"Oh, believe me, you've made your stance on that *perfectly* clear." Lorelei gave a rippling hum of delight. "It's been delicious to hear from all of Ailana's spies just how aggravated our little

Otto is about it! But you can't simply sit back now and pretend that the battle is over."

Saskia's eyes narrowed in suspicion. "Have you been speaking to my First Minister?"

"Really, darling." Lorelei sniffed. "I'd never disrespect you that way . . . unless you think it might work better for me? Is *she* less grumpy and more hospitable in the mornings?"

With a great effort of willpower, Saskia restrained herself from rolling her eyes. That would only count as giving in to the other woman's mischief.

Ailana spoke before Saskia could come up with any answer. "This second Serafin Empire has been a threat to every free nation on this continent since it first formed half a century ago. Until now, though, it didn't have a guiding moral philosophy to motivate its people in new attempts at expanding outward."

"And Otto thinks *Purification*, of all things, would motivate them to fight?" Saskia's lips curled into an unhidden snarl.

"*I* think we all need to shut him down before he can find out," said Lorelei, "and there's no time to lose. If Estarion's high general refuses to fight you himself, the Emperor will send out his own high general, the *Golden Beacon*." Her voice was suddenly venomous. "You've no idea just how dangerous that blond bastard can be. The Imperial armies don't just follow him. They *love* him. He could sacrifice tens of thousands, and they'd still fall at his feet and call it an honor to serve."

"And how exactly do you propose that I stop any of that from happening?" Saskia stared at her, ignoring the sudden increase in noise outside the room as one of her own crows added a squawking rebuke on top of the gryphons' battle cries. "Even I have limits, you know. If you imagine that I can simply drop my protective border, march my five thousand troops into Estarion, and take on the entire empire, even with whatever help you two may or may not choose to offer me . . ."

"You won't need to." Ailana's lips curved into a small, satisfied smile. "My spies have picked up some *extremely* interesting news." As the gryphons outside finally fell quiet, her next words dropped into the silence like pebbles into a deep, dark well. "The Archduke of Estarion has gone missing. Whoever finds and captures him—or kills him—controls the next move in this game."

5

Felix halted with one hand in midair, still reaching for the handle of the library door.

"*Whoever finds and captures him—or kills him . . .*" The words, spoken in Imperial Serafin, had sounded all too clearly through the door.

Had he really imagined, only yesterday, that he could throw himself upon Queen Saskia's mercy? Silently, he sent up a prayer of thanks to all the gods and goddesses of the Imperial pantheon—Estarion's own Elva in particular— for last night's misunderstanding and the disguise that had come with it.

Felix had found the silver moon-mask, as

promised, lying on the floor outside his bedchamber that morning beside a hot breakfast. Now, the cool silver covered his face with an enigmatic—and entirely deceptive—smile carved into its expression. When he'd looked into the mirror in his room after tying the mask's black satin ribbons into place, only his eyes had been left unhidden—and even those had looked oddly unfamiliar through those small, shadowy holes in the mask.

With the hood of his cloak pulled up over his dark hair, he looked every bit the mysterious and powerful dark wizard he was meant to be.

That sight had buoyed his confidence enough that he didn't falter when a squawking crow arrived next, tapping noisily at his door, to lead him insistently out through the maze of the castle. Felix hadn't even lost his nerve when they arrived at this carpeted and gaslit antechamber to find two massive creatures already engaged in battle, their cruel eagle beaks clashing furiously, their muscular leonine bodies locked in combat, and the force of their massive wingbeats sending furious gusts of air that tipped small tables and crockery in all directions.

Until now, Felix had only ever read about the flocks of dangerous gryphons who still lingered in some wild, forsaken corners of the continent. His eyes had widened behind the mask when he'd glimpsed the gleaming leather sidesaddles on this pair.

Fortunately, the furious cawing of his guide crow had made both beasts rear back obediently and then fall into reluctant-looking bows, their gold-furred forelimbs propped on the patterned carpet as they cleared his way.

With their hot breath still panting against his cloak and that fragment of overheard conversation in his ears, Felix squared his shoulders and turned the handle of the library door. With all the arrogance of any dangerous dark wizard, he stalked into a large, circular, and astonishingly cluttered room with a high, rounded ceiling . . . and found himself facing three figures far more dangerous than any snarling beasts.

"Your Majesties." It took all his years of courtly training to move smoothly forward into a bow instead of jerking backwards in recognition. "I beg your pardon for interrupting all of you. One of Her Majesty Queen Saskia's crow-guides summoned me here to begin my work."

"And who is *this* intriguing creature?" purred the predator on his left.

Queen Lorelei of Balravia was universally agreed to be the greatest beauty on the continent. Popular songs about her deadly allure were sung throughout the empire, while theatrical entertainments by the dozen dramatized her many scandals, and moralistic screeds circulated dire warnings about the perils of such dazzling female and fae glamour unchecked by mortal men's control.

With long-lashed cornflower-blue eyes, a scandalously low-cut gown that showed off every astonishing curve of her figure, and poppy blossoms cascading from her abundant blonde curls, she looked the very image of enticement . . . but Felix knew only too well how much could lurk behind appearances, especially at court. The calculation in those lovely blue eyes as they rested upon him made his skin prickle with instinctive warning.

"He's my librarian." Queen Saskia's voice was brusque, but Felix's gaze still turned to her with an irrational sense of relief as she straightened in her seat, setting down her half-drunk cup of coffee with a sharp, decisive movement.

Last night, in the flickering torchlight of her entry hall, his first sight of her—fiercely beautiful, terrifying, and more intensely compelling than anyone else he'd ever met—had seemed to be tinged with the surreality of his exhaustion and the crown of bones she wore.

Today, with sunlight flooding in through the line of windows to illuminate every golden speck of dust in the air, the suppressed magical power that crackled around her figure still gave off a tingling, magnetic charge. Once his gaze had landed upon her, Felix couldn't look away—and she didn't need any adornments to look impressive as she swept to her feet. Her close-fitting crimson velvet gown clung to her own curves as she stepped firmly into place between him and her visitors, her pinned crown of smooth black plaits just at the level of his mouth and her warmth and energy filling the air between them. "There is a reason I keep an actual parlor to receive guests," she added tartly. "We ought to go there and leave him to begin his work for the day."

"You have a *librarian?*" The third predator in the room raised one elegant eyebrow as she looked meaningfully around the great room. It was full of shelves that rose a full two stories high, with ladders, a narrow mezzanine, and a curving staircase that ran along the wall to aid in books' shelving and retrieval—but still, teetering piles of books, newspapers, and manuscripts filled most of the floor, creating an ocean of confusion that almost entirely surrounded the circle of couches.

Apparently, Queen Ailana of Nornne didn't need to exert her famously inhuman ice magic in order to chill the air.

A low growl sounded from Queen Saskia's throat as she stood protectively before him. That sound made Felix swallow hard over an unsettling sensation that . . . didn't feel like fear.

"He's *new.* He hasn't had a chance yet to sort out the mess my uncle left me."

"But can you really trust him to look through so many dangerous old tomes without any supervision? And is it fair to expect so much of him?" Queen Lorelei batted her lashes with faux concern as she rose to her stockinged feet, waving one arm in a gesture that gracefully indicated the disastrous state of the room. "If you'd like, I would be more than happy to send one of my own librarians here to aid him in this great challenge, as a token of our friendship."

"As would I, believe me," Queen Ailana said dryly.

Would a sinister dark wizard allow anyone to speak so dismissively about him without erupting into a storm of magical temper? Felix glanced around the three most notorious rulers on the continent and decided: even the most powerful dark wizard couldn't be foolish enough to think this a battle he could win.

"Absolutely not," Queen Saskia snapped. "You two have had all the chances you'll get to gather information from my library." Proving yet again that, unlike Felix, she had *not* been forced into years of training in courtly courtesy, she shook her head in open disgust. "Enough nonsense! We can finish up our conversation about . . . that other matter in a different room."

That other matter. Of course. Felix let out a long, controlled breath as the world resettled itself around him.

The ferocious Queen of Kitvaria might be standing in front of him now as if ready to defend him from the world, but if she ever discovered his true identity, that equation would be reversed. She was every bit as much a threat to him as the other two queens . . .

So it was clearly a sign that he hadn't yet recovered from the exhaustion of his journey that, even with everything he knew about her, he *still* couldn't stop his gaze from dropping to the curve of her velvet-enclosed waist, so close before him . . . and the lush, tempting area beneath it.

It was fortunate that the folds of his stolen cloak were so voluminous. Even so, Felix shifted back a careful step as he yanked his gaze upwards.

"Ah, well." Queen Lorelei's gaze met his over Queen Saskia's shoulder. Surely, she couldn't have seen where he was looking, not with his eyes partly shielded by the eyeholes of his mask— but the thoughtful way she pursed her lips stiffened his muscles in warning.

Stretching those famously plump lips into a rueful smile, she stepped closer and reached past Queen Saskia to hold out one dimpled, ungloved hand. "Perhaps we'll have a chance to converse again one day. I'm always interested in adding interesting characters to my own court, you know."

At that, Queen Ailana muttered something under her breath, but Felix couldn't make it out. There was no way to ignore the expectation in that outstretched royal hand. He had to take it or offend a fae queen.

Yet, she *was* fae. If she had some magical scheme in mind that she could only enact with the clasp of bare skin . . . ?

Well, then, he would have to hope that his own magical employer would sense it happening and protect him. Bowing respectfully, Felix took Queen Lorelei's right hand in his and politely kissed the air above it.

Her fingers darted upwards to grasp his wrist with the rapidity of a striking snake. Yanking him forward, she turned his hand to study his palm with narrowed eyes and unmistakable, dangerous focus.

Gods and goddesses preserve me. His heartbeat was thundering in his ears even louder than the angry snarls of the gryphons outside as those earlier words echoed once more in his ears.

"Whoever finds and captures him—or kills him . . ."

At least he wasn't wearing his archducal signet ring. That lay safely hidden in the single makeshift traveling case he'd managed to bring, along with the locket that held a miniature portrait of Emmeline and a strand of her soft brown hair. The only other possession he cared about . . .

Felix's breath caught at the realization.

. . . Was the one adornment that *no one* would expect any archduke of the Serafin Empire to wear.

When he was still a very young child, his parents had made him swear never to remove the slender golden loop that pierced the upper cartilage of his left ear. Even the Count had never forced him to break that vow—but he had ruled that every single cut of Felix's short, dark hair had to thoroughly hide that "womanish" adornment.

His portraits had been spread across the continent from the

time he'd first inherited the archduchy, but not a single one had *ever* included that earring.

Still bowing politely over their joined right hands, Felix pulled back the hood of his cloak and carefully swept back his hair over his left ear.

Queen Lorelei's quick intake of breath cut through the air.

He couldn't help glancing up. At this angle, the eyeholes of his mask obscured half his vision . . . but her blue eyes glittered as if she'd had a revelation.

"If you're *quite* finished ogling my employee?" On his right, Queen Saskia had already started for the door with a swish of crimson velvet. "As you both pointed out a moment ago, he does have work to do."

"As do we." Queen Ailana rose from her own seat but waited expectantly behind her companion as their hostess opened the door before them, casting the wrangling gryphons outside back into silence. "Lorelei . . . ?"

"Of course." With a lingering—warning?—stroke of her soft thumb across his palm, Queen Lorelei finally allowed Felix's wrist to slip from her grasp. "I wish you fortune with your task, wizard," she murmured as she leaned down to scoop up her boots from the carpeted floor. "Perhaps we shall meet again soon."

"Good fortune with your own endeavors." Felix rose with practiced fluidity from his bow to watch all three queens glide out the door to finish their joint plans of how best to hunt him down.

The moment the door fell shut behind the last of them, his legs gave out beneath him.

"*Ahh!*" He had to grasp hold of the closest claw-footed couch to drag himself over and then slump onto its cushions, letting out a shuddering breath that rocked through his limp body.

Divine Elva! He'd been in danger of death for months now, but it had never before felt quite so visceral.

Gradually, as his breathing slowed, he became aware that an ancient-looking book lay half-open beside him, its paper binding broken, three fragile-looking pages already shaken loose.

Never, in all his life, had Felix been able to ignore an open book. He scooped up the first page with fingers that still trembled slightly.

It had been printed long ago in the crabbed, old-fashioned script of a past era, which few people in the modern day remembered how to read. Fortunately, Felix had learned early to read that long-gone script as part of his much vaunted classical education.

Even so, the words written in that script seemed meaningless at first—until, as he read further with his eyebrows drawing lower and lower with every line, he realized that the syllables all fell into familiar beats. *Wait.* Could ancient magical spells actually use the same scansion as the poetry he'd spent years analyzing?

Lifting his head, Felix surveyed the vast room of unsorted books and manuscripts and what looked to be the forgotten paraphernalia of at least a century's worth of readers.

Blinking, he recalled Queen Saskia's instructions last night.

"Arrange it all into some reasonable order, set aside anything that looks particularly dangerous or useful, and catalogue the contents. Do you think you could do that?"

Felix had no idea how to maintain his disguise well enough to survive the next few months . . . but for this particular task, at least, his education had finally served him well.

Carefully, he tucked those delicate lost sheets back into their damaged casing and gave the book a reassuring stroke. "Don't worry," he murmured as he rose to his feet. "You won't be mistreated again. None of you will."

Already busy making notes in his head, he strode towards the ordinary, nonmagical satin bellpull that hung by the door, muscle weakness entirely forgotten.

His attempts to sort out his own life might have gone catastrophically wrong, but with a fountain pen, a supply of black ink, and blank paper—a *good deal* of blank paper, he amended—he might just be able to sort out this broken library of magic after all.

6

Naturally, Lorelei's fae portals were every bit as sparkly and excessive as everything else about her. Saskia only just managed to hold on to the shreds of her patience as she watched her unwanted visitors ride their haughty gryphon steeds into the rainbow-colored doorway that Lorelei had summoned for their departure. As the portal finally snapped closed, Saskia drew a deep breath of relief—and inadvertently breathed a dozen leftover sparkles into her nostrils.

Ugh! This was why she never invited guests into her home.

Sneezing uncontrollably, Saskia turned away

from the final shimmering remnants of the portal and started for the closed parlor door and the delicious freedom of her waiting laboratory beyond.

Just before she could reach for the door handle, she was hit by a deeply unwelcome realization: *Mirjana needs to know the news they brought.*

Closing her eyes, she rocked to a reluctant halt. She should have ordered more troll coffee after all.

Unfortunately, she'd learned one thing from all those years of trying to avoid her uncle's assassins: putting off unpleasantness only made it worse. So, she turned her steps and went directly to the tower study she had claimed for those unavoidable moments when she had to either focus on the tedious paperwork that came with rulership or—even worse—face her former lover.

As she rounded the last winding curve of the narrow stone staircase, she reminded herself grimly that she *had* named Mirjana First Minister of Kitvaria for good reasons. It was only difficult to remember those reasons when she had to endure one of these meetings.

A fresh pile of notices was already stacked on top of Saskia's heavy oaken desk when she arrived, every one of them marked *URGENT* in Mirjana's elegant lettering. Saskia pushed them to one side and flicked open the clasp of the heavy rectangular jewelry case that had lain safely hidden behind that pile. As she pulled the case open, she revealed an oval mirror set inside its lid, as well as the Great Seal of Kitvaria cradled safely within.

"*Finally.*" Mirjana's face appeared in the glass of the mirror a scant minute later. As usual, her glossy brown hair was upswept in a lovely waterfall arrangement that glinted with tastefully hidden jet beads above her long, creamy neck . . . which Saskia knew to be just as soft as the silk Mirjana loved to wear. She looked, as she always did, far more queenly than Saskia had ever felt—and her gaze moved with its usual swift appraisal across Saskia's own rumpled appearance. "Is this the first time you've stepped out of your laboratory all week?"

"Actually, I just hosted a royal meeting. The Queens of Balravia and Nornne——"

"Without any cosmetics or jewelry? Not even a necklace?" Mirjana demanded. "You do realize——"

"They weren't here to trade fashion tips." Safely out of sight, Saskia's fingers rattled against the desk. How on earth had she ever imagined Mirjana's endless critiques to be *helpful* when she'd been young and in love? Had she simply been so desperate for romance, after years spent hidden with her protectors, that she'd fooled herself into thinking of Mirjana's lectures as gifts of affection? "They brought news I thought you'd want to hear as soon as possible."

Mirjana's perfectly plucked eyebrows rose. "Is it, by any chance, related to any of the urgent missives I've sent you over the past four days?"

Swiftly, Saskia slid the unopened pile of letters even farther from the mirror's line of sight. "It's related to Estarion. The Archduke——"

"Has talked the Emperor into making your uncle a Knight of the Imperial Order and declared him an official paladin of Divine Elva. I know. Why do you think I've been begging you to return to the capital?"

"*What?*" Every other prickling discomfort was suddenly devoured by a raging storm in Saskia's head. "The Archduke made *my uncle* an Imperial Knight and a paladin? Blessed by an actual *goddess?*"

"We-e-ell . . ." Mirjana shrugged. "Likely, the goddess herself wasn't involved. The Archduke is a modern man, you know—if he's like most politicians, he'll give more lip service to the pantheon than actual belief. I doubt he bothered to pray to Divine Elva himself before making that public proclamation. Still, religious titles do matter to the public as a whole, so—"

"He just told the world that *my uncle* is a perfect symbol of manly honor and was blessed by a goddess *after murdering my parents*." Dimly, Saskia was aware that her voice was rising . . . and it wasn't alone. All around the office, papers and books were lifting off their surfaces, carried by the surge in her emotions into a whirling vortex centered on her chair. "Over the last eighteen years, my uncle bled Kitvaria's treasury dry for his own selfish profit. He tried to kill me and everyone I ever cared for, no matter how many times I told him I didn't want the throne . . ."

"And now you have it at last, for which we're all thankful." Mirjana's voice cut through the storm: clear, precise, and controlled, as the First Minister of Kitvaria had to be. "But I need you here at the capital to *keep* it from now on, not hiding from your responsibilities any longer."

"What are you talking about?" Saskia gave her head a swift shake as she fought for control, breathing hard. She couldn't quite bring herself to let go of the whirling storm of paper in the air, but she wrapped her fingers around her desk to ground herself, and she forced the curve of flight into a wider arc, pushing the storm out of range of her First Minister's judgmental gaze. "I'm not hiding from anything! I just spent weeks on the border fighting for our country. The experiments I'm doing now on silversand and hellbane could make all the difference if the Empire ever manages to break through my barrier and invade again."

"Yes, but the *Empire* isn't the only thing you have to worry about." Mirjana's voice tightened with barely restrained impatience. "In case you've actually forgotten, you have a whole nation of citizens, now, looking to you for direction and protection."

"Which is why I appointed you First Minister." Saskia focused on steadying her breathing and slowing the whirl of paper all around her. "We may have had our own personal disagreements"—to say the least—"but I trust your judgement when it comes to politics. You know I don't need to interfere with every little day-to-day decision. As long as we discuss all of the larger issues, which we can do perfectly well from here . . .”

"Being an actual *queen* can't be done behind the scenes!" Mirjana's mask of patience shattered as she snapped out the words. "After all these years, you still don't understand or even care how ordinary, nonmagical humans work, do you? They're reading your uncle's weaseling complaints in the newspapers and hearing all about his Imperial honors; they need to see you in public, smiling and waving and keeping them all safe."

Saskia barely repressed a full-body cringe at the idea. Still, she fought to keep her tone steady. "I am keeping them safe, and I always will. If what you wanted in a queen was a smiling ninny you could tote around like a puppet, merely to wave at the crowds—"

"What I *wanted*, I gave up on getting from you four years ago." Mirjana enunciated the words with just as cold a precision as she'd used in the final battle she referred to now—the moment their three-year-long romance had ended with bitter finality. "Yet I still, somehow, keep hoping that you'll finally start caring enough about your people—*all* of your people, not only the inhuman ones—to make an effort and become a true queen for their sake."

Enough. Saskia's grip tightened around her desk, and the whirl of paper stilled in midair. She wasn't a teenager anymore, desperate for affection and approval from the most beautiful girl she'd ever met. The vision of herself she'd always seen reflected in Mirjana's eyes—half-feral, heedless of everything that ought to matter, and always, inevitably, in need of instruction—*did not* have to be her truth as an adult.

"I thank you for your report," she said tightly. "I'm sure we'll meet again soon to discuss other topics."

Face tightening, Mirjana took a deep breath and lifted her pointed chin. "As you say, Your Majesty. But remember: your uncle has spent nearly two decades telling everyone you're a monster. Hiding from your own citizens now tells them you think he's right."

Argh! Saskia lunged to slam the jewelry case closed . . . but

Mirjana had already vanished from the mirror by the time she touched it.

Panting, Saskia glared at her own wild-eyed reflection as papers and books showered and thumped onto the floor around her. *So much for proving her wrong.*

She hadn't even managed to tell Mirjana about the missing Archduke.

. . . If he even *was* missing. Could he still be issuing public proclamations if that were true? She should have pressed Mirjana for more details while she had the chance.

She certainly wasn't about to call back her First Minister now . . . but fortunately, Saskia had someone else she could consult. After all, why bother to hire a dark wizard without making use of all his skills?

With a determined swish of her crimson velvet skirts, Saskia abandoned the storm-tossed office and started down the narrow, tightly curving tower staircase. She was only halfway down when the sound of commotion and uproar from the library level reached her ears.

Damn it, *this* was why she'd always hated dealing with dark wizards! Muttering a particularly filthy goblin curse, Saskia lifted her skirts an extra half inch and hastened her steps the rest of the way down and through the richly decorated velvet-and-bronze maze of side chambers. She burst into the library's antechamber just in time to see Morlokk stepping out of the library itself, a thoughtful frown on his craggy face, while Mrs. Haglitz steamed furiously across the carpet towards it, flanked by two worried-looking kitchen maids.

A mini-flock of Saskia's crows swirled with cawing impatience outside the Morlokk-blocked doorway, and Saskia gave up the idea of asking her new librarian for help.

"Very well," she said wearily. "What has he done? And will I need to take care of the body before I can finally return to work?"

"Your Majesty." Morlokk gave her the same pained and

sorrowful look that had reduced her to squirming guilt every single time he'd used it on her as a teenager. Unfortunately, the effect hadn't softened over the years. "Do you truly imagine your household staff too incompetent to manage a single corpse without assistance?"

"Of course I don't." Wincing, Saskia lowered her shoulders, which she had braced for battle, and let the soft, heavy skirts of her gown drop with a whisper of surrender to the floor. "I apologize for the insinuation. I've been having a bit of a . . . discussion with my First Minister ever since my visitors left, and—"

"*Harrumph.*" Mrs. Haglitz rounded on her like a warship abruptly redirected. "If that pert-nosed snip still thinks she can tell *you* what to do, after all these years . . . !"

"Everything's back under control now," Saskia said with grim determination. "I only came to consult with my new librarian about a small, insignificant matter—but I'm happy to deal instead with whatever trouble he's caused for all of you this morning." Really, it would be quite cathartic to let out her raging temper on a deserving source. Remembering some previous dark wizards' tantrums and the way *they'd* treated her staff . . . "It would be a pleasure, believe me."

"Well, then, you can tell him for me that he *won't* be skipping any of my household's good meals, now or ever!" Mrs. Haglitz crossed her arms, and her kitchen maids leapt backwards to cluster behind her short, broad back for shelter. "*He* sent me a note, carried all the way to my office, if you can believe it. A handwritten *note*, saying Cook and I needn't worry about any more of his meals today as he was so hard at work!"

"Ah . . ." Lost, Saskia looked to Morlokk for aid.

He stepped forward, and her crows shot past him, squawking their triumph. "I assure you, Mrs. Haglitz, the Sinistro's message was not intended as an insult. I believe he was, in fact, attempting a kindness in being considerate of your and Cook's time and energy."

"As if we found *feeding this castle* to be an inconvenience? Or does he think neither of us can manage it?!"

Oh, darkness. "I'll make sure he understands the truth," Saskia said firmly, "and I won't let him offend you again, Mrs. Haglitz. But . . ." Frowning, she looked past Morlokk to the open library doorway, from which even more squawking from her crows could be heard. "What's all the rest of this uproar about, then?"

"Ah." Morlokk frowned thoughtfully. "It's a technological issue, actually."

"A *what?*" Her eyebrows shot upwards. Since when had any dark wizards cared about technology? Far too much of *that* was touched with iron for any magical being's comfort, starting with those giant, malevolent trails of iron that Emperor Otto's workers were stretching across the Empire for his new railways.

"He has begun work on the cataloguing of your library," Morlokk said, "and it seems that he's in need of a particular sort of pen that isn't available here in the castle."

"From a particular type of feather, you mean?" Crow feathers were by far the most convenient, as Saskia regularly found them in her flock's wake—but she wasn't surprised that a smugly sophisticated dark wizard would demand something more challenging to procure. "What kind of exotic quill does he imagine he needs just to write a list or two? A *phoenix* feather? Or . . ."

Wait. Brightening, she glanced around the antechamber. "Would a gryphon feather do?" Surely, after all that earlier grappling, at least one or two feathers must have been shed.

"No, what he wants is called a *fountain pen.*" Morlokk sounded just as baffled as she felt. "Apparently, the first model was developed just last year. Sinistro says they're all the rage in the Empire's capital cities."

"Well, he's not *in* the Empire anymore, and he'd do well to remember it." Narrowing her eyes, Saskia started for the library door. "Don't worry about this problem, Morlokk. I'll take care of it myself."

She found her new librarian standing at a makeshift table in the middle of the room, surrounded by the circling and still loudly squawking mini-flock of crows, his face covered by his silver moon-mask but the hood of his cloak tossed carelessly back over his shoulders. Of course, it was impossible to read his expression behind the mask, but his head was tilted with surprisingly courteous attention as the birds all jabbered excitedly at him and showered an assortment of random items into his outstretched bare hands and onto the table before him.

Buttons, ribbons, colorful threads, coins and jewels and . . . aha. So, *that* was what had happened to her missing pearl earring!

Mirjana had given that respectably pale and discreet pair of earrings to her early in their courtship, as part of her determined attempt to civilize Saskia's appearance and manners. Saskia had dutifully worn them to please her lover, at the time, and worn them again at her rare royal appearances on her First Minister's instructions. However, she certainly hadn't felt any regret when she'd discovered the loss of one of them from her jewelry box last month.

Respectable and discreet would never describe anything she wanted for herself.

Still, confusion temporarily overtook her ire as she studied the random assortment of offerings. "What in the world did you ask them to bring you?"

The wizard's shoulders—which appeared to be high and lean—twitched underneath the massive folds of his dark cloak at the sound of her voice. Still, his response was as unexpectedly patient as his attitude towards her crows had been. "I believe they're attempting to help me build a new pen. It is very kind of them to share their treasures, although I'm not sure exactly how to make use of them."

"Ah, yes. Because you want a *fountain pen*, even though no one here has even heard of them before." Saskia crossed her arms fiercely, remembering her purpose. "You don't think an ordinary quill pen is good enough for a dark wizard?"

"*Not* when it comes to the safety of your books." Voice hardening, he drew himself up into a looming figure of shadows. "I'm sure you must have noticed how delicate a good many of these volumes really are."

Saskia had to suppress a grimace as she remembered the way Lorelei had tossed aside that old book earlier, haphazardly scattering pages. "No one has looked after the books in this room in two decades."

Her uncle had made use of his own hired dark wizards when he'd usurped the throne from her parents, but he'd always made a political point of remaining uninvolved with magic himself. This room had once been Saskia's most beloved childhood playground, but during the first seven years after Yaroslav's usurpation, when she'd been held prisoner in this castle, she had been firmly barred from its library. Only her uncle's dark wizards had been allowed to use it—and they'd never taken any care with their stolen magical resources.

Her new librarian nodded firmly in response. "A fountain pen is *far* more effective than a quill pen for this sort of delicate cataloguing. It carries ink in its own reservoir, so it needn't be dipped into open bottles that may be tipped over and spill, ruining your ancient manuscripts."

"That makes no sense." Saskia's brows drew together as scientific curiosity took the fore. "How can it be safe to keep your ink *inside* the pen? Wouldn't it fall out and leak all over everything?"

"Ah, but it's the air pressure *inside* a fountain pen that holds the ink in place." As his words quickened, his hands rose to gesture an enthusiastic accompaniment. Free of last night's gloves, his fingers were long, fair-skinned, and shapely, drawing compellingly graceful arcs through the air. "It's an astonishing new technological development. I've—that is, I've heard that some Imperial archdukes have been amassing whole collections of new models produced by various different craftsmen across the Empire."

"Hmm." Saskia watched his gesturing right hand arc dangerously close to her youngest male crow, Oskar, who was veering excitedly towards him with yet another useless button offering.

Rather than batting or smacking the bird away as any other dark wizard of her acquaintance would have done, the librarian halted his gesture just in time. He even turned over his hand to offer Oskar his palm in a careful—almost apologetic—gesture.

"Perhaps we can find a way to acquire one of those fountain pens for you after all," Saskia murmured.

He certainly deserved *something* for worrying about her books and being kind to her noisy, demanding pets—and Oskar, now perched on the table directly in front of him, was now blatantly nuzzling into his hand in a shameless quest for affection. Saskia's lips twitched as she watched her new librarian hesitate . . . and then give in.

How often was any sinister, masked dark wizard approached for cuddling by a bird?

Oskar's smug gurgle of delight as those long, sensitive fingers stroked gently across his feathers could have all too easily been mistaken for a feline purr.

"Ahem!" Saskia covered her helpless smile with a forced cough. "I actually came about a different matter. I want you to look out for a particular spell as you sort through these old spellbooks."

"Of course." His masked head tilted, but he didn't stop petting Oskar, who was strutting in place with pride while the other crows reacted with outraged jeers. "Does it have a name?"

"Probably." Saskia's lips twisted with frustration. It had been far too many years since she'd looked carefully through any written spells—but there hadn't been any available in her hiding place in the woods, where Morlokk and Mrs. Haglitz had secreted her once she'd finally managed to escape her uncle's prison. As with most witches, her own magic worked most powerfully on a physical, instinctive level, although she preferred to keep it leashed as tightly as possible. Fortunately, her experiments in blending carefully controlled bursts of her own power with magically viable ingredients in her laboratory had been extremely productive.

Still, dark wizards valued written spellcraft above all, and she hated admitting to ignorance in front of anyone. That irritation lent her words a snap as she continued, "That's your job to work out. Unless you happen to know this spell already? I'm looking for a way to locate a particular person, without anything useful on hand."

The wizard's hand stilled on Oskar's back. "Anything . . . useful?"

Saskia shrugged impatiently. "No drops of blood, no hair, no precious belongings, no relatives, none of his most personal secrets to whisper into the wind and track him down . . . you know."

"Of course." Between the silver curve of his round mask and the messily tied knot of his black silk cravat, she glimpsed a flex of fair skin, shifted by his swallow. "Do you at least know this man's name?"

"Naturally." But she wouldn't share that now—not when she'd seen how badly her librarian had reacted to even the slightest mention of Estarion's hated archduke last night. "I'm sure we can clip a few newspaper pictures, too, if that's needed for the spell. The man is such an egotist, I can't count how many portraits he's posed for across the years."

Neither, honestly, could she blame the newspapers that splashed those portraits across the continent; that wistful, fine-boned poet's face was any portraitist's fantasy. No doubt, more than a few viewers were still foolish enough to sigh over Archduke Felix's dreamy portraits despite all he'd ordered done since his ascension. Saskia had always found it particularly embittering that so much delicate beauty had been granted to a man with such a vicious will for dominance.

Squirming and hopping on the table with frustration, Oskar loudly protested the cessation of his petting—and Saskia found her lips curving against her will as she saw the gentle way her librarian's hand still rested against the crow's back.

"What is your name, anyway?" she asked abruptly.

He reared back as if she'd slapped him, his hand falling away from Oskar's feathers. "I beg your pardon?"

"I can't just think of you as Sinistro." She had, of course, with the last few dark wizards she'd hired—but they had been different. She had never wanted to give *them* the gift of her attention for long enough to remember their individual, irritating identities.

"Ah. Of course." That tiny patch of skin flexed again, distractingly. "My name is . . . Fabian."

"*Fabian.*" She tested the single name on her tongue. No doubt it was a professional moniker, taken on at the start of his magical career, but it suited him all the same. She nodded as she stepped away. "Well, Fabian, I trust you'll find that spell for me as soon as possible."

"Of course." His chest rose and fell beneath his cloak. "I'll be certain to keep an eye out for it in the course of my cataloguing."

"And I'll ask Morlokk to see about finding you a fountain pen," she promised, "but now, it's time for both of us to return to work."

As she turned away, her gaze fell on the fraying velvet couch closest to the window. A memory flashed across her vision, bright and bittersweet: a long-ago afternoon spent curled up on that vividly blue new couch. She'd been happily playing with her dolls, utterly convinced that she was working just as hard as her mother, who sat on the facing couch with her curling black hair spilling across her shoulders and her wire-framed spectacles balanced on the tip of her nose, surrounded by notes from her many ethnographic journeys and immersed in creating epic new spellwork.

Only a flash, and then the memory was gone, replaced by the faded reality before Saskia's adult eyes . . .

But for the first time since she'd repossessed this castle, she found herself thinking that she might not mind spending more of her own time in the library, from now on.

7

As heir to the Archduchy of Estarion from birth, Felix had never before served in anyone's employ. However, he was uncomfortably certain that misleading *any* employer would be considered grounds for prompt dismissal . . . and when one's employer was the most terrifyingly powerful witch on the continent, the consequences were likely to be fatal.

Still, as Queen Saskia strode out of the library, surrounded by her omnipresent storm of prickling energy and followed by a swirling crowd of crows, he reminded himself, on a deep, slow breath, that he hadn't *lied* to her any more than she'd lied to him by keeping secret the identity of her prey. Having overheard her earlier conversation with the other two queens, Felix would indeed keep a sharp eye out for any spells that could possibly be used to hunt the errant Archduke down . . . and then he'd bury them so deep within the catalogue that no one else would ever find them.

Even in the role of a sinister dark wizard, though, Felix could never bring himself to harm a book—and this library had suffered enough mistreatment already. So, with a final, reassuring stroke of the inquisitive young crow who had stayed by his side after all the others left, Felix forced himself to set aside his unhelpful feelings of foreboding and fix his attention on the task ahead.

Unfortunately, cataloguing a library of magic was easier said than done . . . especially when he didn't even know the main parameters.

Spells, it seemed, were composed of a whole myriad of elements. It wasn't only their varying intents that differentiated them; there was a whole array of different styles and structures, not to mention all the different languages that had been used. Without his rigorous training in both linguistics and the ancient poetry that had apparently influenced magical spellcasting for centuries, Felix would have been lost and buried in a sea of paper forever. As it was, by his third night of focused study and his fifth used-up quill pen, he thought he *might* be starting to see a glimmer of light ahead . . . but his head ached with the effort of concentration as he fought to make sense of it all.

Was it an indication of the user's greater power when a variant of the same spell was noticeably shorter, without so many rhythmic elements being required? Or did that actually indicate the opposite—a mere beginner's spell?

A real dark wizard, of course, would know without even having to wonder. But—

Wait, what was in his mouth?

Blinking, Felix lifted his gaze from the ancient, faded text he'd been poring over for hours, with the help of both candlelight and a gas lamp, to stare at the half-eaten food in his right hand. It was some sort of cold pastry pocket made of half a dozen fine layers of crunchy, savory dough, all wrapped around a combination of spiced cabbage and meat that—he tested it with his tongue, and his eyes widened—was *delicious*.

Where in the world had it come from? He was almost certain that he had remembered to reassure the cook and housekeeper that they needn't inconvenience themselves by sending him private meals. He didn't remember even hearing any interruptions. His body must have operated on sheer instinct to push his mask high enough to free his mouth and eat as he worked, just now. But—

"*Ahem!*" The sound of a peremptorily cleared throat made Felix nearly drop the pastry in his haste to drag his silver mask back into place. An instant later, Mrs. Haglitz, the forbidding troll housekeeper, shoved aside one of the towering stacks of papers in front of him. Crossing her long, muscular arms, she raised the tip of her green nose high beyond the folds of the voluminous and colorful patterned shawls that covered nearly all of her face as well as her broad shoulders. "Are you actually *trying* to make me drop you into my soup pot, young man?"

"Ah . . . no?" Warily, Felix rose from his seat, slipping the half-eaten pastry pocket back onto the nearly full plate of food that—he now saw—sat beside him. His back gave an aggrieved twinge at the sudden movement after hours of bending, but he ignored it, every hair on his body prickling with warning.

Beside him, the cheerfully cheeky young crow who'd kept him company for the past few days collapsed into a defensive crouch, its feathers ruffled.

"Then tell me what in all the dark mountains' shadows you think is wrong with my staff's efforts!"

"I . . . what?" Felix shook his head, trying to bring the moment into focus. Was this all some strange dream brought about by too many days of thinking about magic? "I haven't a single complaint. Have I somehow offended any of them?"

"Have you—?!" Mrs. Haglitz's pink-and-black top shawl ruffled under the explosive power of her breath. When she spoke again, her voice was sickly sweet and somehow even more dangerous. "Sinistro, tell me truly: Do you find the mattress of your bed too hard? Too soft? Your bedcovers unacceptable in any way? The standards of your meals too low?"

"Of course not." Felix frowned. "Why would I?"

"Well, I'm sure *I* don't know," she snapped, "because we work hard to see to everyone's comfort in this castle—but none of it seems to matter to you!"

Felix had to brace himself to keep his feet from shuffling backwards in cowardly retreat.

"Last night, you didn't return to your bedchamber for so much as a single hour. *I* was told you'd bedded down on the library floor for an hour or two as if you'd nowhere better to go. Not only that, but you've left more than half your meals uneaten!"

"I have?" Felix's eyes widened as he turned to see—oh, there *were* more plates in the room behind him, piled full of even more delectable-looking food that he hadn't even noticed. "I'm sure I told the staff not to worry—"

"*Not to worry?*" Mrs. Haglitz snorted magnificently, and the crow dived under the hanging left sleeve of Felix's cloak for shelter, letting out a muffled squeak.

At the sound of that panicked squeak, Felix lost every impulse to retreat. He curved his arm protectively around the crow, his aching spine stiffening.

"*If* Her Majesty forgot to make it clear two days ago . . ." Mrs. Haglitz began ominously.

"Queen Saskia isn't to blame for my mistakes. Nor is anyone else." As the chastened ball of ruffled feathers tucked closer into his side, Felix hardened his voice to exquisitely polite steel. "If I've broken any of the rules of this castle, I sincerely apologize for my transgression—but I cannot allow anyone else to suffer for it."

Surprisingly, the housekeeper didn't respond with outrage to his statement. Instead, her big head cocked under the folds of her many shawls, and her voice softened slightly. "You think you need to protect Her Majesty—or that little pest hiding under your arm—from me?"

"I'm certain Queen Saskia can defend herself." Felix kept his own tone steady, feeling the bird's rapid heartbeat pulse against his arm. "However, I won't assign responsibility to anyone but myself for my own failings."

Emmeline had tried to take that on for him far too many times when they were children. They'd both known that the Count saved his most brutal acts of physical discipline for Felix—but she had never understood that Felix suffered even more when he had to watch her be punished for his mistakes.

"Hmm." With a sudden, decisive movement, Mrs. Haglitz uncrossed her arms and pulled the veiling shawls off her head for the first time since they'd met. Mossy green branches mingled with strands of thick grey hair and orange and red leaves in the long mass that showered over her broad shoulders and continued well below her waist. Her wide green face, finally revealed, was creased with wrinkles and cracks so deep, Felix spotted a patch of small brown mushrooms growing inside the one closest to her tall, pointed left ear.

Her eyes, though, commanded all of his attention: undeniably ancient and infinitely weary, those green and gold depths left him dizzyingly off-balance. "Young man, I don't know what sort of life you've found for yourself in the outer world, especially if you've had to spend it hidden inside the moon-forsaken Empire, but I'll tell you now: in this castle, no one is punished for failures they can't help. Her Majesty would never stand for that kind of cruelty."

Her Majesty had not become notorious across the continent for the mildness of her own behavior . . . but Felix closed his lips behind his mask to keep that comment to himself.

"So be it." Mrs. Haglitz sighed, shaking her head at him. "If you aren't looking down your nose at our hospitality or the food you're offered . . . why exactly have you been sleeping in here and starving yourself since you arrived?"

Felix shrugged uncomfortably. "I don't require that much food, really." As a child, he'd had to learn to go without; he hardly noticed a few missed meals nowadays.

"Mm-hmm." Her tone reeked of skepticism. "And you don't need any proper sleep, either?"

He had learned how to live without that, too . . . but something in her expression made the reassurance stop in his throat.

"I thought as much." She slapped her discarded shawls over her left forearm with a loud *smack*. "In that case . . ." The housekeeper turned and surged towards the door. "Come with me. You're going to eat a good meal at a proper table, and then you're going to have a full night's sleep. *In a bed.*"

Felix winced. "Truly, I can't!" Helplessly, he waved his free hand at the stacks of books and papers that surrounded him. "Can't you see the state this library is in? I promised Queen Saskia that I would sort it out for her."

"And you will—but there's no use trying to do it on an empty stomach, much less when you're half-dead on your feet from exhaustion. Her Majesty knows what a mess this was left in. D'you really think she'll expect it to be finished in a week?"

"Ah . . ." Uncertainty clenched at Felix's throat. How long *would* this take someone who knew what he was doing? Someone who wasn't lying about his skills and experience?

Mrs. Haglitz snorted. "I don't think she'd prefer you to botch the job."

"I won't," Felix vowed. He might have misled his new employer about too many things, but he did know how to study and absorb vast quantities of information.

And perhaps it *had* been too long since he'd slept and exhaustion was beginning to overwhelm his better sense . . . but as he found himself seated at a mouthwatering feast ten minutes later—with a smaller second plate set out beside him for the delighted crow, and a pair of goblin footmen cheerfully pointing out all of the different food options laid before him in the elegant dining room—Felix found himself thinking dreamily that he might be able to fit himself into this new role after all.

If he were truly fortunate, the rest of the world might even forget that the man he had once been had ever existed in the first place.

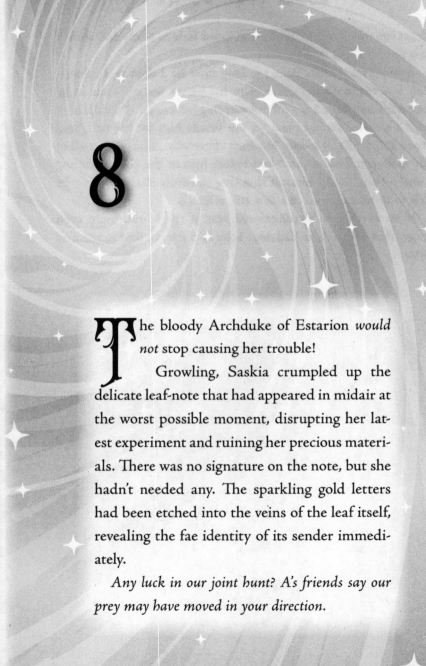

8

The bloody Archduke of Estarion *would not* stop causing her trouble!

Growling, Saskia crumpled up the delicate leaf-note that had appeared in midair at the worst possible moment, disrupting her latest experiment and ruining her precious materials. There was no signature on the note, but she hadn't needed any. The sparkling gold letters had been etched into the veins of the leaf itself, revealing the fae identity of its sender immediately.

Any luck in our joint hunt? A's friends say our prey may have moved in your direction.

By "friends," of course, Lorelei meant "spies"—Ailana's coolly efficient network of spies, spreading across the continent like transparent ice to ferret out secrets for the Queen of Nornne. Perhaps Saskia ought to have felt grateful to have this particular secret shared with her . . . but the entire purpose of erecting a magical barrier of epic strength between Kitvaria and Estarion had been to give her time *off* from thinking of that damnable Archduke. Now, her carefully created silversand and hellbane concoction, stymied at the moment of would-be magical catharsis, had fallen back into the cauldron with a sad and squishy *plop* of surrender, left gooey, unactivated, and unusable . . . and Saskia had already read two different urgent notes about the Archduke earlier that day.

It would be helpful if all of her various interrupters could, at least, get their warning stories straight.

According to Lorelei's latest botanical interruption, the Archduke was slinking around the border of Kitvaria now, like a venomous serpent hunting for a vulnerable entrance point. According to the two earlier missives from Mirjana, though, he was busy sending delegations of priests and diplomats—including Saskia's godsdamned *paladin* of an uncle!—to plead with the Emperor for the use of an elite squadron of Imperial Gilded Wizards to tear down her lovely barrier. *That* news had sent her rushing back to her laboratory, to redouble her trials for a new magical line of defense.

Even if her barrier was destroyed—or the Archduke found his own way through it—she wouldn't make any invasion easy. How many of his own soldiers would the man truly sacrifice for the sake of her uncle's cause?

If only Yaroslav would be sensible enough to accept defeat, for once in his petulant, entitled, and malicious life . . .

But then, the Archduke wasn't to blame for her uncle's continued survival. *That* was Saskia's doing. If she'd had the strength of will to murder him when she'd had the chance, none of this would be a problem now.

Snarling at the memory of her own weakness, Saskia set herself to the tedious work of cleaning her equipment. Even after the failure of her intended activation, the contents of the cauldron were still too magically unbalanced to be dumped into any ordinary cesspit or compost heap—and if any lingering remains were left to curdle in the cauldron, her next experiment might well be her last.

Fortunately, Saskia had been handling volatile magical materials ever since she was a child—and in those twelve halcyon years after she'd escaped her uncle's grip, before she'd been forced to take the throne, she had learned under Mrs. Haglitz's unyielding eye how to scrub and polish anything to perfection. She was just cleaning off her hands, using a special mixture she'd created to neutralize all types of magical residue, when a familiar knock sounded on the door.

"It's safe to come in, Morlokk!" she called, without removing her hands from the bowl of cleansing cream. "You won't be set on fire or transformed into a toad by anything in here now."

"You reassure me greatly, Your Majesty." Her majordomo stepped into the cavernous room, holding a sheaf of papers in his giant hands. As a girl, when she'd first escaped into his and Mrs. Haglitz's protection, the strength of those hands had promised safety; now, she looked at the pile of letters he held and winced even before he intoned, "These are for you."

"Was today's post really so urgent that you had to bring it down?" Avoiding his gaze, Saskia turned to wipe off her hands with a clean towel and unfastened her laboratory apron without haste. "You know I already went through Mirjana's most urgent messages this morning . . ."

"These are *invitations*," Morlokk said, "and they've been piling up for the past week while everyone's waited to find out whether you will be hosting your own seasonal celebration." He set them down with painstaking care on the newly cleaned table before her. "You will need to make a final decision today, if Mrs. Haglitz is to make all of her own festive preparations in time."

Sighing, Saskia hung up her apron and turned back to accept her doom. Creamy sheaves of stationery embossed with gold leaf competed for the role of the most swooping handwriting and the most flowery artificial scents. Her nostrils flared with distaste as she lifted up the first, which smelled overwhelmingly of out-of-season jasmine. "Does no one even remember that we're still at war? Why is everyone suddenly in the mood for feasting and celebrations?"

Morlokk's tone was patient. "If you'll recall, we are approaching the time of Winter's Turning, and you are Kitvaria's crowned queen. Do you really not remember your own parents' annual celebrations?"

At his words, a wholly different combination of scents filled her memory: beeswax candles everywhere, used for the priests' rituals, along with tangy smoke from the many pine fires, cinnamon from the vats of hot mulled wine, and the most comforting fragrance of all: her mother's vanilla perfume pressing against her skin as Saskia was hugged good night.

She'd been sent to bed at the usual time, of course, but she still remembered lying awake, vibrating with curiosity as the festivities continued late into the night below her in the grand, crowded ballroom of their city palace. How could she possibly fall asleep when wild, vibrant strings and woodwinds were sending joyful, mischievous invitations whirling up through the floorboards of her room? Everyone else was so happy downstairs: her parents the smiling, circulating hosts, beloved by everyone around them, and even her uncle for once smiling, a favored guest . . .

Her fingers clenched the delicate envelope, crumpling it against her palm. "I don't have time for that sort of frivolity this year. You know I have real work and a kingdom to defend."

"Unfortunately, your First Minister . . . well." Morlokk coughed into one big fist. "I believe she may have anticipated your response." Reaching into the pocket of his silk waistcoat with his free hand, he removed a small, sealed note covered in Mirjana's all-too-familiar script and handed it to her between the tips of his thumb and forefinger. "She instructed me to give this to you if you refused to accept any of these invitations."

Gritting her teeth, Saskia accepted the unwanted offering. This note, at least, didn't smell of anything but the plain black ink that Mirjana always used . . . but that was the only comfort she could take as she ripped open the seal.

There was no greeting at the top of the terse note, only a warning and an ultimatum:

> *The high priest and nobles will all rebel if the Queen of*
> *Kitvaria doesn't publicly honor the gods and her highest*
> *nobility at this traditional time of year. Choose which*
> *noble house to honor by accepting their invitation or*
> *follow in your own parents' footsteps and announce that*
> *you'll host a celebration in the capital, as every one of*
> *your ancestors did.*
>　　*Now.*

Darkness take the gods and everybody else, too. Squeezing her eyes together, Saskia took a long, steadying breath.

She had only attended one royal Winter's Turning celebration since her parents' murder, but she would never forget the avid gazes of the gathered priests and invited nobles as she'd stood against her will behind her uncle, flanked by guards on either side. Yaroslav had held the crown for almost two years by then; everyone had heard his gloating explanations, spread far and wide by journalists and gossips alike. He had *had* to step in to save the kingdom from the taint of her parents' "failed" rule: a taint that, according to her loving uncle, had come to toxic fruition in her blood.

Looking back, she supposed he must have felt some pressure to produce her in public and prove that she was still alive; even the most conservative and anti-magic of Kitvaria's nobles might well have been moved to protest the idea of executing a child.

But not one of them had stepped forward at that celebration to show the slightest sympathy for her. Only their gazes had clung to her like sticky sugar-water, hungrily awaiting any thrilling displays of the dangerous, uncontrollable magic that had corrupted her from birth—a sad result, her uncle claimed, of all the time her mother had imprudently spent consorting with the nonhuman creatures of their realm in her years of ethnographic work.

Who knew what concoctions the old queen might have ingested among those creatures, or which scandalous, inhuman rituals she might have participated in while carrying her child? None of the nobles had any means of knowing, that much was true . . . but they'd all been more than ready to believe the delicious worst.

Nausea rippled through Saskia at the memory. She swallowed hard.

It wasn't enough. Bile rose inexorably through her chest.

The sound of all those whispering voices in her ears . . . her mother's perfume and her uncle's smile . . .

Saskia's head spun as she dropped the note to the table. "I need air!"

Morlokk's sorrowful sigh sounded behind her, but he didn't even try to stop her as she fled.

Saskia managed to hold the nausea in check as she thundered up every flight of the narrow, curving staircase, one hand resting against the cold stone wall to keep her balance. At least the exertion helped; by the time she reached the final door, at the very top of the south tower, she was almost too breathless to even feel the stinging bile in her throat.

Her magic turned the lock by instinct before she could reach out with her fingers. Panting, she stumbled out onto the roof of the south tower—and lunged immediately for the battlements.

As she hung over them, she sucked in deep, desperate breaths of the sharp, cold air, her fingers clenched convulsively around the ancient stone. When she finally felt safe enough to straighten, she tipped her head back, shutting her eyes against the too-bright sunlight and letting the wind sweep across her face and neck to flay and cleanse her.

Distantly, she was aware of the rush of wings through the air as her crows swirled in a protective cloud around her, summoned by the intensity of her emotions and her magic. She didn't need to listen to their angry, worried caws to know they were ready to soar into battle by her side . . . but this time, none of them could help.

For once, she couldn't fight at all.

Saskia might not have attended a royal Winter's Turning since she'd fled her uncle's clutches, but even she knew they were more than simple entertainments; they were, along with Spring's Ease, the public rituals that led the calendar for the whole kingdom.

She'd agreed to take the crown for the sake of everyone she loved. She wouldn't fail them now. But she was no longer the child who had innocently believed in the loyalty of her parents' guests. If she were to walk into that grand ballroom again, with all the same people in attendance, this time wearing the crown upon her head—to feel every gaze turn upon her and know that, even as they bowed or curtseyed, they were all secretly wondering how many of her uncle's sickening claims about her were true . . .

"Your Majesty?"

That hadn't been the voice of a crow. Saskia startled hard, and the flock around her squawked a cacophony of protest at the disruption. At first, she couldn't make out anything past the shifting black chaos that surrounded her; then she realized that the new arrival was cloaked in black as well.

Darkness take it. The last person she could ever allow to witness any vulnerability on her part was a dark wizard; they were constantly jousting for power and only too ready to dismiss her authority.

She released the battlements as if they'd burned her. "What do you want?"

"Ah . . . nothing, actually. I only . . ." He broke off, clearing his throat. "Forgive me for the interruption. I'm afraid my crow—that is, *your* crow, but it's spent the last week keeping me company, no doubt on your command—anyway, it was quite insistent that I follow it up here. I assumed that you were summoning me."

Saskia's shoulders sagged with her long sigh. "Not this time." She swept out her right hand in a slow, gentle half-circle, prompting the crows between them to flap out of the way. With the rest of the flock no longer blocking her view, she could see young Oskar balancing on the dark wizard's shoulder with his roughly textured black claws wrapped around the thick fabric of—what was his name?—oh, yes, *Fabian's* cloak. "All of the crows were summoned," she explained wearily. "Oskar must have decided to bring you along as his chosen companion."

"I . . . see." There was a long moment of silence as they regarded each other, for the first time, in the open air. Sunlight glinted off the silver mask, hiding his expression, while his hooded figure cast a long shadow across stone.

Saskia was only too horribly aware of her own disordered appearance. The purple kerchief she'd worn over her hair in the laboratory had managed to stay—just barely—on her head, but at least half of her hair seemed to have come loose from the topknot underneath. Now it lay in careless, untidy hanks across the shoulders and back of her plainest gown. Thank the gods, she'd at least remembered to remove her stained apron before she'd fled the laboratory and her responsibilities.

She could almost hear Mirjana's voice in her ears: "*In the* civilized *world, it's essential to present a polished and fashionable appearance at all times . . .*"

"*Does* he think of me as his companion?" Those weren't words she'd expected to hear from a dark wizard, but they broke through Saskia's bitter memories like a cool wind sweeping through them. Fabian had tilted his hooded head to peer at the crow still perched on his shoulder, and his voice was full of doubt.

Saskia snorted a laugh. "Why else would he have left the flock behind to hang on your sleeve for the past week?"

"But . . ." He raised his left hand towards his occupied shoulder, and Oskar let out an impatient grunt, leaning forward for the petting that was clearly his due. "You really didn't ask him to stay with me?"

"Why would I?" Baffled but reluctantly charmed, she watched Oskar nuzzle demandingly against Fabian's bare hand . . . which appeared to be smeared with large splotches of ink. "Have you been suffering from those ink spills you were worried about? I thought your special pen would have arrived by now."

"Oh, it did." The wizard's fingers curled against Oskar's beak as his voice lowered in unmistakable embarrassment. "It's only . . . a bit messy to fill. That is, it was the first time. But it will soon become easier! This is a different model than I had tried before."

At the price that Morlokk had reported paying for that *fountain pen*, it was a wonder Fabian had ever had the chance to try other models with his previous employers. Still, Saskia found her lips curving in amusement as she shook her head at him. "Is my entire library of magic covered in puddles of ink now?"

"Absolutely not!" His shoulders stiffened to attention. "Would you care to come and see what I've done so far?"

A refusal rose immediately in Saskia's throat.

As she'd told Morlokk, she had work to do. More than that: she had an excruciatingly painful letter to write, acquiescing to her First Minister's demand. No matter what Mirjana had said in that note, they both knew that Saskia had no idea how to choose among noble houses in order to accept one of their invitations. No, she would have to give in to necessity and tradition and host her own event as queen . . .

But *not* in the grand ballroom of her parents' city palace.

Here on the top of her tallest tower, the wind was cool, the air was clear, and she could finally think again. So, she knew exactly what to do—and could allow herself to take a moment to relax before she outraged everyone by doing it.

"I have a feast to plan," she told the dark wizard. "We'll be hosting Winter's Turning here at Kadaric Castle this year . . .

"But I'm certain I can come down and visit the library for a few minutes first."

9

Felix had never been more grateful for his concealing mask and cloak than when he'd emerged onto the tower roof to find Queen Saskia with her head thrown back, lips parted, a cloud of crows swirling around her and energy crackling so intensely through the air that it lifted the hair at the back of his neck.

It should have been a terrifying sight: the wicked witch of Kitvaria no doubt summoning a terrible storm of magic to rain down upon her enemies.

But it had stopped his breath for quite a different reason.

Even now, as he led her down through the

twisting staircase towards the library he'd rashly invited her to visit, Felix couldn't escape the memory of her pale throat tipped back and exposed to the sunlight; her dark lashes swept against her cheek as she squeezed her eyes shut in some extreme of emotion or magical effort. It was beyond rash to even allow himself to imagine that pose in a different context; in the months of numbness since Emmeline had died, he'd barely even remembered the existence of such matters. And yet . . .

Intimacy with his wife and oldest friend had always been a comfort. It might have begun as a requirement upon their arranged wedding, but over the four years of their marriage, it had become a shared game that brought them both pleasure, escape, and relief—as familiar, as gentle, and as achingly sweet as Emmeline herself.

That hot, hungry bolt that had lanced through him in the open air above the tower felt as different as a lightning storm, ready to break him open.

"*Caw!*" With a firm rap against Felix's hood, the crow on his shoulder—Oskar—alerted him to the open doorway he'd almost walked past.

Felix rapidly corrected course, not only by physically turning his body but by turning his mind to the challenge ahead.

It would be impossible to describe the current state of Queen Saskia's library as *impressive*. Still, as they stepped into the vast room together, he braced himself to give a calm accounting of his work. He'd learned long ago to bear disdain; he wouldn't flinch now, no matter how scathing her assessment.

He wasn't prepared, though, for the small sound of wonder that came from her throat. "You've done so much!"

"I have?" Blinking, he looked around the densely cluttered chamber, trying to see it through fresh eyes.

A solid fifth of the curving, floor-to-ceiling bookcases on the lower level of the circular library had been emptied in his quest to sort and catalogue the random selection of handwritten and printed spellbooks, history books, scientific journals, newspaper clippings, printed ballads, and more. Now, dozens of carefully balanced stacks of books and paper filled the room, even covering the faded chairs and couches where the three dangerous queens had awaited him a week ago. Six neat stacks of his own lists sat on the study table, next to a tightly sealed inkwell and his single, precious pen; a single cleared walkway led to that table from the door.

"I am aware," he said, "that it's nowhere near ready for your use—"

"But you've made real progress." She swept out one hand in demonstration, and the crows who'd clustered behind her took that as their signal to flock past her and race towards the empty bookcases, squabbling and pecking at each other in competition for the best perches on the shelves. Felix's own crow abandoned him to join the race with a noisy squawk, and the queen had to raise her voice to continue. "It's clear that there's a purpose behind all of these divisions, and that's something no one has been able to say about this library since my uncle stole it eighteen years ago."

She was, nigh-on miraculously, pleased; she might be far less so when she actually realized how simplistic his categorizations so far had been, with no true education in wizardry to ground them. Still, Felix forced himself to say, "I can explain how I've divided them, if you'd like to oversee my work."

"Must I?" She grimaced. "I have more than enough work of my own, at the moment. What I *would* like, though"—she slid him a glance that looked shockingly mischievous—"is a look at that expensive pen of yours, after hearing so much about it."

The dangerous heat that had been simmering inside his gut ever since he'd stepped onto the tower roof leapt into flame at that look.

His wits, which had kept him alive at court for years, shut it back down *immediately*. The Witch Queen of Kitvaria might be capable of many previously-unheard-of things, but she was certainly not interested in flirting with him now. Perhaps she was in a whimsical mood, after whatever great spell she'd been working on the roof; more worryingly, she might be hinting at real anger over the cost of his acquisition.

Either way, he had to remember that she was infinitely more likely to kill him than to kiss him, no matter what his treacherously reawakening body might wish him to imagine. So, as Felix walked past her to the study table, he set his teeth against the impact of that inevitable storm of energy and kept his body as firmly under control as if he'd been performing his usual role at court under Count von Hertzendorff's icy oversight.

It was hard not to give in to enthusiasm, though, as the noise of the crows finally began to subside and he lifted the wonderful new pen to show her. "You see? There's not a single spot of ink visible from the outside—and no spatters on your books or papers, either."

"Hmm." She leaned closer to examine it, dark eyes narrowing with a focus as sharp as any blade. "Is that wood encasing the ink? Won't it seep through?"

"No, it's ebonite—a new type of rubber, only developed a few years ago. It looks like wood, but it's far more secure. Feel for yourself." He laid the pen in her cupped right hand and breathed through the prickling sensation of her skin brushing against his.

The distraction vanished with a splash of icy cold as he recognized the marks of old scars on her fingers and palms. "Are those burns?"

There were *so many* of them. Had someone hurt her—*marked* her—on purpose?

Poisonous old memories stirred from the compartments where he'd locked them long ago . . .

But she shook her head dismissively. "Oh, those are just from my laboratory work." Closing her fingers around the pen, she held it up to study from different angles. "Which end do you write with?"

"Here." Shoving down the old memories before they could take over, he showed her how to remove the cap, revealing a shining steel nib, far sturdier than any hand-carved quill. "Would you care to give it a try?" He scooped up a spare piece of paper and laid it on a bare section of the table before her. "You have to use a slightly different angle than you would ordinarily, but . . . no, that's not quite—here, let me show you."

Stepping up behind her, he wrapped his right hand gently around hers. He redirected her movements to draw a firm line of ink, his attention wholly focused on instruction as he leaned over her to help—until her warm, lush body shifted with a deep breath against his cloak.

He froze, every sense flaming into life with sudden, excruciating awareness.

Heat radiated from the skin of her hand, held in his clasp. And where their bodies met, her smaller, curving figure surrounded by his . . .

Elva protect me!

Felix took a lunging step backwards as he released her, opening up a good two feet of space between them. Still bent over the table, she remained unmoving for a silent moment as his heartbeat thundered against his chest. Then she set her jaw more firmly and scribbled a firm, decisive line of script across the blank paper.

He didn't even try to read what she wrote. He was too busy remembering how to breathe.

When she finally straightened, she was wearing a cool and distant look, as if in her mind, she'd already retreated far away from the importunate overtures of her second-rate librarian and his cluttered library.

"Forgive my impertinence," Felix said hoarsely. "I—"

"There is nothing to forgive." She closed the pen and handed it back to him, her smile perfunctory. "I see your point. This *is* a better way to write—and I appreciate your help as well as your care for my books." Her gaze passed smoothly over him to land on the stack of manuscripts on the floor beside him, still waiting to be categorized, and her mask of politeness abruptly fell away. "*Wait.* That pile, there . . . are they—?"

Felix shifted aside to clear the way. "They are all in the same handwriting, but I haven't found any name for the author. I haven't yet had the chance to look through them carefully enough to decide on a grouping. They seem to cover a wide variety of topics, so I suppose I could distribute them throughout the library, but . . ."

"*Don't.*" The word rang with power as she reached out to brush the tips of her fingers across the bound manuscript at the top. Was he imagining the way her fingers trembled as they touched it? "These were my mother's notes."

"Your *mother?*" Felix's eyebrows rose behind his mask. "I didn't know Kitvaria had had a scholar—or a wizard—for a queen."

"Oh, she wasn't raised to rule. She never even wanted to." The current queen's lips twisted as she spoke, her fingers resting lightly on the stack of manuscripts. "Mama planned to spend her life adventuring and exploring different cultures across the world . . . but when my father fell in love with her, he promised full support of her work—an equal partnership. So she stayed in one kingdom after all and devoted herself to ethnography within it. She used to visit for months at a time with all the different groups around the kingdom, trolls and goblins and humans alike, and she learned from every one of them."

Felix tried to imagine either of his impeccably proper parents— much less the Count—choosing to abandon the glittering court in Estaviel City to camp in the woods with trolls. It was impossible. "Your father didn't mind?"

"Well, he missed her, of course, but he knew she was doing important work. He always said her studies, when they were finally collated and published, would revolutionize the way that humans across the continent thought about their neighbors. And of course, she used to take me with her on her expeditions whenever she could, although . . ." Queen Saskia's voice drifted off.

"Although?" Felix prompted, a moment later.

This time, the curve of her mouth held only bitterness. "*Although* my uncle always made a great, noisy fuss in front of everyone about the so-called dangers of those journeys. At the time, I was young and idiotic enough to think him actually concerned for my sake."

Felix's chest constricted at the pain in her voice. His own childhood had been upturned when his parents had died. How much worse would it have been if they'd been murdered . . . and by a relative he'd loved?

It took all of his self-control not to step forward and offer comfort. He knew, though, that the powerful Witch Queen of Kitvaria wouldn't welcome it from him—especially not so soon after he'd outrageously laid his hands upon her person. So, he kept his lips sealed behind his mask and his feet firmly planted on the floor as he watched her battle to regain her self-control.

Giving herself a brisk shake, Queen Saskia released her mother's notes and stepped backwards. "Regardless, I'm glad you've kept these all together. You are still missing one important volume, though, from the full collection."

"I am?" Felix frowned. "I haven't spotted any others in that handwriting yet."

"That would be because I hid the final book." She crossed the library floor in long strides that sent her autumn-leaf-colored skirts swishing around her determined figure and brought a wave of crows rising from their perches to fly after her. They circled her, cawing, cooing, and rattling with interest, as she dropped to her knees behind the elaborately carved and curling staircase that led from the first level of the library to the mezzanine and second level of shelves above. "If I can still find the hinge, after all these years . . . *aha!*"

Something clicked inside the base of the staircase. As Felix watched with fascination, a miniature door popped open in the smoothly grained wood, which he could have sworn to be unbroken. Queen Saskia reached deep inside the hidden compartment and drew out a thick sheaf of papers, bound only by a crimson ribbon.

"*Good.*" She let out the word on a sigh and gave the top sheet an absent-minded stroke with one thumb before rising to her feet.

Her crows swarmed eagerly to investigate both the treasure in her hands and the open compartment from which it had come, while Felix hung back, waiting.

"I couldn't save my parents," Queen Saskia said, "but I managed to protect this one legacy, at least: my mother's greatest work. She wanted to reframe how every wizard is taught, to take account not only of our human traditions but of other species' magical traditions as well. It was to be an entirely new approach to wizardry . . . and if my uncle's men had ever come across it, he would have ordered it burned as a matter of principle."

Her lips compressed for a long moment as she looked down at the papers, ignoring the pestering of her crows. When she looked back up, her dark gaze met Felix's through the eyeholes of his mask and pierced him with its intensity. "I hadn't planned to take this from its hiding place until this library was fully in order again and my temporary librarian's post was ended. But, Sinistro . . ." She tilted her chin in a nod of respect. "I think I may trust you with it, after all."

It wasn't heat, this time, but a helpless lurch of tenderness that Felix felt as he reached forward to carefully take the papers from her hands. "I will be honored to keep your mother's words safe," he murmured, bowing deeply.

He meant that promise with all his heart . . . but guilt twisted in his gut as he straightened, examining the manuscript in his hands and realizing exactly what it might mean for him.

A New Approach to Wizardry, from First Principles Onwards, read the title in a confident, looping script that was only slightly faded by the years.

Queen Saskia had truly honored him with her trust . . . but she'd also handed him exactly what he needed in order to successfully continue to deceive her.

10

Saskia was certainly *not* avoiding her own librarian. That would be absurd. She was simply extraordinarily busy.

Not only did she still have innumerable challenges to surmount in her fight to erect new magical defenses against the Archduke of Estarion's scheming, she was currently weighed down with the nightmare of an upcoming feast to both plan and dread—especially as it had somehow transformed, in the hands of Mirjana and Mrs. Haglitz, into a horrifying two-day event with an ever-growing number of gossiping guests desperate to invade her privacy.

So if she hadn't happened to stop in the

library again over the past week, that did *not* in any way imply that she was, of all insulting notions, *nervous*. Wicked queens, obviously, did not suffer from nerves.

. . . And they absolutely did not ever find themselves shivering at the mere memory of that moment of arcing, snapping heat and physical connection and that sudden, breathtaking sense of possibility and—

"Saskia, darling?" Across the small, round table where they sat in a sunny parlor with green walls covered in ivy chains and scented blossoms, Lorelei batted long, glittering eyelashes with exaggerated concern. "Have we broken you with too much social chatting?"

Saskia landed back in the present with a thud. "Don't be ridiculous," she said flatly and downed the rest of her insipidly flowery tea in one lukewarm gulp. "I am perfectly fine. *Obviously*."

On her other side, Ailana cleared her throat delicately. "Then . . . are you by any chance ready to answer the question we just asked?"

The question . . . Saskia rapidly searched her memory. *Oh, yes*. That was what had sent her down that chain of distraction in the first place. "No progress whatsoever," she reported.

If there *had* been any progress in his hunt for a useful spell of finding, her librarian would have sent a note to alert her. He certainly wouldn't have waited in hope for her to visit him—not after the way he'd leapt away from her with unhidden horror the last time they'd met, repulsed by the same accidental intimacy that had sparked wildfire through her own skin.

The vivid memory of that frustration lent her words a harsh edge. "Are you absolutely certain that the Archduke is missing? According to my First Minister, he seems to be astonishingly busy conspiring against me from his palace in Estaviel City at the moment."

"Oh, he doesn't need to be at the palace to do that," Ailana murmured. "He may well have left plans with his Chief Minister—

or be keeping up a private means of communication as he quests after something else in secret."

"*Quests?*" Saskia snorted, setting down her empty teacup with a clatter. "He's hardly a knight of old. That man has no interest in anyone but the most proper and civilized of his fellow nobles, and there's no need for him to visit any of them in secret. All *he's* ever sought to do is stomp on the weak and impress the Emperor with his bigotry."

"Which is all the more reason to be concerned about any secret quests on his part." Ailana took a small, ladylike sip of her own tea and then dabbed her lips neatly with one of Lorelei's lacy napkins.

"But—my goodness!—do you really mean to say that your infamous network of spies still haven't had any luck, after all this time?" Lorelei blinked at Ailana with exaggerated shock . . . and incorrigible mischief lurking in her tone. "From the desperate way they're whispered about by everyone, I'd thought they must be infallible!"

Ailana's face tightened. "My spies are *excellent,* as they proved when they informed me of his departure, which has been kept so deep a secret from the rest of the continent. But even the best intelligence workers can hardly be expected to work miracles— and as far as any of them can tell, Archduke Felix simply vanished from sight. The only glimpse anyone *may* have had came from a farmer who thought he *might* have spotted the Archduke riding towards the Kitvarian border. That is why I came hoping to learn . . ."

She turned expectantly to Saskia. "How many of your spies have you sent out looking for him so far?"

Saskia closed her eyes for a brief moment of deep exasperation. "Unlike your web of informants, Ailana, I don't work for you—and I didn't come here to deliver a report and be judged upon it by either of you." She'd had quite enough of *that* from her First Minister, who had breezily—and with maddening condescension—dismissed Saskia's single attempt to broach the idea of the Archduke being anywhere in the world but his own palace.

Saskia had voluntarily arrived at this meeting at Lorelei's home in Balravia only because she'd known that the others would foist themselves upon her again if she didn't accept their invitation. The last thing her castle needed was even more visitors.

"Oh, but we're all working together, you know," Lorelei said soothingly. "We'll *all* suffer if the Empire continues to expand."

"But you're not the ones it has its eyes on at the moment." Saskia's shoulders sagged as exhaustion nearly overcame her. "You wouldn't believe how cunning the Archduke has been with some of his latest overtures. He hasn't only been reaching out to Emperor Otto for help. My First Minister told me yesterday that he's sent messengers to all of the other free kingdoms around me, trying to negotiate for any of them to allow his armies to march across their land, undisputed, to approach Kitvaria from a magically unprotected border."

"Those *bastards!*" The word hissed out between Lorelei's teeth as her eyes glowed a sudden, shimmering gold. "Are they actually considering it?"

"According to Mir—to my First Minister, the Archduke is claiming that it's his sworn duty as Kitvaria's loyal ally to reclaim the throne for my 'poor' uncle . . . despite the fact that Yaroslav stole it from my parents in the first place."

That was why she was so exhausted that she'd struggled to focus on their conversation today. Braving the wrath of Mrs. Haglitz, she'd stayed up all night in her laboratory, fighting to conceive of any possible way that she could extend her current magical border to at least five times its current size . . . despite the fact that the epic endeavor of creating such a massive shield in the first place had nearly drained her of life as well as magic.

That part didn't matter now. All that mattered was that she finish this meeting and find a way home to get it *done*.

But her colleagues weren't moving on so quickly. "Those rotting bastards!" Fresh shoots of ivy curled upwards in furious tendrils around Lorelei's gauzy chiffon skirts. "They're so narrow-minded, they'll support *anyone* over a woman, won't they? They're all so godsdamned threatened by the notion of any of us daring to hold a throne without a man to 'guide' us . . ."

Ailana's voice was measured but as cold as ice. "Anyone who allows an Imperial army to cross into their lands, regardless of the excuses given, will find it surprisingly difficult to be rid of that army again afterwards. I wonder how many of your neighbors have thought through those consequences over the clink of Estarion's gold and the charm of the Archduke's messengers?"

The Queen of Nornne tapped one elegant brown finger against the rim of her own teacup as her eyes narrowed. "I wonder . . . when was the last time you met any of your neighboring rulers in person, Saskia?"

Saskia gave an irritable shrug. "Oh, decades ago, I'm sure. I was a child the last time there was a continental conference that brought everyone together."

"I remember that conference well." A dangerous sliver of blueish-white frost formed across the deep brown of Ailana's eyes. It disappeared a moment later as she gave a firm nod. "Well, clearly, you'll have to invite them all to your Winter's Turning feast this year. It's the only way to handle this properly."

"*What?*" Saskia cringed. "Surely they'll have their own feasts to host, won't they?"

"They'll make time to attend yours if they know what's good for them," Ailana said. "Trust me to make certain of that."

"And you won't have to worry about any danger coming with them, because we'll both be there, too, of course," Lorelei added. "The Queens of Villainy stand together against all enemies from now on."

"I . . . thank you?" Saskia looked longingly at the empty pot of tea that sat before her. Surely there must have been *some* caffeine hidden amongst that colorful pile of scented leaves and blossoms, if only she could feel it in time to sort through all the different potential consequences of this political jousting. For once, she truly wished that Mirjana was by her side to interpret social cues for her.

No troll coffee or First Minister magically appeared to save her, though, so she was left to make her own decision. "Of course you're both welcome to attend my Winter's Turning," she said on a sigh. Why not? Mirjana had sent out endless invitations. Within a few weeks, seemingly *everyone* would be packed inside Saskia's home, whether she liked it or not. "But I haven't actually asked for your assistance, so—"

"You don't need to. Not anymore." Ailana's voice was implacable as she caught Saskia's gaze and held it. "We all know what it is to stand alone as a ruler. None of us can survive that way forever. That's why we've chosen to form this alliance and work together from now on."

"And trust me, darling, it's no trouble! I *love* parties. I cannot wait to see that lovely library of yours again . . . not to mention your lovely new librarian." Lorelei winked. "Have you managed to get any glimpses behind his mask yet? I'd find out everything I could about him, if I were you. I did like the look of his shoulders under that cloak—and it is *so* satisfying to ferret out all of a man's secrets, isn't it?"

"Lorelei . . ." Ailana let out a tightly controlled sigh.

Saskia sealed her lips shut and ignored that impertinent line of questioning entirely.

Unfortunately, she couldn't ignore her own conclusions. If the other queens could help protect more of her borders, then she had a responsibility, as Queen of Kitvaria, to accept that assistance . . . at least until she found a way to protect them on her own.

Still, she refused to be the weak link in their alliance. So, she would have to pay another visit to her librarian after all and hope that he'd forgotten that piercing moment when attraction had nearly overcome her good sense for the first time in nearly a decade.

She found him, of course, in the library. He sat at the study table in the center of the room when she entered, so engrossed in his note-taking that he didn't even look up from his work. For the first time since they'd met, his all-concealing silver mask was shoved halfway up his face, angled to give him an unobstructed view of whatever he was studying so closely . . . *ah.*

He was reading her mother's final manuscript and taking intent notes on it with the famous fountain pen.

Was he shocked and outraged by the words laid out before him? Saskia drew closer, stepping softly across the carpeted floor. She had chosen to trust him with it in a moment of unusual optimism, and yet . . .

Memories curled through her like seeping smoke.

So many dark wizards in the past had been outraged by the radical nature of her mother's work. She still vividly recalled one employee of her parents who'd been reduced to such ranting fury by its inherent challenge to the notion of human superiority in magic—in his view, its attempt to *taint* future human magic by "corrupting" it with inhuman influences—that he'd had to be escorted out of the castle under armed guard.

Saskia had recognized him, only a few months later, among the traitorous wizards who'd aided her uncle in his coup. So, she held her breath now as she stepped stealthily closer to observe her own dark wizard . . . and to hunt for any signs of would-be betrayal.

There was no fury in what she could glimpse of his expression. True, his face was tilted away from her towards his work and shadowed by the propped-up mask, but still, she could make out the clean lines of his jaw and the sensitive lips that were pressed together now in unmistakable concentration.

His long fingers lifted a sheet of her mother's manuscript with every bit as much painstaking care as she had seen him use before to stroke her crows' rough feathers. Was this man ever less than gentle?

His lips parted absentmindedly a moment later, the tip of his tongue flicking out to moisten them. He set down the fountain pen and carefully fastened its cap before lifting a half-full coffee cup from the table to sip. He continued to read intently . . .

But Oskar, who had been napping on the table in a pile of rumpled black feathers beside the cup, woke at the disruption and let out a sleepy call of welcome to Saskia.

"Mmmf!" The wizard lurched forward in shock, slapping his free hand to his lips to protect the papers before him from any spattering of coffee. He jerked again as his hand met bare skin. Then he slid his long fingers in a rush across his lean, close-shaven cheek and yanked the silver mask back down over his chin with a groan of frustration.

"Truly, you have nothing to fear." Giving up on silence, Saskia strode the rest of the way to his table, following a path laid out between new piles of books. "I'm sure your appearance is terribly dire and desperate, but I believe I might just survive the sight without swooning pathetically."

Any other dark wizard would have been incensed at such teasing; *her* dark wizard let out a half laugh that sounded pained. "I can't imagine you swooning over anything. But, Your Majesty . . ."

"I saw nothing you wouldn't wish to reveal," she assured him. Was there, after all, something more to his insistence on masking than the usual dark wizardly mystique? A scar of some sort, perhaps, that made him self-conscious? She gentled her tone as she continued, "You really ought to have some way to safely eat and drink, though, if you are to spend so many of your waking hours

at work. Now that I've seen the lower half of your face and survived it, do you think you could possibly shift to a half-mask?"

"Ah . . ." He paused, taking a breath that looked strained.
"Perhaps. Yes. If . . . that is, you really saw nothing that alarmed
you?"

He sounded so earnestly concerned that Saskia had to bite
back a rueful snort. If he had any notion of the sights she'd witnessed across her life, he wouldn't have the slightest fear that
she'd be disconcerted by the angular line of his freshly shaven
jaw, much less by any old scars he might be hiding . . . although
she might well find herself lying awake tonight, haunted by the
memory of those sensitive lips parted as if for a kiss.

Focus! It was her lack of sleep distracting her, no more. Snapping back to full alertness, she lifted her chin and did her best to
erase all thoughts of his lips from her mind. "You're perfectly safe
to reveal the lower half of your face from now on," she promised,
"but I actually came here with a different purpose."

"Of course." He rose from his seat on the other side of the
table. "Do you wish a progress report on your library as a whole?
Or were you thinking particularly of your mother's own work?
I've been considering various different options for how best to
arrange the binding of her final manuscript, but—"

"I'll leave all of that in your good hands." Her voice was firm,
but the final knot of tension in her chest released in a rush of
warmth and relief at his words. Clearly, he hadn't been so shocked
or infuriated by her mother's manuscript that she would have to
fear losing his loyalty after all.

Truly, she should have known better, by now, than ever to
have worried. A dark wizard who spoke to everyone he met with
kindness, respected all the nonhuman members of her staff,
and looked after her most impudent young crow with unfailing
sweetness was a rare and precious find. She wouldn't let herself
forget that again.

"Actually," she said, "I came here to ask about a different type of progress. Have you had any luck so far in finding any useful spells for locating a lost stranger as you've sorted through the library?"

"*Ah.*" There was a surprisingly awkward moment of silence. Saskia couldn't see the wizard's expression behind the silver mask, but every line of his body seemed to have rigidified within his cloak. "I have been carefully looking out for such a spell," he finally said, his voice strained, "but unfortunately . . ."

Click. The door to the library opened behind Saskia, and the sound of Morlokk's polite throat-clearing cut off the wizard's next words.

"Ahem. Apologies, Your Majesty and Sinistro, but I must inform you both that an unexpected visitor has arrived."

"Oh, no, really?" Saskia groaned as she turned to face her majordomo. Hadn't she done more than enough socializing for one day? "Surely you and Mrs. Haglitz can deal with whoever it is. Unless it's really unavoidably urgent . . ."

"I'm afraid this particular visitor cannot be handled by either of us." The weary crags in Morlokk's face seemed to deepen with his words. "You see, a second dark wizard has come in answer to Your Majesty's advertisement, and he is *quite* insistent on remaining even though we both informed him that you'd already filled the post. In fact . . ."

Morlokk let out a heavy sigh as he finished. "He claims that you have been tricked into making a terrible mistake."

11

Felix's throat closed as Morlokk's sonorous voice filled the room. *"You have been tricked . . ."*

He had known from the beginning that he couldn't maintain his disguise forever. Somehow, though, he still hadn't been prepared for this moment to come.

He grasped hold of the table before him as his gaze clung to Queen Saskia's vividly compelling face, waiting for fury to overtake her first shock.

He didn't have to wait for long. As her dark eyes flared wide, she let out a growl that reverberated through his bones. "Of all the arrogant, insulting, *unbelievably* disrespectful bastards—!"

Oskar leapt to his clawed feet on the table between them, his feathered head bobbing as he frantically scanned the room for enemies.

"Your Majesty"—Felix fought to keep his voice steady—"if you wish for my resignation—"

"Don't be absurd," she snapped, without even glancing back at him. "*You* can stay here in peace. I'm going to go teach *that* dark wizard a lesson about who makes the decisions in this castle!"

With a sweep of her heavy velvet skirts, she stormed for the door. Morlokk held it open for her, bowing his head politely. The majordomo bowed again to Felix, with scrupulous courtesy, before following his mistress out of the library . . . but Felix felt the speculation in that thoughtful gaze like cold water splashing over any deceptive sense of relief.

He was moving across the crowded library floor an instant later, stepping swiftly around the piled stacks of books and papers while Oskar shook out his feathers and then flew to overtake him. Still, the library antechamber was empty by the time they reached it. Felix turned in place on the thick, patterned carpet, trying to guess which staircase and direction the others would have taken. "Elva guide me . . ."

"*Caw!*" Oskar zoomed ahead to the farther door—and with no better guidance, Felix followed after.

The queen must have been summoning her crows again. More and more joined them in the steep stairwell as they descended, some of the birds squeezing in through arrow slits in the stone walls while others circled down from higher levels of the castle. Most of them shot past him immediately, unburdened by the long, tangling cloak that Felix wore or the unevenness of the old steps. Oskar, at least, stayed carefully within reach, but even he cawed with impatience.

"Trust me," Felix muttered, lifting the folds of his cloak higher, "*I* would prefer to move more quickly, as well."

Every instinct warned him that he needed to witness what was about to happen, so that he could prepare himself to flee . . . or simply give himself up to execution.

No. Even as that thought flicked through his mind, he dismissed it.

Felix had been desperate enough when he'd first arrived at Kadaric Castle to accept his own death as a risk worth taking. Coming here had been only the final toss of a coin before his surrender to inevitability.

In the past few weeks, though, he had felt what it was to control his own life for the first time. He had worked harder than ever before, and something deep inside him had been awakened by it: a free-flowing source of energy and even, astonishingly, confidence. Felix might be wearing a disguise, but beneath that silver mask and in Queen Saskia's library, he felt more keenly *himself* than ever before.

He refused to give that up without a fight, so he scooped up the folds of his long cloak to *run.*

Together, he and Oskar emerged a minute later at the back of the grand hall where Queen Saskia had received him upon his first arrival. This time, Felix found himself standing in the shadows behind that massive, intimidating throne, shielded not only by Morlokk's looming figure, planted as ever by the queen's side, but also by the cloud of angry crows that circled the throne while the queen's voice and waves of furious energy rolled through the air like thunder.

". . . If you think you can intimidate my staff and imagine your own desires to be more important than my time—!"

"Your Majesty is clearly overwrought." The deep male voice that spoke oozed with a false sympathy that made Felix grit his teeth behind his mask even before he heard the next words. "Of course no one could blame you for being so overburdened by your new responsibilities that you couldn't wait for my arrival or tell the difference between a mere dark wizard and a *master.* But *I* am here now to solve your problems, and I am more than ready to take matters in hand."

Ready to take matters in hand . . . Felix had to hold back a flinch at the too-familiar words. He'd been only eight years old when he'd heard them uttered by the Count, in Felix's first introduction to his new regent. Even then—having been sheltered all his eight years of life beforehand—he'd sensed the cold warning that accompanied that statement, and he'd felt a shudder of foreboding.

Queen Saskia showed no such fear. "So you think I have no notion of how to judge a wizard—or make my own decisions?" Her voice was no longer raging. Instead, it had dropped to a near purr that made Felix's skin prickle.

The other man chuckled, an oily sound. "Oh, Your Majesty. What training has any witch ever had in true wizardry? Of course you all have your own sorts of powers, enough to frighten the nonmagical, but if you think *I* couldn't overcome them with a thought, *well* . . ."

Felix couldn't see the derogatory gesture the man used to finish his statement, but he didn't need to. As Oskar flew to join the rest of the flock behind the queen, Felix stalked forward to take his own place, unhidden, between Queen Saskia and Morlokk, anger burning through his fear. "You will *not* threaten the queen."

He wasn't a child anymore. He wouldn't stand back and quietly allow a new tyrant to take over yet another home.

Beside him, Morlokk let out a barely audible sigh . . .

But the dark wizard who stood before them let out a chortle that sounded like delight. "Aha! My so-called *competition*." The cloaked figure stood disrespectfully close to the stone steps that led up to the throne, his broad chest puffed out beneath the folds of his black coverings in an attitude that Felix had seen far too many times before from his own brutal brother-in-law just before an act of physical retribution.

The wizard's hood tilted with a moment of inspection . . . and then, following his muttered command, balls of fire appeared above the beefy palms of both hands, sizzling with heat. He grinned fiercely below a crimson half-mask decorated with bumpy, painted scales to mimic a dragon of old. "Excellent! A duel will settle this matter for good. Your Majesty, prepare to have your decision made for you."

Oh, gods. Felix froze in place. What had he been thinking, to challenge this man? He couldn't win a duel of magic. He barely even understood the basic structures of the spells that he'd been studying . . . and he knew for a fact that he had no magic of his own that could bring any of those spells to life.

Every young child in the Empire who possessed a spark of magic was carefully identified by the inspections mandated by law, regardless of their station in life. They were then removed from their families for lifelong training in Gilded Wizardry. Needless to say, Felix had passed—or, rather, failed—that early inspection without a hitch.

And yet . . .

I've dealt with pain before. And he couldn't—no, *wouldn't*—dishonor his employer by turning and running now. So Felix said with perfect calm, "Her Majesty makes her own decisions. I merely follow her instructions—whatever they may be. If she wishes me to fight against you . . ."

"*Her Majesty,*" Queen Saskia snapped, "wishes to be finished with all of this nonsense! Fabian, you may return to the library. I appreciate your loyalty, but there was no need for you to attend this meeting. And as for *you*—!"

Her voice abruptly cut off as a crack of thunderous sound filled the room. Balls of fire hurtled through the air from the dark wizard's suddenly outflung hands, aimed directly at Felix.

Oskar screamed with rage from his place behind the queen.

Felix set his jaw and *braced* . . .

And the balls imploded, half a foot from his chest, with a popping sound that sucked half the air from the room and left his ears ringing.

"*How dare you?*" Queen Saskia's whole figure seemed to lengthen, shadows multiplying behind her, as she surged to her feet. Her crown of bones cast an unnaturally growing shadow that swept across half the hall as she loomed furiously over the bulky, cloaked figure. In that moment, she was every bit the terrifying dark queen of rumor and legend. "Every member of staff in this castle is under *my* protection. You think you can attack any of them before my eyes and *survive the encounter?*"

"Now, Your Majesty." The wizard had the sense to fall back a step on the flagstones, raising his now-empty hands. Still, his tone was heavily indulgent. "No one expects you to understand the rituals and rules of dark wizardry, but—"

"I don't need to understand *anything*," Queen Saskia spat, "except that *you've* just made a mistake that every other dark wizard will whisper about in horror for decades—because *no one* will be allowed to hurt any of my people again!"

She flung up her arms. Her crows flocked behind and above her, like an oncoming storm of retribution. All the prickling energy in the room gathered around her, just waiting to be released . . .

And waves of almost unbearable heat swept through Felix's cloaked body as he watched, his mouth falling open behind his mask.

It was incredible.

She was incredible.

He wanted to fall to his knees before her in awe . . .

So he was almost too late in stepping forward. "Wait!" he blurted, his voice hoarse.

Queen Saskia's sigh was full of aggravation as she stilled with her hands still raised in preparation. As she turned towards Felix, the dark wizard before them opened his mouth to speak; an impatient flick of one finger on her part sealed his lips shut.

"What now?" she demanded.

"Your Majesty, you don't need to kill him for my sake!" Felix swallowed hard over his dry throat, fighting to think clearly through the overwhelming, intoxicating waves of power that emanated from her towering figure. "He didn't actually succeed in hurting me. And—"

"But he dared to *try*," she snarled. "You may have a surprisingly soft heart, Sinistro, but I do not—and I *will not* allow any challenge to the safety of my staff *or* to my authority to go unpunished. A message must and will be sent to any other dark wizard who thinks he can attack my staff to overrule my own decisions."

"But how can he send that message if he's dead?"

The wizard turned to lunge for the door—but another flick of the queen's finger fixed his feet irresistibly to the ground.

"Ahem." On Felix's other side, Morlokk cleared his throat, reaching out with one giant hand for Felix's arm. "Perhaps, Sinistro, you should withdraw, so you needn't disturb yourself by witnessing . . ."

"*Wait*," Felix repeated, stepping closer to the throne.

The dark wizard was physically convulsing, now, with his efforts to escape; furious whimpers and what might have been attempted spells sounded through his sealed lips, but they didn't concern Felix at this point. All his focus was on the woman who stood above him, vibrating with power and fury. She was the most dangerous, beautiful, astonishing creature he had ever met . . . and she was ready to kill to protect *him*.

It would be suicidally foolish to even dream of running up those stone steps to kiss her with all the exhilarating passion she inspired. But he kept his gaze fixed steadily on hers as her power thickened in the air, and he said, "Men like him would only take his death at your hands as a challenge. They'd want to prove their own strength to all their peers by being the one who could finally beat you."

Magical or not, he knew that type of aggression only too well after growing up with Radomir at his side.

Queen Saskia's dark eyes narrowed as she held his gaze. "What would *you* decide for me, then?" she finally asked, her voice poisonously sweet.

Felix didn't miss the lurking danger in the air. But he'd spent too many years of his life in suffocated silence. He already cared too much, too foolishly, to stay silent now. So he said firmly, "Your decisions are your own, always—but if you would choose to accept my advice this one time? *Humiliation. That's* what they fear most of all. If you make this one a laughingstock, others will be far less tempted to put themselves in the same situation."

For a long moment, Queen Saskia didn't answer. Then her lips curved into a gleamingly satisfied smirk that made Felix suck in a breath—and fight down an entirely inappropriate physical reaction.

"I will accept your good advice this time, Sinistro." Turning back to the desperately wiggling dark wizard, she tilted her head, considering him for a moment. Then she said, "You wanted to be the most powerful person in this castle, didn't you?"

She dropped her hands, with the finality of a theatre curtain falling at the end of an opera . . .

And where the dark wizard had stood, a tiny mouse squeaked desperately as it wriggled out of the abandoned cloak.

She sneered down at him with magnificent disdain. "I would suggest that you take your leave now, while you still can, because my crows are nearly ready for their midday meal."

The flock behind her cawed their enthusiastic agreement. The mouse turned and fled for the door . . .

And Felix let out a long breath as he accepted the inescapable truth:

His life might not be at risk from Kitvaria's witch queen at this moment, but his heart was in grave danger of being lost to her forever.

12

If only Saskia could turn every irritation into a mouse, life would be so much easier. Unfortunately, by the time sunset began to settle around Kadaric Castle that evening, she had to throw down her laboratory notebook in defeat. She simply couldn't concentrate on her work, and the fault lay in her own misbehaving nerves, which hadn't settled since that absurd confrontation earlier.

The sight of those fireballs flying towards Fabian's chest . . .

Of course she'd stopped them in time. But what if she hadn't been there?

Ugh, what nonsense! As a dark wizard

himself, Fabian was no doubt more than able to protect himself. He would have handled that attack perfectly well without her if Saskia hadn't happened to leap into action first.

And yet . . .

She was on her feet, sprinting for the library, the moment she finally realized the only possible reason for that maddening compulsion she'd been fighting against for hours: *of course*, this was all about protecting her kingdom. What else could it be?

"I need that finding spell sooner rather than later," she explained five minutes later as she strode into the library, only slightly out of breath. "But I don't want you to rush through your own important cataloguing work, so I'll simply join in the hunt myself."

His eyebrows—nearly as dark as her own—rose high over the thin black half-mask he'd swapped into since their last meeting. Then he bowed, graceful as ever, behind the long study table. "As you wish, Your Majesty."

"I *do* wish." She firmly swept up a pile of ancient newspapers and manuscripts from the chair across from him. "It's the only practical solution."

It certainly was. Practically speaking, with every minute she spent in Fabian's quiet, steady presence, she felt calmer and more certain of herself. It might have been decades since she'd practiced any written spellwork, but she was perfectly capable of poring over these old books now. By the time half an hour had passed, she was even enjoying the process.

"Good gods. Take a look at this!" Breaking the studious silence, she pushed a leather-bound book across the table and pointed at the lengthy personal ruminations that its writer had included before the ingredients of his spell. "Do you think he actually expected anyone to take that advice seriously? Or was it all an elaborate practical joke?"

Fabian's head tilted as he read . . . and then, frowning, he read it again. "That hardly seems typical preparation for spellwork."

"Much less hygienic *or* good for a caster's concentration!"

She snorted. "I'll wager he was cackling as he wrote that up, just waiting for all those poor, earnest young wizards to plaster themselves with mud and dance around naked in the cold for his amusement. He certainly never did that himself!"

For the first time since they'd met, Saskia saw Fabian's lips quirk into a near smile. His gaze rose to meet hers. "One can only hope not," he said gravely.

Grinning, Saskia retrieved the book and then settled back into her chair for another hour of work and companionship. Neither of them was lucky enough to actually find the right spell in that hour, but they did take turns pointing out different ones of interest . . . and by the time she left, feeling warm and relaxed, she could hardly remember all the agitation that she'd felt earlier that day.

As she returned to the library again and again for snatched hours of work across the days, she had the satisfaction of seeing her serious librarian grow more and more comfortable in her company. Of course, he never treated her with less than full respect—but as time went on, he stopped holding himself so carefully in her presence, as if no longer awaiting a sudden threat. Better yet, more and more often, he allowed her to glimpse the dry humor that lurked behind his grave façade.

And oh, that façade was so pretty . . .

No!

Saskia caught herself, a week after her first visit, gazing not at the crumbling spellbook in her hands but at Fabian's all too appealing profile, half-masked, with every angle lit by the warm glow of a nearby gas lamp. Snapping her gaze back to the pages spread before her, she bit back a groan of self-reproof.

The man had literally *leapt away* from her the last time they'd been close enough to touch, as if she were the monster her uncle had always named her. She might have earned his trust since then, but that didn't mean he wanted more than friendship between them—and he certainly didn't need her gaping at him like a lovestruck fool when he was trying to work!

Setting her teeth together, she forced her gaze back to the book on her lap and the task it represented . . . which was, *of course*, the only reason she was here in the library in the first place.

Her fingers tightened on the delicate pages.

"Your Majesty?" Fabian lowered his own book, frowning. "Is anything amiss?"

"Nothing at all." She stretched her lips in a forced smile. "Just . . . reminding myself of my own restrictions."

His eyebrows rose.

To Saskia's intense relief, the door opened before he could speak again.

"*Here* you both are." Mrs. Haglitz nodded firmly as she surged inside to set down an overloaded tray on the table between them, nudging books and manuscripts out of the way. "Now, mind you don't waste any mouthfuls of this good meal, either of you! And as for you, Your Majesty . . ." She pinned a minatory glance on Saskia, who tried not to squirm beneath it. "I'll expect to see you soon afterwards."

. . . For even more Winter's Turning preparations. "Of course." Saskia sighed, her shoulders slumping.

At least worrying over *that* impending nightmare would provide some distraction from her too-tempting librarian. And as the festival approached, every day of the next three weeks did indeed prove increasingly full of interruptions. Letters flooded in from dignitaries across the continent, all too willingly accepting her invitations but following up each and every acceptance with lists of special requests and petty demands that she couldn't have cared less about.

Fortunately, Mrs. Haglitz and Morlokk were both on hand to help siphon off the nonsense. Even more fortunately, Saskia now had a second refuge in the castle to which she could retreat when everything became too much.

She could even tell herself, truthfully, that she was there to do important work.

As it came to her final few hours of freedom before the hordes descended on Kadaric Castle, she turned her steps once more towards that quiet, soothing refuge . . . and carefully tamped down the bubbling excitement that wanted to rise with every step that took her closer to her librarian.

"Your Majesty." As she stepped into the room, Fabian turned from the bookshelf he'd been emptying, his lips curving beneath his half-mask. "You've found time to help me again today?"

"Yes, *please*." Saskia collapsed into the comfortably faded and nicely cushioned chair that had appeared in her usual place and become her favorite seat over the past dozen sessions. The moment those cushions met her back, she felt the knotted muscles in her shoulders finally begin to ease. "Bring me books, any books. As long as they have nothing to do with seating arrangements, I can take on anything!"

"Ah." His teeth glinted as his small smile widened into a grin. "You *have* been undergoing torture. I understand."

"I'm not certain that you could." As he walked towards her, his arms full of books and his dark cloak sweeping gracefully against the floor, she forced herself to ignore the teasingly exposed hollows of his cheeks under that half-mask . . . and the way an unexpected dimple had appeared along with that rare, mischievous grin. "Until the last two days, even I couldn't have imagined that *anyone* could possibly care so deeply about where they sat at supper. If it were up to me, I'd send them all up to their rooms to feast on their own and impress themselves with their own consequence."

"Mm." His soft-looking lips briefly compressed, that fascinating dimple deepening. "I'm not sure how many diplomatic negotiations could be managed with no casual conversations or meetings allowed."

"That's what everyone keeps on telling me." Accepting the small pile of books that he handed her, Saskia set all but one of them onto the table in the spot that he'd kept clear for her.

"Perhaps I should simply hire an actress to wear a mask and crown for the whole of tonight while I stay in here and get much more enjoyable work done."

It was astonishing just how expressive a man could be with half of his face covered. His rueful amusement was unmistakable. "Even from the very little that you've told me, I doubt your First Minister would approve."

"She might prefer it, actually." Saskia sighed as the tension began inexorably to creep back into her tightening shoulders. Mirjana would be arriving soon after lunch, in plenty of time to cast her eye over all of the preparations . . . and over Saskia, too.

Flipping open the book in her lap, she resigned herself to her fate. "I can't stay for long this time, I'm afraid. I've been informed that it will be a many-hour-long process to transform my appearance into the image of a proper, respectable, and *civilized* ruler."

"Why in the world would you wish to do that?" Fabian halted a foot away from his own seat, staring down at her. "Forgive me, Your Majesty, but that seems entirely counterproductive."

"Really?" Frowning, she closed the book. "How so? The whole purpose of this dire house party is to convince the nobles of Kitvaria, as well as my fellow rulers across the continent, that they've nothing to fear from me. I need to prove I can fit in perfectly among them."

"Are you certain?" His eyebrows rose. "I would have thought . . ."

The silence dragged out between them as she waited for him to complete the statement.

Finally, he shook his head with a grimace. "Never mind. You wouldn't want my opinion. I was only ever trained in diplomacy, not in governance."

"Then you had far more relevant training than I ever did—and I would welcome your opinion." She would also dearly love to know how he'd come by any such training as a young dark wizard.

Obviously, he must have been raised outside the Empire. That was the only way any natural magic-worker could remain free of abduction by the Imperial state and escape a bleak childhood of "training"—or rather, forced indoctrination—in one of the cold Gilded Academies.

But had he been born into a noble house in one of those free kingdoms, expected to ignore his own magical powers for the sake of an exalted family name? Or . . . ?

Her musings—familiar by now, after weeks of drifting, casual conversations and increasingly hungry curiosity—were cut off by his low sigh as he sat down across from her. Setting his hands flat on the table between them, he said, "In my own personal opinion . . . no, wait. I have a question. Did you become the Queen of Kitvaria by being courteous and civilized in your appearance and your diplomatic approach?"

Saskia snorted, which was all the answer merited by such a foolish question.

"And did you successfully defend your kingdom from invasion afterwards by respectable, civilized means?"

"You know I didn't."

"What I *know* is that you've successfully created a reputation that's caused everyone on the continent to whisper your name in fear . . . and the High General of Estarion to withdraw his forces from your border. So I wonder: Is that reputation something you truly *wish* to change at this point?"

Narrowing her eyes, Saskia considered the point that he was making. "Everyone agreed that my scandalous powers were required to seize the throne from my uncle, for the sake of the kingdom. Now that he's gone and I wear the crown, though, the highest Kitvarian nobles and a fair few of my fellow rulers find the thought of a wicked queen . . . unnerving."

His head tilted. "And do you wish to settle their nerves by hiding your powers and your nature now? I don't believe the queens of Nornne and Balravia have ever taken that particular approach."

No, they hadn't, had they? Lorelei and Ailana would laugh in the faces of anyone who asked either of them to *fit in* and hide their strength.

Saskia's fingers rattled against the book in her lap as she considered the other two so-called Queens of Villainy . . . and her own First Minister.

Unlike any of them, Mirjana *was* accustomed to being liked and admired. She had been raised in the Kitvarian court, the daughter of an influential family with diplomatic and marital links all across the continent. She knew down to her bones how to fit in with respectable continental society, and she'd been attempting to pass on that knowledge to Saskia from the first time they'd met.

If Saskia followed Mirjana's advice tonight, she might well manage to pass as an ordinary queen for an evening, to put both her nobles and her fellow rulers at ease.

And yet, when it came down to her own deepest needs . . .

The last time Saskia had walked into a royal Winter's Turning, she'd been surrounded by guests who openly wondered whether her innocent appearance was a mere disguise. Did she really want to repeat that experience?

No.

In her castle, in her own damned kingdom, she would hold her head high and leave them no room to even *consider* that question.

"You give excellent advice as always, Sinistro." She set the book she'd held, unread, upon the table. "If you'll excuse me, I need to change a good many of the last month's careful plans *very quickly*—and see that the skulls are set back up along our entry path in good time for boiling."

Hours later, Felix was so immersed in the late queen's magical primer that he entirely failed to notice either the knock that sounded on the library door or the soft thuds of footsteps against the carpeted floor. It was only when a throat was cleared, pointedly, just before his study table that he finally realized he was no longer alone.

"Your Ma—oh!" He'd become so accustomed, by now, to Queen Saskia's regular visits that it took him a moment to wipe the foolishly delighted smile from his face. He blinked as he reconciled his instinctive, hopeful expectation with the actual figure who loomed over him . . . and then he gave a respectful nod, capping the fountain pen that he'd been using to take notes. "Mr. Morlokk, good evening. May I be of service to you?"

"Not to me, Sinistro, but to the queen." Morlokk's rumbling voice was as calm as ever, but as the majordomo's gaze passed over the open manuscript, Felix had to fight a guilty impulse to cover it from view.

There should be nothing suspicious about Her Majesty's librarian choosing to study her mother's work, and yet his hand still twitched towards the elegantly inked title of the closest page ("A Structuring of Spells"). He clenched his fingers into a fist to stop it . . .

And Morlokk's gaze missed nothing.

Felix carefully relaxed the muscles in his jaw beneath his half-mask. At moments like this, he missed the security of the full silver mask, difficult though it had made eating and drinking across each day. "I am always happy to be of service to the queen. Is there a particular book she'd like me to send her, to show any of her guests? Or . . . ?"

"She requires *you*," Morlokk said gravely. "She sent me with the reminder that you are not to spend this night sequestered while the rest of the castle celebrates the season. You are invited and expected to join in with the official festivities."

"What?" Felix's eyebrows soared at the very idea. To step out into a castle crowded with nobles and rulers from across the continent, every one of whom would have seen his image regularly printed in newspapers even if he *hadn't* met them personally . . .

Worse yet, if any other dark wizards were visiting, they might well want to test his supposed powers in another of those "rituals of dark wizardry" that the last one had treated him to.

Felix gathered his wits with an effort. "That will not be necessary, I assure you. I am a member of staff, hardly an invited guest. I am more than happy to continue my work here, so—"

"Invited *and expected*," Morlokk repeated, with the infinite patience and inevitability of the rock-encrusted mountains he resembled. "Her Majesty made it clear that no refusal was to be tolerated, no matter how admirable your work ethic. You will present yourself tonight for the opening festivities, the Winter's Turning ritual, and the feast of celebration afterwards."

"But . . . *why?*" Felix asked helplessly. He waved at the towering stacks of books around him. "Surely, Her Majesty would be better served by—"

"Her Majesty's decisions are not ours to question." Morlokk's tone was as unruffled as ever, even as he spoke the most blatant untruth Felix had heard in weeks.

He hadn't yet put together all of the intriguing details of Queen Saskia's past, but she clearly treasured every one of her staff members—and Morlokk and Mrs. Haglitz, in particular, held more influence over the dangerous Queen of Kitvaria than anyone else in the world.

Still, her majordomo continued implacably, "We must all serve the queen according to her wishes. Before her guests leave tomorrow, she wishes her dark wizard to be witnessed by everyone."

"I see." Felix expelled a long sigh of surrender. *Of course.* Had he really spent so long away from court that he'd forgotten the very basics of diplomacy? Or was it his hopelessly growing infatuation that had sent his thoughts racing so recklessly elsewhere?

Naturally, Saskia didn't care whether or not he, himself, happened to be at her party; she was only making a show of force by ensuring that all of her invited guests saw the ominous *dark wizard* in her employ. That was simple good sense.

He'd spent all of his life, until the last few weeks, being a walking and talking political symbol; he could certainly manage another evening of it for her sake.

No more excuses. Felix straightened his shoulders as he rose to his feet.

Whether she knew it or not, Queen Saskia had saved his life more than once already. He wouldn't hide from any challenges that she asked of him now, no matter how many risks he had to run.

Without looking away from Morlokk, he reached out to slip the page of notes he'd been making into the folds of his cloak. "If you'll excuse me," he said, "I must prepare myself." He wouldn't leave any too-revealing notes behind—and he couldn't possibly step into that gathering without a mask that covered his entire face.

Oskar had flapped off some time ago—probably in hopes of stealing extra food from the bustling kitchens deep below—but Felix had no doubt that the crow would be back soon to find him. With luck, the loyal creature would be just as willing to follow Felix tonight into this kind of battle as he had been four weeks ago, when it was magic they had faced together.

With a full mask, a black cloak, and a sinister bird on his shoulder, even Felix could look the very image of a dark wizard . . . couldn't he?

"Sinistro." Morlokk gave him a respectful bow before stepping aside to clear his way.

Felix expected the majordomo to follow after him. But when he looked back from the library doorway a moment later, he found Morlokk frowning thoughtfully down at the study table and the manuscript Felix had left unguarded behind him.

Felix's stomach curdled with unmistakable warning.

13

A roar of sound emanated from inside the castle's grand ballroom that night—the sound of Saskia's invited guests and would-be judges. Outside, where she stood in a private passageway that no guests could access, everything was safe and still except for the swirls of eerily cool vapors that swept out from underneath the closed ballroom doors, teasing and tickling at Saskia's feet in their tight green snakeskin shoes.

They were trying to tug her forward, where everyone knew she had to go.

Her crown of bones sat heavy on her head. Her rings bit into her fingers as she clenched them into fists. She could already smell the too-familiar scents of pine and cinnamon in the air.

You're the queen. You're not a child anymore.

There's nothing to be afraid of.

Beside her, Mirjana let out a weary sigh as she tried—and failed—to sidestep the curling vapors. "Are you really sure that all these theatrics were necessary? If we had simply held with tradition and our original plan to *soothe* your guests with comfortable familiarity . . ."

For once, Saskia was grateful for an instinctive snap of irritation. It broke her out of the haze of remembered panic. "The original plan wouldn't have worked," she said firmly, drawing her first unobstructed breath since she'd seen the waiting ballroom doors. "If we want our glorious neighbors *not* to roll over like pet dogs before the Archduke, the last thing any of them ought to be allowed to think is that I am either harmless or predictable. No, we need them to be even more frightened of me than they are greedy for Estarion's gold."

"As you say." Mirjana's voice was tight. "You are the queen, and I must follow your lead. Just know that I stand ready to help if needed."

The pinched expression on her lovely face showed exactly what she was thinking . . . but Saskia lifted her chin, remembering a different face, earlier that day, and steady brown eyes that had never once lacked faith in her.

"Well, then." With a twitch of one finger, she sent the heavy doors swinging open into a raucously loud, dark world of smoke and magic and swarming, untrustworthy visitors. "Let us begin this royal celebration."

Felix had acted as either guest or host for well over a decade's worth of glittering Winter Festivals in the Serafin Empire. Not a single one of them had prepared him for the cavernous world he stepped into along with a chattering stream of guests.

Open fires shot crackling, pine-scented flames high into the darkness from half a dozen giant pits placed around Queen Saskia's vast ballroom. The crystal chandeliers remained unlit, but white vapors, glowing with impossible, internal light, curled high around the rafters and snaked through the air around the shadowy forms of the gathered guests—who alternately flinched or shrieked with delighted horror whenever the cool tendrils brushed against their skin or hair.

Lilting violins and wind instruments played a hauntingly compelling tune, but Felix could make out neither the musicians nor even the direction from which their music came—and a clawed goblin's hand tugged at the sleeve of Felix's cloak just as he was turning in place to search for them.

"All well, Sinistro?" Krakk, one of the goblin footmen, grinned up at Felix, his bulbous green eyes reflecting red from the light of the ribbon of vapor that hovered just above him. On his other hand, he balanced a massive tray of steaming clay mugs with seeming effortlessness. "A drink to warm your gut for Winter's Turning?"

The scent of hot, cinnamon-laced wine wafted upwards, and Felix took a deep, appreciative breath. Even Oskar, half-asleep against Felix's neck after his earlier feasting in the kitchens, lifted his head with a small purr of interest. Still . . .

"Not just now, thank you," Felix said on a regretful exhalation. "Perhaps, if there's any left when this is all over . . ."

Even in this darkness, he couldn't risk removing his mask for an instant. He'd recognized too many of the other guests already.

There, surrounded by his own crowd of noble followers, stood the blond young King Hravic of Prsklava, downing a large cup of mulled wine. After drinking a similar amount of the sparkling champagne at the Winter's Festival he'd attended in Estaviel City last year, Hravic had cornered Felix with a long and rambling, unstoppable rant about the injustice of his latest mistress's complaints. It was an experience Felix wouldn't have cared to repeat even if he didn't have to fear recognition.

Speaking of recognition . . . in a neighboring group, familiar, tinkling laughter made Felix take a quick, instinctive step in the opposite direction. *That* particular Kitvarian countess, then in her thirties and quite intoxicated, had spent one Winter's Festival when Felix was seventeen making a determined and public attempt at seduction, with no interest in his polite but firm refusals. He'd managed to escape before matters could shift from deeply uncomfortable to desperate, but even now, the sound of Countess Markovic's laughter made his jaw tighten.

The crowd before him was thickly shifting, but as Felix hesitated, waiting for an empty space to clear, Oskar rose to his feet on Felix's shoulder and shook out his feathers with a grumpy mutter. Spreading his wings wide, he emitted an arrogant demand so loud, it cut off every conversation around them.

"Cawww!"

Felix winced at the ringing in his ears. Still, it worked: other guests first glanced their way out of curiosity, then shifted swiftly aside with widened eyes and respectful nods. Apparently, the sight of Felix's tall, hooded, and masked figure, carrying a crow for a herald, was more than ominous enough to clear his path.

It was a very different reception than he'd experienced at any previous Winter Festivals . . . and as his initial trepidation faded away, he had to guiltily admit that he enjoyed it.

Slowly and deliberately, he paced forward, allowing the cloak and the mask to do their shadowy work for him without a single word being spoken. Oskar's strong claws gripped his shoulder in support as the bird cocked his head back and forth, clicking loud warnings at everyone who dared step too close.

In truth, Felix had no particular path or direction in mind—but if he had to, he would be perfectly content to spend the next few hours simply circling the room in menacing silence. At least no smiling and nodding was required of him for once; no listening attentively to pompous strangers without ever letting the interest fade from his expression . . . or having the slightest power to effect any of the political favors they craved.

In this moment of liberation, Felix could almost believe himself to be an actual dark wizard, too powerful and dangerous ever to be constrained by social standards.

Ha! He made a rueful face behind his mask at the thought . . .

And then a familiar, prickling energy shot sudden sparks across his skin. It rolled forward in an irrepressible tidal wave from the far corner of the room.

Felix spun instinctively around to meet it.

The lilting music screamed its way upwards in an arpeggio of warning—and then vanished as double doors flung themselves open. Those doors hit the stone walls with resounding *thuds* that echoed through the crowded darkness. The whole ballroom fell abruptly silent, every gaze fixed on that corner entrance, where bright light from the outer passageway highlighted two women.

Both of them were strikingly attractive. Both of them, to Felix's surprise, were familiar. But only one of them made the breath stop in Felix's throat as he took an involuntary step forward, every sense exulting in that intoxicating energy.

Queen Saskia's pitch-black hair was unbound beneath her towering crown of bones, and it spilled in thick, shining waves across the silk shoulders of her absinthe-green gown. Felix swallowed hard as his gaze traced the bodice, cut far deeper than any he'd seen on her before. Cradled within the shadows of that dangerously alluring V was a large, egg-shaped pendant that pulsated with shifting purple and black overtones.

Gemstones flashed on Queen Saskia's fingers as she stepped forward and swept out her arms. Crows and bats rose up behind her like a storm cloud, answering her call. When she opened her crimson-painted lips, her voice sounded—magnified tenfold—from every angle of the ballroom:

"*Welcome to Winter's Turning.*"

She dropped her hands . . . and the storm broke over her, black clouds shooting towards the two high chandeliers, making guests duck and gasp in their wake.

Every candle in those chandeliers lit with a triumphant blaze, flooding the gathered crowd with light as the Witch Queen of Kitvaria stalked into the ballroom that now unmistakably belonged to *her*.

Grinning fiercely behind his mask, Felix started forward to pay tribute to his queen.

Saskia breathed deeply and slowly through her nose as she stepped into the ballroom, fighting down the waves of tremors that wanted to accompany those too-familiar scents of pine and cinnamon. Guests were already surging towards her, their gazes avid and their hands outstretched.

Her mask of confidence felt so thin, it was about to shatter—but Mirjana stepped up to her side, lips stretched into a wide, warm smile, and smoothly took control. "Ah, Your Majesty King Franz. How glad we are to see you here! My beloved ruler and I were both ecstatic when we received your kind acceptance."

Ha! Saskia thought. Smiling thinly, she inclined her chin in a minimal nod of greeting.

The grey-haired and medal-bedecked King of Visknya aimed a toothy grin directly at her bosom. "Finally! It's a pleasure to meet my nearest neighbor at last. We've all been eagerly awaiting our invitations to visit ever since you took the throne."

"Oh, really?" Saskia's smile tightened. "I'd heard that you were busy entertaining visitors of your own from the Archduke of Estarion, on behalf of my uncle."

"Ahem!" Clearing her throat hastily, Mirjana closed her hand around Saskia's elbow and turned her towards the next hovering visitor. "And of course, Your Majesty must remember the Countess Markovic."

"Oh, I certainly remember *you*." The Countess, a buxom woman in her early forties with a pink taffeta gown, curtsied deeply as she aimed a melting look up at Saskia through her long eyelashes. "You always looked so sweet whenever you appeared at court, Your Majesty. Of course, I *never* believed any of those terrible rumors! And I told all of my friends not to believe them either. We always hoped that you would become our queen one day, no matter *what* we had to pretend to survive at court until then."

Straightening, she shifted closer in an overpowering cloud of jasmine perfume and reached out to put one soft, clinging hand on Saskia's shoulder. "Now that you're finally on the throne where you've always belonged, you must tell me everything about yourself—all the *real* stories of your childhood and where you so mysteriously disappeared off to all those years ago."

"Must I? Really?" Saskia's voice was dry enough to catch flame.

"Perhaps later," Mirjana said firmly, and reached for her elbow once again.

Saskia took a quick step backwards, freeing herself from both of them. "Thank you, First Minister . . . and Countess. I believe I can stand upright without assistance."

"Naturally." Mirjana bared her teeth in a smile, her eyes glittering dangerously as the Countess gasped beside her in wordless, fluttering offense. "I am only here as your humble servant. Do tell me which introduction you would prefer to have next?"

Damn it, there was an order of precedence to this nonsense, too, wasn't there? And if she got it wrong while Mirjana was watching and just *waiting* for her to make an embarrassing mistake that proved how inept she really was on her own . . .

A sparkling shower of rainbow lights erupted in the center of the ballroom. For the first time ever, Saskia's body went limp with relief at the sight.

"Actually . . ." Her lips curved into a satisfied smile. "I don't believe I'll need any introductions for our latest honored arrivals."

"Who in the world—?" Mirjana began.

Her words cut off with a snap as the sparkles faded. *No one in this ballroom could mistake the new arrivals for anyone but exactly who they were:* the *other* most notorious queens on the continent.

"Saskia, darling!" Lorelei caroled as she slid off the back of her riding gryphon.

In honor of the festival tonight, Bluebell was clad in a diamond-and-sapphire-encrusted riding saddle and harness. His golden eyes blazed above his fearsomely hooked beak as he pawed the ballroom floor with big, clawed lion's paws. Still, even his magnificence paled into the background as Lorelei danced forward, her gown a shimmering, swirling, magical creation that tricked the eye into thinking it a different color with every instant. "We are *so* sorry to be late! Did you miss us horribly until now?"

"I don't recall discussing either of those invitations!" Mirjana hissed into Saskia's ear.

"Why would we need to discuss them?" Saskia whispered back, even more quietly. "They are my closest allies."

"They *are?*"

Ailana's cool voice interrupted them, rolling like rime across the room. "How delightful it is to see so many good friends gathered together." Still sitting atop her own gryphon, Frost, she slowly turned her gaze across the room . . . and an icy wind followed in its path. Royals and nobles alike shivered as the taste of snow suddenly filled the ballroom, but the Queen of Nornne's expression remained perfectly calm. "Of course, *all* the free kingdoms of this continent must stand together against the Empire's threat. I'm certain everyone here must understand that simple fact by now."

"Oh, I'm sure no one would ever be stupid enough to make Saskia, Ailana, and me *all* furious through any petty betrayals,"

Lorelei said gaily to the gathered, frozen crowd. "We may not have the overinflated muscles of the Emperor's famous Golden Beacon, but we Queens of Villainy are a force to be reckoned with! And unlike that hopeless prig of a general, *we* simply have no limits." She winked lavishly . . . and for one overwhelming moment, the scent of rotting, putrid vegetation filled the room. Even Saskia had to fight the urge to gag.

A second later, the overpowering stench was gone, and Lorelei clapped her hands together as warmth returned once more to the air. "But we're not here for boring political conversations, are we? We're here to celebrate Winter's Turning! Saskia, darling, *when* will the official ritual finally begin, so that we can all move on to feasting and dancing?"

Mirjana stepped forward, almost visibly drawing a mantle of authority around her. This time, though, Saskia didn't need anyone to speak on her behalf. "The ritual will begin soon," she told Lorelei and the listening crowd. "I need only greet my guests before we all begin. Would you and Ailana care to join me?"

As Lorelei beamed and Ailana nodded in gracious assent, goblin footmen hurried across the room to take the gryphons' harnesses and lead them away to a quiet corner of the castle. No doubt the beasts would cause havoc there with their constant dueling . . . but this time, Saskia was too glad for their riders' presence to begrudge a few broken plates or furnishings.

Lorelei and Ailana might be even more dangerous than their steeds—and every bit as focused on their own, more subtle jostling for dominance—but tonight, she wouldn't begrudge them any of their scheming, either. With her fellow queens by her side, the idea of fearing petty judgements from anyone else in this ballroom suddenly felt beyond absurd.

"Your Majesty." Mirjana's whisper in her ear tightened her spine with new tension. "If I might have a private word with you, outside the ballroom?"

Oh, Saskia knew exactly how that *private word* would go.

"I couldn't possibly leave my honored guests," she said with as much regretful sincerity as she could muster. "However . . ." Her gaze swept the wide-eyed group around her—and landed on the one hooded and faceless figure whom she had come to wholeheartedly trust.

"Sinistro." She let out the word on a sigh of relief. "Mirjana, may I present my new librarian? Fabian will escort you on your own social rounds tonight, while I look forward to our conversation later. You'll still stand by my side for the ritual itself?"

Mirjana's jaw tightened in a way that heralded a scathing and soul-withering lecture to come . . . but under the scrutiny of so many watchful eyes, she lowered her head in a respectful nod. "Of course." She left with a sweep of skirts to take the cloaked arm that Fabian held out to her with perfect, courtly grace . . .

And when Saskia turned back to her guests, this time, she felt no fear.

14

Felix grimaced behind his mask as the First Minister of Kitvaria took his arm . . . not, unfortunately, for the first time.

He had never made the connection, in his conversations with Queen Saskia, between the "Mirjana" she referred to and the smoothly confident daughter of a previous Kitvarian ambassador to the Estarian court. Back then, he'd known her only under her surname, but he'd met her at least half a dozen times at various gatherings. They'd never spoken of any matter deeper than the latest opera or weather pattern, but he'd always seen the sharp intelligence in her eyes . . . and if he'd even imagined the possibility of serving as her escort, he would have fled the moment he recognized Mirjana's face.

Fortunately, he still remembered the courtly rules that had been drilled into him ever since he'd learned to speak. "Your Eminence." As he drew her smoothly across the floor, moving at just the right speed for polite bows and greetings, he asked, "Was your journey from the capital comfortable?"

"Out to these godsforsaken mountains? On *those* roads?" She let out a sharp laugh that was entirely unlike the diplomatic tones she'd spoken in before.

The mask shadowed his vision too much to allow a sidelong glance, but he felt the sudden tightening of her grip on his arm. When he turned, he found her looking across the crowd at Queen Saskia and her companions, her expression unreadable. She looked back too soon, catching his gaze through the mask . . . and he stilled at the sudden intensity in her words. "May we have a moment of privacy, Sinistro?"

Oh, Divine Elva. If she'd recognized him already behind his disguise . . .

He barely heard his voice over the thrumming in his ears. "Of course. Shall we?"

Smoothly, he shifted direction, aiming them towards a quiet corner of the room. She matched his steps, with no apparent urgency in her movements.

The moment they reached the corner, she released his arm and turned to hide her face from the rest of the room, doubly blocked by his cloaked figure and by Oskar on his shoulder. Felix dipped his head politely lower, so that she could speak without raising her voice.

If she accused him, he wouldn't deny anything. He would . . . no, he wouldn't run. He couldn't shame Queen Saskia so badly in public. No, he would simply confess, but then . . .

"Sinistro," said the First Minister of Kitvaria, "I will not make you choose between your loyalties to our mistress and our nation. But I must ask, for Kitvaria's sake alone: exactly what sort of relationship *does* Queen Saskia have with Ailana of Nornne, in your opinion?"

"Ah . . . I beg your pardon?" Felix blinked behind his mask as Oskar, indifferent to low-voiced human conversations, settled in for another nap on his shoulder. "That is, I believe they are allies."

"*Allies.*" There was an odd tension to her tone as she repeated the word. "So, has the Queen of Nornne visited our queen often, then? And in private?"

Frowning, Felix shifted backwards, careful not to let Oskar slip. "I'm afraid I couldn't answer such a question. I am Her Majesty's faithful servant."

"As am I!" Passionate intensity rang in Mirjana's voice. "That's why I'm trying to *protect* her—and with her insistence on hiding out here, in the middle of nowhere, you're the only observer I can safely ask. You must have heard the rumors by now: the Queen of Nornne's heart is as hard as ice. Not one of the women to whom she's shown favor has lasted longer than one night in her bed— and she's never allowed a single one into her heart."

She shook her head, her expression haunted. "If Ailana *has* taken it in mind to court our queen, I promise you it won't be because she's finally fallen in love. It only means she has some hidden scheme in mind, and poor Saskia's been drawn into her web."

Felix had relied on his instincts to stay alive every day, back in his own archducal court. All of those instincts were shouting at him now.

"I have never seen any signs of an intimate relationship between our queen and the Queen of Nornne," he said at last.

. . . But he would swear in Divine Elva's name that the woman before him *had* enjoyed one with Queen Saskia in the past and would like to do so again.

Her Majesty had spoken only rarely to him about her relationship with her First Minister. Most of her comments were wry references to the disappointment that she imagined she somehow posed to Mirjana, among others, in her new role as queen. Felix had never guessed at any other connection between them . . .

But as he looked now, as if for the first time, at Mirjana's fine-boned, delicate beauty, he swallowed down a sigh of resignation.

He had already known that his hopeless infatuation could never lead to anything. But that theoretically understood impossibility had never felt quite so tangible as it did now, gazing at Queen Saskia's beautiful and effortlessly powerful former partner, who had clearly been born ready and eager to manage a nation . . . and who, just as clearly, saw only one potential romantic rival in this crowded ballroom.

"I thank you for your honesty *and* your discretion." Taking a deep breath, Mirjana resettled her slim shoulders. Her smile as she looked up into his mask was perfectly polished. "Kitvaria appreciates your service—and if you ever find that our queen no longer requires you in her own private library, you may always look to me for assistance."

"You're too kind." Felix's lips felt numb as he shaped the expected words. "Shall we return to the others?"

"Of course. I'm so glad we understand one another." She placed one hand lightly on his cloaked arm, and they stepped back into the crowd together.

With Ailana and Lorelei flanking her rounds of the ballroom like flamboyantly lethal tour guides, Saskia endured the rest of the formal introductions with minimal amounts of agony. Better yet, within half an hour, it was time for everyone to stop talking and assemble into the traditional patterns of expanding circles. As the ritual of Winter's Turning finally began, she swallowed down a sigh of relief.

Even she didn't dare to break this trembling silence. The whole room had fallen silent and still with the torchlit entrance of the priests and priestesses. Now, all of the most brash and scandal-hunting rulers bowed their heads in a hush that might have been sincerely reverent . . . in less sophisticated company.

Mirjana stood once more at Saskia's side for the presentation of the priests, her head piously bowed. In a quick, sidelong glance, though, Saskia had seen her First Minister's gaze darting busily around the gathered circles of guests, taking in every detail and storing it up for later. Knowing what she did about her fellow rulers, Saskia was certain that Mirjana was not alone in feeling obligation rather than exaltation at the enactment of the divine ritual.

Personally, Saskia had never felt any great attachment to the ancient gods and goddesses who'd shaped the world so long ago. Whether or not They somehow still existed, vast and invisible to mere mortal eyes, she had more than enough pressing concerns of her own without bothering about Their divine squabbles.

However, her parents had followed the Empire's single good example by accepting all faiths in their kingdom. She wouldn't fail in their example now, even if the sight of Divine Elva's priestess did make her teeth clench uncontrollably.

Stepping to the center of the innermost circle, the priestess raised her antlered staff with a throbbing, deep-pitched chant of offering, and Saskia aimed a slitted glance upwards in sheer irritation.

Oh. Her mouth dropped open. The priestess was staring directly at her . . . but not with human eyes.

Saskia didn't have to be an expert in the divine to know exactly what those glowing, golden eyes signified. She'd *seen* the real woman beneath the goddess a minute earlier, with a dark, shadowed human gaze beneath that giant fur headdress. Now, a different face had been transposed over those human features, an overlaid mask so bright with radiance that Saskia's eyes stung with the contact . . . but she couldn't look away.

As the antlered staff rose even higher in the air, Saskia's chest pulsed with the pressure of the golden light that shot out from it, like the heat of the sun itself.

Saskia couldn't breathe as that infinite golden gaze swallowed hers, absorbing everything she was and ever had been. The helpless, overwhelming immersion lasted forever and ever . . . and then the goddess finally turned Her avatar's head, and Saskia fell free, gasping for air.

Her relief lasted only an instant. Then she followed the divine gaze.

Oh, no.

Golden radiance shot through the air between Her staff and the tall, cloaked and hooded figure who stood in the second rung of the circle with a rumpled-looking crow snoring on his shoulder. The figure's masked face was hidden from view, but his hands were clasped before him in what looked like true worship . . . and he had no idea of what was aiming at him.

Fabian! Saskia stepped forward with a jerk, breaking the inner circle of worship.

The priestess's head whipped around. Summoning all of her power—*useless, pitiful against a goddess*—Saskia braced herself for divine fury and retribution.

Instead, Divine Elva gave her a smile of pure, undiluted, jaw-dropping mischief . . .

And then She was gone.

Shaking, Saskia fell back into place. Through the ringing in her ears, she could make out the priestess's ongoing—unbroken?—chant as it finally drew to a close. The woman's age-lined face was serene as she sang, her posture unshifted from her original pose.

"Saskia?" Mirjana hissed into her ear. "What's wrong?"

"I . . ." Saskia shook her head, wordless. Across the circle, Fabian's hood was still bowed.

No one else in the room seemed to have been affected. Apparently, that divine visitation had been reserved for her alone . . . as had that message.

What in the world had Divine Elva been playing at by pointing Fabian out to Saskia in such a way? She might think She was an all-knowing goddess, but if She was deluded enough to imagine that Saskia didn't already notice her librarian every single day and dream *far* too often of him at night . . . especially of that moment, weeks ago, when his cloaked body had curved around hers and his warm fingers had closed around her own and if she'd only turned her head—

Wait.

Saskia's racing thoughts slammed to a sudden, horrified halt. She did know one thing about this particular goddess, didn't she? Divine Elva had been the patron deity of Estarion back when it was still an independent nation, before the new Serafin Empire had been formed and swept up all those individual deities from across the continent into a single Imperial pantheon.

. . . And it was the godsdamned *Archduke of Estarion* who had ordered Yaroslav to be named a holy paladin of Divine Elva.

When Saskia remembered the way Fabian had flinched at her mention of the Archduke on his first night here . . .

How close a patron *was* Divine Elva to the hateful current archduke? Would She work to advance his plans even here?

Perhaps Elva had appeared tonight in kindly warning to stand back, away from oncoming danger—but if She expected Saskia to accommodate any schemes that threatened Kadaric Castle's gentle, kind-hearted, and thoroughly *off-limits* librarian, She had no idea of just how wicked a queen Saskia could be.

She had already defied her uncle, the Empire, and all the respectable folk of the continent. She was more than ready to defy the gods, too.

As her fingers curled into fists by her side, Saskia ignored

Mirjana's speculative looks and endured the rest of the ritual with a throbbing pulse. This evening couldn't end quickly enough.

She needed to get back to her laboratory and then the castle library . . . this time, for a wholly different search.

Sheltered by his hood and mask, Felix counted down the minutes of the lavish Winter's Turning feast. How long until he could safely slip away from the gathering?

Thank Elva for the ritual that had come beforehand; the peace and stillness granted by Her priestess's familiar, comforting chants had given him the time and space he'd needed to settle his rioting emotions. All he wanted now was to fall into bed and stay there, in the dark, until he could finally forget all of the deluded hopes that had been dashed earlier this night.

Still, his assigned mission, once released from escort duty, was to loom in a menacing manner, so loom he did as the guests devoured their midnight feast over bright gossip and dagger-like political maneuvering. For once, it was no challenge to go without any food of his own. Even if he hadn't been wearing the inhibiting silver mask, he wouldn't have been able to summon any appetite.

Queen Saskia sat between her First Minister and King Hravic, who looked far less intoxicated and more alert than he had at Felix's last Winter's Turning celebration. Still, Felix wasn't surprised that Mirjana had felt secure enough to give Hravic that place beside her queen. Saskia wasn't bothering to even pretend any interest in his rambling discourse about the exploits of his favorite hunting dogs. Instead, her face had drawn tight with fierce contemplation, her body poised like an arrow waiting to be shot—and even as Felix halted, caught by the sheer intensity of her focus, she lunged to her feet, her chair scraping noisily against stone.

"A happy Winter's Turning to you all, and good night!" Without further ado, she turned and strode to the farthest door. It flung itself open before her with a crack like thunder. Emitting a raucous chorus of triumph, her crows and bats—who had been perched around the hall and ceiling through the feast—soared after her in a dark, shifting wave, leaving the room behind them echoing with shock.

... Until the Fae Queen of Balravia broke the silence with a clap of delight. "Well! I do like an early night sometimes. Don't you? *So* much more time to—"

"Ahem." Mirjana rose smoothly to her feet, clearing her throat. "Honored guests. Her Majesty would like me to convey . . ."

But Felix didn't stop to find out which polite reassurances and thanks Mirjana *wished* her queen had thought to add to that farewell. Released from duty, he strode for the closest servants' door. His steps sped up with every passing moment as he took each twist and turn that led to the safety of his tower room. He didn't even stop to gather up any light before lunging into the cool air of the narrow, twisting staircase, finding his way up the uneven stone steps by no more than feel and memory.

He *needed* the privacy of his room. He couldn't wear this mask or cloak even a minute longer. He needed to push open his window and breathe in the cold, high mountain air. He needed—

"Oh, how delightful! I'd been hoping to find a moment alone with you."

Felix rocked to a halt only just in time as the Queen of Balravia appeared on the darkened staircase just above him in an ecstatic shower of colored light.

Oskar shot to his feet, squawking in panic.

"Your Majesty!" As the tips of Oskar's unguarded claws pierced his shoulder, Felix nearly squawked as well. Clearing his throat, he bent into as deep and respectful a bow as he could manage without either knocking Oskar from his perch or physically crashing into Lorelei. With the fae queen's shimmering magic lighting the narrow stairway, the stone walls suddenly felt far too close around them. He took a clumsy, lurching step backwards, to a lower step, as he straightened from his bow. "Forgive me if I missed a royal summons or—"

"Oh, no, I meant to find you in *just* this way, I promise. It is so much easier to talk in private, don't you think?" She batted long, blonde eyelashes over implausibly innocent blue eyes, shedding sparkles across her cheeks. "Of course, any man who wears a mask so often *must* understand having secrets to keep!"

Smiling enticingly, she leaned closer to him in her gauzy, swirling, changeable gown . . .

And Felix took another firm step downward. "In that case, we had better go to the library."

"Oh, no, really?" She gave him a theatrical pout, but her eyes shone with unhidden mischief. Without further complaint, she followed him down the steps and through the darkened private passageways, far from the guests' brightly lit wing. "You *are* clever, aren't you? It's no wonder Saskia is so possessive of you."

Felix's foot halted mid-step for a perilous instant . . . but then, with a grimace, he forced himself to keep going. He hadn't survived all of his years at the Estarian court to give in to shameless manipulation now.

The tension in his shoulders eased slightly as he stepped into the comfortably familiar clutter of the library, where he had at least some pretense of control. Stacks of books still formed a maze across the floor, and the fire had been long since banked for the night, but the colorful light cast by Lorelei herself was enough to guide him down the familiar paths to the sideboard where an oil lamp sat. The fae queen waited in the doorway, but Felix could feel her watching his every move.

"*So* careful," she mused as he lit the lamp. "No flamboyant spells to make this whole room bright as day, to impress Saskia's honored guest?"

Felix winced. "I'd never dare cast any spells in this library before it's fully catalogued." He might not be a true dark wizard, but he'd read more than enough magical texts by now to know the dangers of recklessness. A magic-worker as powerful as Queen Saskia needn't concern herself with such issues, but the more he'd read, the more he'd come to understand just how rare the queen's level of power truly was.

"Mmm. Fair enough, I suppose." As she picked her way delicately through the paths between the books, her speculative gaze swept across the room. "And yet, I truly can't recall any other dark wizard ever openly admitting to any sort of fear or weakness."

"I'd call it *caution*," Felix said as evenly as possible, "and I'd add that some of us have nothing to prove. If you'll forgive me, Your Majesty, I believe my own employer has already decided my qualifications more than sufficed." The words sent a sharp pang of guilt through his chest; he stiffened his shoulders, forcing it down.

"Darling Saskia certainly has . . . which, of course, is why I wanted so badly to speak to you." Reaching the sideboard where he stood, Lorelei beamed up at him. "I'm just so interested in your work! I can't have any dark wizards in my own court for tedious political reasons—*you* know we fae haven't always had the easiest of relations with your kind—but visiting Saskia's library left me *so* curious about the sorts of spells you cast." She clasped her hands before her chest as she tipped her head back to look up at him. "Won't you tell me all about them? How *do* written spells even work?"

Her blue eyes were wide, her enthusiasm infectious . . . and Felix felt a cold sliver of unease run down his spine. Carefully, he took a half-step backwards, breathing slowly. Oskar had already flapped off to an empty shelf and buried his beak in his feathers. There was no one Felix could look to for support. "Of course I can explain how they function," he said, "but for a deeper understanding, I would happily ask Queen Saskia for permission to loan you an introductory text, or . . ."

"Oh, no, I'm not here to read dry old texts!" Rolling her eyes, Lorelei waved off the idea. Then she stepped even closer, until her shimmering skirts brushed against his legs and her small hands were pressed against his chest, curling around the fabric of his cloak. "I want *you* to tell me *everything*, and then—"

This time, Felix didn't even hear the door open.

"*Lorelei.*" Queen Saskia enunciated every syllable with icy clarity. "I want *you* to remove your hands from my librarian. *Now.*"

15

ll evening, the cage Saskia had erected around her temper had been bending and shuddering under too much pressure, but her interaction with an actual goddess had—she'd *thought*—been the final blow.

Now, she knew she'd been wrong.

This—escaping at long last into the comfort and refuge of her library only to find *her* librarian, already threatened by Divine Elva, now being groped by her so-called *ally*—was the blow that shattered the crumbling remnants of her cage, leaving nothing but red-hot fury behind.

All of her burning focus landed on the fae across the room, whose small, dimpled hands were *still* pressed against Fabian's chest as if they belonged there. Saskia's precious laboratory notebook fell with a *thunk* onto the floor. She didn't cast it a single glance.

She needed both of her hands free for battle.

"Darling!" With a tinkling laugh, Lorelei finally—*finally*— stepped back, but first, she gave Fabian a godsdamned *pat on his chest,* as if to offer reassurance . . . or perhaps a hidden message. Was she setting up an assignation for later? Wait, was *he*—?

Fabian stepped backwards with a long, lunging stride that spoke of nothing but relief to be free.

Saskia took a shuddering breath. She couldn't let herself think about the depth of her own relief. Not now. Not when Lorelei was dancing towards her with a smile so smug, it practically screamed of fabulous secrets and bawdy jokes she wasn't yet ready to share.

"My *dear* Saskia," purred Lorelei, "what perfect timing! Your lovely librarian was just about to pr—that is, to teach me everything he knows about written spellwork. Would you care to listen to the lesson, too?"

"*What?*" Saskia stared at her, momentarily thrown off-balance. "Why in the world—?"

Fae or not, Lorelei knew more about spellwork than almost any wizard on the continent. In the first full meeting of the Queens of Villainy, she'd given her expert opinion on various spells in this library after no more than a passing glance. Why would she need Fabian to explain any of it now? Unless . . .

Saskia's eyes narrowed. Was this some deceptive new flirtation technique? Did Lorelei imagine that pretending ignorance would somehow make her more appealing to Fabian, as it would have to that crowned fool who'd sat beside Saskia at tonight's feast? If so, Lorelei certainly didn't know Saskia's librarian.

She wouldn't be given the chance to rectify her mistake.

Taking a prowling step forward, Saskia raised her hands . . .

And Fabian said, "Everything's fine! I would be happy to explain the principles of written spellwork, if Queen Lorelei would still care to hear them. It all comes down to choosing a basic structure and understanding the rhythms of classical Serafin pentameter."

For the first time since Saskia had stepped into the room, Lorelei's eyes widened with unguarded surprise. She whipped around to stare at him, open-mouthed.

Fabian's face was hidden behind his enigmatic mask, but his voice was calm and confident as the infamous Siren of Balravia gaped at him. "There are three essential elements to every spell, no matter which structure is chosen. The first element, which sets the spell's intent—"

"That's enough." Despite everything, Saskia had to bite back a smile at Lorelei's gobsmacked expression. The fae queen looked more disgruntled than Saskia had ever seen her—but Fabian had gifted Saskia with the moment she needed to wrest her own temper back under control. Fury still thrummed through her body, but under his steady gaze, she forced herself to lower her arms and tamp down her waiting magic. "Lorelei, you may play your games with any other man you like, but my staff is *off-limits*."

"That's—!" Lorelei cut herself off, her eyes narrowing. "Wait. All of your staff? Or just this delicious creature, in particular?"

"*All* of them," Saskia gritted. "I protect what's mine. *Always.*"

"Hmm." Lorelei looked between the two of them for a long moment—then shrugged carelessly. "Oh, very well! I'll find my night's entertainment elsewhere if I must. But Saskia, just so you know . . ." Fearless as ever, she flitted to Saskia's side and put one light hand on Saskia's braced shoulder, ignoring the dangerously bunched muscles underneath. "I really meant it," she breathed into Saskia's ear, "when I said before that your librarian is *intriguing*. I'd work to ferret out all of his mysteries as soon as possible if I were you!"

At that, Saskia couldn't hold back a low growl of rage—but Lorelei was already dancing away, laughing as she left the room.

The library door fell closed behind her, leaving Saskia and Fabian alone in the close, warm circle of light cast by the oil lamp.

Tension still palpably vibrated in the air. Even Fabian's familiar was gone, no doubt snoozing somewhere among the shadows of the shelves.

So no one else would witness her loss of control if she stalked directly to him, pulled his head down to hers as she'd been longing to for weeks, flung aside that damned mask, and finally—

No! With a snarl of frustration, Saskia turned and strode back to the spot where she'd dropped her laboratory notebook. Pages lay scattered around it on the carpeted floor, casting years of careful records into disorganization. A burning pulse beat in her forehead as she knelt to gather them up, barely conscious of the soft sounds of footsteps moving towards her.

Would the frustrations of this night never end?

Fabian sank down to the carpet beside her, his cloak fanning out to brush her skirt. Saskia let out a long, shuddering breath, the knots in her chest beginning to loosen under the warmth of his presence.

Just another few minutes, she promised herself. Once she'd collected all of her notes, she could bury herself in work until she was too tired to think anymore and she could fall into sleep like a deep, dark pit, safe from every political or physical alarm of this long night. She could keep hold of herself for a few minutes longer.

So, as Fabian lifted a sheet of scribbled notes from the ground with his usual steady, gentle care, she took a deep breath and then reached past him to continue her own part of the work.

She'd misjudged her timing. He straightened as she leaned. Their bare wrists brushed against each other . . . and held.

He didn't move away.

Saskia froze, her arm still stretched out in midair. Her gaze was still aimed at the paper-strewn floor between them, but every inch of her body pulsed with awareness of the tingling contact between the lightly haired top of his warm, lean wrist and the smooth, vulnerable inner skin of hers.

She didn't move to break the contact.

Neither did he.

She hardly dared even breathe, lest she break the shimmering possibility of the moment. If she did, and he lunged away from her again, the way he had the first time they'd touched . . . or as he had from Lorelei, just now . . . !

She couldn't bear the uncertainty any longer. Slowly, reluctantly, she tipped her head backwards.

Fabian's eyes were dark and shadowed behind his mask, but she could hear his quick breathing and see it, too. His cloaked chest rose and fell before her with his shallow pants of breath.

That was most certainly not revulsion . . . and something inside her caught fire at the sight.

This flame had been banked for weeks, only waiting to be set free. Saskia's tongue darted out to moisten her dry lips as she considered her options—and Fabian's cravat shifted with his convulsive swallow.

His gaze followed her movements as if pulled by a string.

Her lips curved with triumph. *Finally.*

She would never force her attentions where they weren't wanted . . . but she would damned well seize the opportunity that had been gifted now.

Slowly, deliberately, she slid her hand against his skin until she held his wrist between her fingers. Her grip was purposefully light; he could pull away with ease at any moment.

Instead, he shifted infinitesimally closer, his breath growing harsher.

She could easily reach up and lift his concealing mask out of her way—but no. For the first time in years, Saskia felt the urge to slow down and *play* . . . and she couldn't think of a more enticing partner in the world than her soft-spoken, ever-restrained librarian.

How far could she push him before he lost all of that restraint?

Attuned to every shift of his breath, she tilted his wrist until his palm faced her. Then she stroked the forefinger of her free hand lightly across that sensitive skin.

He shivered, eyes falling closed. Heat bloomed deep within Saskia at the sight of his pleasure.

This was the most addictive form of power she had ever tasted.

Slowly, carefully, she traced the lines across his palm, keeping her touch tantalizingly light.

Letting out a low groan, he leaned even closer.

Stilling, she waited until he opened his eyes again and met her gaze. Then she lifted his hand and gave a darting, teasing lick to the vulnerable center of his palm, where so many lines met.

"*Saskia!*" His low, rough cry mingled protest and demand . . . and marked the first time he'd ever spoken her true name rather than her royal title.

The fire within her surged at the sound of it, breaking free of the last of her restraints.

She grinned up at him, feeling as wild and free as the girl she hadn't been for years. "Yes?" she said politely.

Then she popped the tip of his long forefinger into her mouth, bit down lightly, and sucked *hard*.

"Gods!" His whole body jerked.

She ran her teeth against his skin as she slowly released him, savoring the salty tang. "Should I stop?"

"No," he said hoarsely. "*Please* don't stop. But I need to touch you, too."

"Hmm." Saskia had to bite her lip to hold back uncharacteristic, bubbling laughter. Instead of letting it out, she raised a single eyebrow in mock-haughty consideration. "I don't think it's quite time for that yet."

"But—"

"*Sit back,*" she told him sternly . . . and the flames inside her shot even higher as he followed her order without protest. "That's better."

His legs were *so* deliciously long! She climbed over them to straddle his warm thighs, the thick folds of his cloak bunching beneath her. He'd propped himself up with his hands on the floor, fingers flattened against the thick carpet for balance. Reaching beneath the silver mask, she tipped his chin back, and gloried in the quick pant of his breath as he allowed it. "It is time," she said, "to lose your cravat."

She'd never untied one before, but she had always been a fast learner. She whipped off the long black cloth only a moment later, while his arms visibly clenched on either side with the effort of keeping his hands off her.

She could never get enough of this kind of power! Saskia savored the tingling pressure of the air between them as she studied the bare skin of his neck, still tipped back and entirely at her mercy. At this time of night, his fair skin was intriguingly stubbled with dark flecks of hair . . . and it flexed before her with his swallow.

She couldn't wait to explore every inch and learn which bits would make him *moan.*

Sliding her right hand into his hood, she closed her fingers around the soft, thick curls at the back of his neck. Then she curved her other hand around one firm shoulder and leaned in, savoring the catch of his breath and the sensation of his pulse speeding up against her fingers.

She *had* always loved conducting thorough experiments.

As Saskia dragged her lips and teeth on a teasing, wandering path along his newly exposed throat, taking his reactions as her guide, her world became a blur of heat and discovery and the glorious sensation of his rapidly hardening figure beneath her . . .

Until the library door opened once more and Mirjana's harried voice sounded just behind them. "Saskia, you know you can't just—what in the world is going on here?"

Curse it! Saskia froze with her lips still pressed against Fabian's warm, stubbled throat.

Her ex-lover had always known how to deflate her self-confidence in an instant. But as she slowly, reluctantly drew back, preparing to turn and face the withering disapproval of her First Minister, the man beneath her suddenly shifted.

A moment earlier, he'd been reclining in graceful submission, head tipped back and lost to the pleasure of her touch. Now, his back straightened and his brown gaze, fully alert, fixed on hers with a message that she couldn't mistake: she wasn't alone in this. His strength was hers.

Fabian was ready to support her in this coming confrontation.

Saskia vowed, at that moment, that it wouldn't be necessary. He'd trusted her enough to be vulnerable in her arms. She *would not* allow him to be harmed for that now.

Lifting her chin, she rose to her feet with careful precision. By the time she finally turned to face Mirjana, her own face was as cold and set as the perfect statue of a queen. "I believe it is customary to knock before entering a room after midnight."

"A private bedroom, perhaps. But a *library*?" Mirjana let out a high-pitched, sharp-edged laugh. "Did you even recall that this castle is full of guests? All of whom we're currently trying to convince that you're *not* wildly out of control?"

Scalding heat rose in Saskia's chest, but before it could spill from her lips, Fabian spoke, his voice as quiet and courteous as always. "Out of *whose* control, exactly?" he inquired as he rose to stand beside her.

Saskia bared her teeth in a ferocious smile, tamping her emotions back down again. "What an interesting question. Would you care to give it an honest answer, Mirjana?"

"Hardly." Her First Minister's delicate nostrils flared, but she didn't spare Fabian so much as a glance. "I am not accountable to your *librarian*, and I don't appreciate being addressed in such a way by your latest plaything. You and I are partners, so—"

"We are *what*?" Saskia gave a spurt of disbelieving laughter. "It's been years since we were last together in any romantic way! We are certainly not—"

"I made you *queen!*" Mirjana snapped, color rising to flush her fair cheeks. "*I* was the one managing all the threads of the rebel movement by the end. I hunted you down in the first place, drew you out, and taught you how to talk to humans again! And I was the one who made you finally see sense and take the throne nine months ago. If I hadn't forced you into doing your duty, you'd still be hiding in that forest with your magical friends now, playing at witchcraft all day long and pretending there wasn't a kingdom that needed you!"

"You think I went into hiding for my own selfish amusement? *My parents—!*" Saskia cut off her words—too raw, too danger-ous . . . *too late.*

All of her hard-won shields had been used up this evening. Now, memories—held barely at bay ever since she'd first started planning this cursed night's events—came roaring in to over-whelm her, replacing the people, the room, and even the carpet around her with too-vivid sounds and sights that she could never forget, no matter how she tried.

Her parents' screams echoing through the palace walls . . .

Their blood had spread *so far* across that carpeted floor. Uncle Yaroslav had the carpet replaced, but every time Saskia had been forced to visit that room from then on, she could have sworn she still saw an overlay of blood. And then . . .

The scents of cinnamon and pine smoke at that next Winter's Turning . . .

Her uncle's openly calculating gaze as he'd debated exactly when he ought to kill her, too . . .

"Your Majesty." Fabian's fingers closed around her arm, warm and steady, pulling her back. "It's very late. Perhaps it would be best to—"

"Saskia!" Mirjana stepped forward, speaking over him. "Don't you dare go running off again now. We have important matters to discuss, *without* your librarian's involvement. When it comes to high-level governmental issues—"

"Enough," Saskia rasped.

Only a few minutes earlier, she had blazed with power and certainty. Now, she felt like an empty husk; a petty imposter swathed in too-revealing clothes, ready to topple at the slightest breeze.

The pages of her laboratory notebook still lay scattered on the floor. She trusted Fabian to look after them. She didn't trust herself on anything at this moment.

Still, she wouldn't leave him unprotected. "Go now, Mirjana," she said with all the force that she could muster. "It's too late for any more discussions tonight."

"But—"

"I'll go, too," she said wearily. "I promise."

"But . . . Your Majesty?" In Fabian's suddenly lowered and tentative voice, she could hear once more the vulnerability he'd gifted her earlier. The skin of his bare throat was still temptingly exposed beneath his silver mask. His black cravat lay crumpled by their feet.

If she only moved a step closer . . .

Aching and empty, she took a slow step back. "It's too late," she repeated under Mirjana's narrowed gaze.

Winter's Turning was officially over.

16

The next morning, all of the visitors in their pomp and finery climbed into their carriages—or onto their riding gryphons, as the case might be—and set off for their own busy cities and palaces, leaving Kadaric Castle as silent and nearly empty as before, surrounded only by vast, boulder-strewn mountain peaks and sky. Within the next few days, almost every domestic routine fell back into place as neatly and easily as if none of the wild spectacle or emotional tumults of Winter's Turning had ever taken place.

Felix wished that he could forget so easily.

His own duties, of course, remained unchanged. As the days passed and snow began to fall outside the window of his tower room, he rose every morning to eat a hot breakfast, pull on his concealing black half-mask and cloak—which he appreciated even more as the temperatures outside dropped further into winter's icy clutches—and walk, under Oskar's noisy, busy chaperonage, down the familiar winding stairs to the library, where the fire would be lit and waiting for him . . . along with the seemingly endless quest to learn how to do his own job.

Each new discovery he uncovered about a previously unknown aspect of magic necessitated a full reconsideration of all of his careful sorting systems. He tried not to consider it a failure every time he was forced to overhaul them. After all, each new amendment to those systems counted as *progress*, painful though that might feel.

It was the only sort of progress he was making.

He still jumped at every new creak of the door . . . because one singular routine *had* changed since Winter's Turning.

Queen Saskia, who had visited at least once a day in the month before that ritual, had been nowhere to be seen ever since. She wasn't avoiding the library itself—Felix knew that much from the books he found waiting for him every morning on the study table, accompanied by scrawled notes in her spiky handwriting, thoughtfully alerting him to their original locations.

No, she was clearly avoiding *him*. Apparently, whatever incomprehensible impulse had overcome her on the night of Winter's Turning—*hot, demanding lips and teeth at his throat, passion and power and glory*—had been dismissed by the next morning. Whether it had been her First Minister's horror at Saskia's choice or simply the light of a new day that had reminded her of how much better she could do, her reaction now was unmistakable:

Regret.

Felix's hand tightened convulsively at the thought, and his fountain pen twitched, black ink spattering across his tidy notes.

Damnation. Blowing out his breath, Felix closed his eyes for a brief but intense moment of self-flagellation. Then he carefully wiped off the nib of the pen. He was just setting down the handkerchief he'd used when the door to the library opened . . . and the pen fell helplessly from his hand onto the papers beneath it, uncapped, as he lunged to his feet, forgetting everything.

But it wasn't Queen Saskia. Instead, Mrs. Haglitz stood in the open doorway, her long arms crossed, her many shawls draped around her shoulders, and her head unveiled as she frowned at him.

"I . . . madam." Felix jerked into a belated but respectful bow. Under the pressure of her examination, he felt stripped bare, despite all the layers of his own clothing and the half-mask on his face. Guiltily, he cast a quick glance at the table beside him, but he didn't spot any uneaten meals that could have caused her ire this time. "May I help you?"

"Tsk! Even worse than I'd expected." She shook her head at him, setting the dangling mushroom by her left ear wobbling in disapproving accompaniment. "Well, then. Best put away that fancy pen of yours, lad, and come with me."

Felix blinked. "Where—?"

But she was already leaving, so he scrambled to cap his fountain pen and hurry after her with Oskar flapping in his wake.

This time, she led them not to the small, oak-paneled dining room where Felix had eaten several times before, but down a meandering set of steps to a vast underground kitchen paved with ancient-looking flagstones, with at least a dozen different cookstoves set against the plain stone walls and fragrant sheaves of savory herbs and dried meat hanging from the high ceiling. An opening in one corner served as a fountain, shooting a steady stream of water from an underground stream into a broad stone pool. Felix shivered reflexively at the realization of just how deep they must be inside the mountain.

Still, the air felt remarkably warm, with fires crackling cheerfully inside two different fireplaces at opposite ends of the room. A plain wooden table sat before the closest fire, with long, sturdy benches laid on either side. Two of the goblins sat at one end, munching charred treats that Felix tried not to recognize as toasted rats; at the other end of the table, Morlokk sat with a delicate porcelain cup of tea in one massive hand and a newspaper spread out before him. He looked up at first with only polite acknowledgment—and then he saw Felix, and his thick eyebrows shot upwards as he pushed himself to his feet.

"Sinistro?"

"Oh, do sit down," Mrs. Haglitz said to them both, and gave Felix a firm push in the right direction.

Obediently, he sat down on the same side of the table as the two goblins, who greeted him with cheerful waves but continued their own low-voiced conversation in a language he hadn't learned, a mixture of chirps and croaks and low whistles interspersed with uproarious laughter. Morlokk sank back into his own seat more slowly, his eyes on Felix's half-masked face.

"I don't wish to interrupt . . ." Felix began.

"And that's enough nonsense out of you!" Mrs. Haglitz bustled over to a long counter covered with a variety of pastries and meals-in-progress and began to chop thick slices with decisive *thunks* of a sharp knife. "No one"—*thunk*—"ever has to be alone and lonely in *this* castle"—*thunk*—"even if *some* people have it fixed in their ridiculous heads that they're doomed to be alone forever. *Pah!*"

A clay plate slammed onto the table in front of Felix in perfect unison with her exclamation of disgust.

"Thank you," Felix said meekly, and breathed in the fragrance of her gift. Gorgeous layers of flaky pastry surrounded the crisply baked apple slices on his plate, generously infused with cinnamon, vanilla, and nutmeg. The sight and smell made his mouth water even before Mrs. Haglitz set down a sturdy mug of thick, dark coffee to accompany it. Felix dug in with enthusiasm while Morlokk returned to reading his newspaper, Oskar dived head-first into his own offered plate of kitchen scraps in one corner of the room, and Mrs. Haglitz went back to work on her various meals-in-progress, muttering irritably under her breath.

"This is truly delicious," Felix said a minute later, as he forced himself to take a break, halfway through, and wiped off a lin-gering fleck of pastry from his lips. "Did you bake it yourself, Mrs. Haglitz? Or did Cook—? Where *is* Cook?" He glanced around, frowning.

"She's off for the week visiting family," said Mrs. Haglitz. "De-serves it, too, after all she did for Winter's Turning. I thought she'd go into hysterics about some of those guests' demands! They're lucky she didn't send any of her snakes slithering into their beds overnight, and serve them right. Still, to hear the way she fretted about taking any time away, you'd think our queen would starve to death without her. I *told* her, I did all the cooking for our Saskia for years, not to mention feeding this fellow." She nodded at Morlokk, who turned a page in the newspaper with a discreet rustling of paper. "The day I let anyone in *my* household go without a meal . . ."

Morlokk gave a weary sigh but didn't look up from his reading material. "You do know she didn't mean it as an insult."

"Hmmph!" Mrs. Haglitz whacked her rolling pin hard onto a towering pile of dough.

Sensibly, Felix ducked his head over his plate and chose not to enter into that particular argument.

He'd never sat on a plain wooden bench to eat before, but he found that he quite liked the sensation. It felt friendlier, some-how, to share the long, scarred bench with the two cheerful little goblins, even as he sensed Morlokk's wary gaze regularly shift-ing between the newspaper and him, as if waiting for him to do anything suspicious. Considering what he'd gathered about the

usual behavior of dark wizards, Felix wouldn't be surprised if
Morlokk were anticipating a literal explosion.

Still, the warmth of the room, the sweetness of the pastry,
and the undemanding companionship of the gathering all combined to make him feel better than he had in days. As his tension eased, he slowed his eating, trying to draw out every last
mouthful ... and his drifting thoughts finally caught up with
Mrs. Haglitz's earlier grumbling.

"Wait. What you said about people who thought they had
to be alone forever ... were you referring to me? Or to Her
Majesty?"

"*Ahem.*" Morlokk cleared his throat and shook out his newspaper with a snap. "Mrs. Haglitz ..."

"Oh, shush. You know just as well as I do that he doesn't mean
any harm to our girl. I'll wager he came running here to hide
from *someone*, but he's no danger to *her*. Are you, lad?"

Felix, whose fingers had tightened convulsively around his fork
at that too-keen analysis, shook his head. "I would *never* wish to
harm Queen Saskia."

"Of course you wouldn't. Any fool can see that. And besides"—
she looked pointedly at Morlokk—"there's no point having both
of them moping around all day long, filling up the castle with
their misery, is there?"

"We-e-ell ..." Morlokk winced. "Perhaps not, but I still don't
think—"

"What do you mean?" Felix stiffened. "What's amiss with the
queen?"

Was she ill? Was *that* why she hadn't visited him? He set down
his fork, legs tensing in preparation to stride off in search of her.
Did she really think he wouldn't want to help in any way he could?

"Why do you think I brought you down here? *Someone* needs
to sort you two out, for all of our sakes." Mrs. Haglitz gave an
impatient huff as she sank down onto the bench opposite him,
cradling a large clay mug of coffee in her other green hand. "Now,

here's what you need to understand about Her Majesty," she began.

"*Must* he?" Morlokk grumbled under his breath beside her. "Really?"

"Shh!" Mrs. Haglitz placed her elbows comfortably onto the table to either side of her mug and continued, "I've known our girl longer than anyone else in this castle. The first time *I* met her, she was a babe at her mother's breast, and she had quite a temper then, too, I can tell you! But she was the sweetest little creature, big eyes taking in everything around her without a jot of fear.

"She came along on all of her mother's field trips, even then. She must've been rocked to sleep by a dozen different kinds of aunties before she ever learned to crawl. And the way she'd giggle whenever anyone played peekaboo with her, no matter how sharp their teeth or long their claws—! *Well.*"

Mrs. Haglitz paused to take a long sip of her coffee, lowering her eyelids swiftly . . . but not quite swiftly enough to hide the sudden, telltale moisture inside them.

Felix held his tongue in respectful silence, but she gave him a fierce look as she set the cup down with a thud. "Her mother, the late queen, was a *fine* woman, no matter what nasty rumors got spread around after her murder! I knew her for years, and I can tell you, I *never* saw her be anything but respectful and good-hearted to everyone she met."

"She was an excellent scholar, too," Felix said quietly. "I've been studying her work in the library. It's astonishing, and it deserves to be more widely known."

"Hmm." Morlokk raised his gaze from the newspaper to study Felix, his gaze unreadable. "Many dark wizards wouldn't agree."

Felix frowned, but Mrs. Haglitz swept firmly past that conversational detour. "I didn't know her husband myself, but I know she thought the world of him, and that was good enough for me. Creatures all over Kitvaria mourned their passing . . . and life got worse for all of us, too, with that villain trying to make himself a big man by cozying up to the Empire and stomping down on everyone he could.

"I can't count how many times I thought of little Saskia and worried over how she might be doing . . . but when she finally showed up at my door, seven years later, fleeing to the only folk in the kingdom she could trust?"

Mrs. Haglitz shook her big eyes slowly, the lines in her face looking deeper than ever. "That bright, brave girl didn't only lose her parents. She had to listen again and again to her uncle telling all the world that *she* was a monster and to blame for their deaths—that he'd *had* to kill them to protect the kingdom and stop her from inheriting and tainting it with her wrongness."

So *that* was where all those rumors of her monstrousness had come from! Felix breathed slowly and evenly through his teeth, fighting to control a rage he hadn't felt in years.

How had he not known about this? He was two years younger than Saskia, it was true; he would have been only five at the time of her parents' assassination—but if he'd been trained to be a true Imperial Archduke rather than a mere puppet, the recent upheavals of Estarion's closest neighbor would have been included in his earliest lessons. Even if he'd simply been allowed to read all the pages of the damned *newspapers* once he was an adult, like any other citizen of the Empire . . . !

His fingers flattened against the table, pressing down hard enough to hurt. It wasn't enough to quell the roiling in his gut.

"She'll do anything to protect the folk she loves," said Mrs. Haglitz. "She'd burn down the world for any of us—but she'll never, deep down, believe she deserves any real happiness of her own. And *that's* what you need to understand about Her Majesty."

Beside her, Morlokk let out a low, unhappy huff of air . . . but this time, he didn't disagree.

"Thank you," Felix said, and meant it. Nausea still twisted inside him, but deeper still, a core of certainty was beginning to form.

If Queen Saskia genuinely didn't wish to repeat the intimacy they'd shared, that was entirely her prerogative. But if, instead, she was avoiding him because she believed that raw, exhilarating pleasure and affection were joys that *she*, of all people, didn't deserve?

Well, then, Felix was going to shift his area of focus in this castle and become a most disobedient servant.

17

The first hint Saskia had that her sweet-tempered librarian was up to mischief came when she crept into the library late that night. As had become her recent habit, she waited until she was certain that he had left it for the evening, using her crows as baffled spies on her behalf and ignoring their grumbling as well as she could.

Why *wouldn't* she want to visit when Fabian was there? None of them could understand it. After all, whenever *they* visited, he gave them strokes, snacks, interesting buttons, and other small trinkets that he came across. In turn, they unanimously adored him, although Oskar jealously maintained his own superiority in Fabian's affections, beating off other too-friendly contenders with fierce squawks and pecks.

The real problem, of course, was that Saskia shared those feelings—and was *far* too likely to attempt more intemperate stroking of her own if she didn't force herself to keep her distance. There was no explaining that sort of dilemma to her crows, though, so they were still muttering complaints at her through their bond as they scattered off to follow their own pursuits for the night and she slipped through the library doorway into the big, darkened room.

Rather than turning on any of the waiting gas lamps, Saskia breathed a lick of flame into her cupped palm and set it hovering in the air above her head, moving with her amidst the piles of carefully stacked books. By this time, she was familiar with the general reasoning behind those piles; she moved without hesitation to the large stack set against a newly emptied bookcase, still clearly waiting to be sorted the next day.

Until a week ago, she'd spent her free time hunting for a spell of finding to deal with the obstreperous Estarian Archduke; now, with his divine ally in mind, she was on an even more urgent hunt for any book or ancient manuscript that might help her defend Fabian against a goddess.

When she glimpsed a single sheet of paper on top of that waiting pile of books and manuscripts, she assumed it was merely another piece of the collection. Then she recognized the elegant, restrained handwriting of her librarian, and her brows furrowed.

Fabian kept all of his notes carefully sorted on his study table. Had he left this one here by accident?

Calling down the ball of flame, she scooped up the sheet of paper and held it up to the light.

Lightning at her fingertips
Stars in her eyes

Leaving me blinded,
Shot through with glory.
  ~F.

A crow feather was sketched in black ink underneath . . . beside a crown of bones.

Saskia's breath stopped in her throat as she stared at that crown.

Did he—had he *meant* her to see—was she only imagining—? Or—?

Why couldn't she think properly?

She had to breathe.

Saskia let her held breath out in a rush, and the paper fell from her loosened fingertips.

She dived for it without a second thought—and the ball of fire dived, disastrously, with her. The next few minutes were lost to an undignified scramble in both physical and magical terms, but when she finally straightened, breathing hard, she held the undamaged paper in her hand. The flames had all been safely extinguished, with only the tiniest bit of charred leather on two bound books to mark that the incident had happened at all.

Perhaps she ought to leave a note of apology about the damage?

No. What could she possibly write to him after reading *that* message?

"*Shot through with glory . . .*"

Was that really how she'd made him feel?

It didn't matter. It *couldn't* matter, for his sake. In fact, she should leave this poem here, in case he hadn't meant her to see it in the first place.

But somehow, she couldn't quite let it go—so it stayed, carefully folded and tucked into the bodice of her gown, as she gathered up every book she could carry, too flustered to worry about relevance. It pressed against her skin, a rustling reminder with every breath as she carried her foraged pile down to her laboratory. There, days ago, she had rearranged one corner into a comfortable nest of purple satin cushions with a new commonplace book for notes on her private investigation.

That she was using a new fountain pen of her own to make those notes was, of course, a matter of mere common sense. How else could she keep her writing tidy in this nest, without any flat surface on which to set an inkwell?

The fact that every time she uncapped her new ebonite pen, a flash of sense-memory overwhelmed her—his arms curving around her, his warm breath against her hair, the bergamot scent of his shaving cream against her skin—was an unfortunate side effect, no more.

Gods, but she loved the way he smelled!

She swallowed convulsively and flipped open the top book in her pile. The folded paper in her bodice shifted with her swallow.

"Shot through with glory."

He had looked it, hadn't he? His head tipped back, his body one long, beautiful line of arousal, given over completely to her mercy . . .

"Fuck!" Groaning, Saskia closed her eyes and pressed her fingertips hard against her head as if she could physically fight those scalding memories back into the tightly locked cabinet where they belonged.

Her sweet, gentle librarian deserved a lover every bit as gentle as himself—a lover who *deserved* to cherish a treasure like Fabian in her bed. Saskia had made a mess of far too much in her life and hurt too many people already. She *would not* add Fabian to that number! So she set her teeth together and forced herself to concentrate on the page before her.

It was frustratingly difficult to research any methods for battling a goddess. Oh, there were plenty of mentions of Elva in various magical tomes, but they were all devoted to extolling the power and glory of Her many and varied aspects. According to theologians and wizards alike, She was even personally responsible for the unleashing of wild magic into the world, when She had graciously allowed it to spill through Her cupped palms as a divine gift to humans and animals alike.

Saskia found it bitterly ironic, in that case, that She had been the patron goddess of Estarion since its founding. Oh, they might still officially worship Her there with fancy shrines and priestesses, but once Estarion had joined the Serafin Empire, that theoretical worship hadn't stopped any of their archdukes from executing Imperial policy by stealing every magical child from their families, to be squeezed and restricted in Gilded Academies until there wasn't a trace of wildness left in them.

Still, Saskia supposed that gods and goddesses were no more likely to be logical in Their affections than humans ever had been . . . and she wasn't feeling particularly reasonable herself. So she scribbled notes through the night with her new fountain pen, and she didn't give up her search until the sun began to rise, marking her deadline to return her borrowed books before her librarian could catch her at it.

Dragging herself out of sleep only a few hours later felt like clawing her way out of a deep, muddy pit. When Saskia finally managed to rise from bed and shuffle back downstairs to her laboratory, her eyelids felt thick and unwieldy, and her head spun with every step. Usually, her first cup of coffee did a better job of waking her, but this time, the coffee waiting outside her room had been surprisingly watery, with a bitter aftertaste that left her feeling even worse than before. Her feet carried her towards her work desk by sheer force of habit as the room swayed gently around her.

Once she arrived, she had to blink her bleary eyes several times before she could be certain of what she saw there.

Her laboratory notebook waited on the center of the desk, just as it had every other morning since Fabian had returned it, reassembled, the day after Winter's Turning. All her shelves of carefully sealed jars and beakers waited in their own usual places on the shelves nearby without a single speck out of place.

But four long stalks of dried rosemary and thyme, tied together by a black ribbon, lay on the desk beside the notebook. She lifted them instinctively, holding them to her cheek and breathing in the spicy, pungent scents of comfort and safety.

Saskia's eyes fell shut. As she breathed in that familiar blend of aromas, she found herself transported back to the warmth of Mrs. Haglitz's cozy kitchen, in that isolated cottage where she'd been welcomed with open arms, treated like a child rather than a monster, and taught—with steady, unwavering patience—to give care and attention to every task and always do her very best.

Had these herbs actually *come* from Mrs. Haglitz's kitchen in this castle? Why would she . . . ?

Saskia's thumb brushed across a small slip of paper hidden behind the black ribbon that bound the herbs together. Her eyes flashed open, her sleep-addled brain clearing in a sudden, desperate rush.

This slip of paper bore no message—only a single letter:

F.

The bottom dropped out of Saskia's stomach, leaving her hopelessly untethered as she stood, gripping the herbs in her hand and staring at that small, neat signature.

How could Fabian possibly have known that she would love this particular scent combination?

And how in all the gods' names was she meant to resist a man who offered her such comfort?

A light knock sounded on the laboratory door, and she startled. "Just a moment!" Her heartbeat tumbled into a gallop as she swiftly laid the herbs back onto the desk beside her notebook, exactly where she'd found them. Her free hand fluttered towards her hair. It was still loosely bound in its nighttime plait, but that restriction never lasted for long. Thick, flyaway strands burst out rebelliously in all directions, and . . .

No. She forced her fingers away before she could set any of it to rights. She was *not* setting out to seduce Fabian, no matter what her traitorous heart might desire. It didn't matter if she looked a mess when he arrived. She should *want* to scare him off.

It should *thrill* her.

"Oh, come in, then!" she snarled, hating everything.

The door opened, and Morlokk stepped inside, bearing a small silver platter with a pot of coffee and an empty cup, and raising one eyebrow at her tone.

Saskia let out a deep, shuddering breath, her shoulders sagging. "Oh, Morlokk. It's you."

"Indeed, Your Majesty." He placed the platter on the shelf she kept empty for that purpose. "Mrs. Haglitz felt you might require more coffee than usual, after taking so little rest . . . *again*."

Saskia grimaced but reached for the pot anyway, driven by the low, persistent throbbing that had just begun in the back of her skull. "I haven't been staying up late for my own entertainment, you know," she muttered as she poured the coffee.

This was far more like it—thick and dark and rich, with a scent that nearly made her moan. Clearly, Mrs. Haglitz had made this pot herself.

"Mmm." Morlokk's tone reeked of skepticism. "I was, perhaps mistakenly, under the impression that you had hired a librarian to deal with any research that was necessary."

Saskia fixed her gaze intently on the coffeepot as she set it back into place, careful not to let her sleep-clumsy fingers expose her more than the shadows under her eyes probably already had. "He has quite enough work to do already, trying to organize that mess my uncle left."

"And you *don't?*"

Saskia might be willing to take a stand against the Serafin Empire and a literal goddess, but even she recognized some limits. Choosing common sense over pride, she held her tongue, took a long, life-giving sip, and didn't try to argue the point.

Morlokk's sigh, as he left the room, spoke volumes. Saskia did her best to ignore it, along with her increasingly distracting dizziness, as she buried herself in experimentation for the rest of the day. According to Ailana's latest missive, the Archduke of Estarion had failed in his attempt to bribe Saskia's neighbors into allowing his army safe passage into her kingdom. Thanks to the queens' display of unity at Winter's Turning, not one of her royal neighbors would dare to openly aid the Empire in any attack. Even so, Saskia wasn't naive enough to think that the Archduke would give up on reclaiming Kitvaria as a client state. Nor would her uncle.

She had to be ready to defend her kingdom if—no, curse it, *when* her magical barrier inevitably failed, whether the Emperor overruled the arguments of his high priest and sent a squadron of Imperial Gilded Wizards to destroy it, or the Archduke and her uncle found a different way to sneak around it. Regardless, Saskia *could not* be taken off guard again, the way she had been as a careless child, thinking she and her family were safe.

But, gods, she really was exhausted. Even the arrival of another pot of coffee in the middle of the afternoon couldn't cure the heaviness in her bones . . . especially as this pot, left without a word outside her laboratory door, had clearly been made by the same person who'd mucked up her first cup at breakfast. The taste of the watery brew was so bitter, it made her wince—but she swallowed it down anyway as fuel for her work.

As the clock ticked towards midnight, she moved slower and slower, until she finally found her eyes drifting irresistibly closed as she leaned against the wall with that damned bouquet of herbs somehow held once more in her right hand, wafting the too-tempting scents of comfort and peace and . . .

"*No!*" Saskia launched herself off the wall like a bird of prey taking flight, ignoring the protest in her aching back and the sickening spinning in her head.

She was responsible for the safety of this castle and this kingdom. She would not give in to physical weakness now.

Pulling off her apron with one hand, she stomped towards the stairs . . . and only realized halfway up the winding staircase that she was still holding the herbs.

"Gah!" She started to pivot, to return them to her laboratory. Her foot slipped on the ancient, uneven stair—and she caught herself just in time, panting with effort.

This is ridiculous. No, she hadn't slept much for several days, but what of it? The world still shouldn't be swimming this way before her eyes.

Perhaps, if she let herself fall asleep in her study nest for a single hour . . .

"*. . . Still pretending there isn't a kingdom outside that needs you?*"

Mirjana's imagined judgement rang in her ears, and Saskia groaned, shoving herself back upright.

She'd never wake up in a mere hour if she let herself sleep now—and she couldn't afford to go running down and up stairs in her current condition.

Pressing her lips together, she reached over her shoulder to tuck the stalks into the back of her gown. They were far too scratchy to be comfortable, but that was good: the itchiness would keep her awake and alert through the rest of the journey.

Another few deep breaths, and the staircase nearly stopped spinning around her. She pressed both palms against the close walls to hold her steady.

Every step upwards was a milestone. Every breath hurt.

Should she really be this dizzy?

Focus on what matters.

She'd run through this castle half-blind with fear and panic once before, waiting every moment for her uncle's guards and mages to capture her. She could walk at a steady pace through it now that she was mistress of the castle *and* the kingdom.

Running through the woods and tangling branches, chest burning, breath loud in her ears . . .

"*. . . Little monster, we can't kill you yet . . .*"

Her parents' blood . . .

Saskia staggered out of the staircase, into the foyer that led to her library. Every footfall thudded an agonizing echo in her skull. What were all of her crows doing here, in this room, now? She'd forgotten to send them ahead of her to check that the library was empty. They should still be—

Crows fluttering around her inquisitively as she wakes in the woods, dirty and hungry and lost and so, so cold . . .

Gods, she was cold . . .

"Your Majesty?" That wasn't the voice of a crow speaking to her. "Oskar brought me down to—*Saskia?*"

She couldn't see him through the crows in her past and her present and the blackness sweeping inexorably over her . . . but she felt the warmth of his gentle, familiar fingers as they closed around her arms, and she knew that she was finally, finally safe.

"Fabian," she whispered, and she let the darkness take her.

18

askia!"

Not ten minutes before, Felix had been lying in bed when Oskar had abruptly gone wild, battering at the door and cawing loudly enough to wake the dead. Felix hadn't been asleep, though; he'd been lying awake with every muscle tensed, imagining every possible reaction Saskia might have to the gift he'd left in the library for her tonight, from delight to excoriating scorn.

He had never imagined *this*.

As she crumpled against him, he caught her automatically, hands slipping from her upper arms to lock into place around her waist and back while her agitated crows swarmed the air around them, flapping and cawing desperately. Her body was warm, but she was shivering; dread sank through him as he pressed his cheek against her forehead and felt the too-familiar touch of burning skin.

"No, no, no!" He scarcely heard his own desperate words as he gathered her up, pressing her as close as if he could absorb the fever from her body. "Not again!"

Emmeline's fever had raged for days, resisting every medical treatment from leeches to healing chants. The Count had thrown every possible resource into saving her, and Felix had prayed to every god and goddess in the Imperial pantheon as he'd sat beside her. Even so, less than a full week later . . .

"No!" Felix snarled, and the crows jerked back in shock at the ferocity of his tone. "Get Morlokk and Mrs. Haglitz," he told them as he lifted Saskia in his arms and strode towards the library door. "Now."

Later, he would work to soothe hurt feelings among the flock. Right now, he had a queen to save.

He had to haphazardly kick and shove piles of books and papers off the closest couch in the library to make space for Saskia's prone body, but for once, he didn't hesitate to mishandle documents. When something rustled against his left arm, though, as he lowered her onto the couch, he paused. Had one of those papers somehow fallen *inside* her gown?

His eyebrows rose as he recognized the bouquet of herbs he'd left for her that morning, now sticking out from the back of her collar. She'd been carrying his offerings with her.

Emotion welled through him at the sight, threatening to erupt, but he couldn't stop to absorb it—or leave the herbs in their current position. She might not know, in this state, that they were scratching her back, but he absolutely would, and he couldn't bear it. Still, the moment he'd removed the herbs and carefully arranged her body atop the couch, he lunged to turn on a gas lamp and then *run* for one of the bookshelves he'd already begun to refill. He was tearing through the first volume on that shelf when the door crashed open and Morlokk burst into the room.

"Sinistro! What's happ—are you *standing there reading* while she suffers?!" The ogre's voice rose to a ferocious bellow that shook the library.

Felix wasn't even tempted to glance up from his book. "I am *trying* to find the right spell of healing," he gritted.

There had to be at least *one* option that could be successfully performed by a nonmagical human . . . but so far, he hadn't found any.

Every single book in this section included at least one healing spell—but every single author surrounded that spell with pages of long-winded warnings about how dangerous the spell might be if applied without exact knowledge of the illness being treated. The wrong spell might not only exacerbate the problem but even kill the patient—and as some of the most powerful and sophisticated workings in existence, they *all* required extreme levels of magical strength from the wizard who cast them.

"Damn it!" Panting, he dropped the first volume to the floor and scooped up the second with hands that trembled uncontrollably.

"So you didn't do this to her yourself?"

"*What?*" Felix finally swung around to stare at Morlokk, his jaw dropping open in disbelief.

"Never mind." The ogre closed his eyes, big shoulders sagging. The majordomo looked shockingly disheveled without a cravat or a jacket over his massive chest and crumpled shirt. "Tell me exactly what happened."

"I don't know!" Felix darted a glance at Saskia's shivering figure, and his jaw tightened. "Oskar brought me here just as she arrived. She fell into my arms."

Morlokk rubbed at his forehead with one fist. "And she didn't say a word that might explain it?"

"Only my name." Felix's voice nearly cracked on that final word.

The way she'd said it, with such mingled yearning and relief . . .

The memory of Emmeline whispering it, just before *her* end . . .

Swallowing, he flipped open the spellbook in his hand to skim through it with all the focus he could summon. He would not stand by, helpless, again and lose another woman he loved.

In the corner of his vision, he saw Morlokk bend over the couch to scoop up the queen's body with infinite care. She looked horribly weak and defenseless as she lay cradled in his arms. Their pose was almost a perfect copy of the hateful images circulated within the Empire, showing ogres menacing human women—but Felix could feel the other man's agony almost as keenly as his own.

Saskia's human parents might have been murdered long ago, but she was still a beloved daughter to more than one person in this castle.

The other one burst into the library as Morlokk straightened. "You've got her. Good." Mrs. Haglitz's words were as brisk as ever, but for the first time since Felix had met her, she was only wearing a single shawl around her shoulders. It lost its purchase as she strode towards Saskia, and she let it fall to the ground with an impatient shrug. "Now, what's she done this time? Worked herself into dropping, or . . . ?"

"She has a fever," Felix reported tightly. He was still gripping the book in his hands, but his gaze fixed on Saskia's lolling head as Mrs. Haglitz turned it back and forth for inspection. "She could barely keep her balance, even before she swooned."

"*Swooned?*" Mrs. Haglitz's eyes narrowed. "Something's not right here." Tipping Saskia's head back, she pried open the queen's mouth and took a long inhalation through her pointed green nose. "Faughh!" Gargling in the back of her throat, she stepped back so quickly that she nearly tripped over the closest stack of books . . . and then collapsed onto the couch as if she'd been pushed there.

"What is it?" Felix demanded. The troll's green skin had faded to a sickly grey with what looked like horror. "If you can tell me which illness has struck her down—"

"That's no mere *illness*," Mrs. Haglitz rasped. "She's been poisoned."

There was a long moment of pulsating silence before Morlokk spoke. "That's not possible."

Mrs. Haglitz had always riled at any disagreements with her pronouncements—but this time, alarmingly, her response sounded as weak and faded as if she'd given up already. "It *shouldn't* be possible, but I can smell the poison on her. Moon forsake me, how could it have reached her? I've been in charge of all of her meals since Cook left. Could I have accidentally sent it to her?"

"*No.* You would never hurt her. We all know that!" Setting down his book, Felix crossed the room in two swift strides. He dropped down to his knees on the floor before the housekeeper and took her weathered, mossy green hands in his own. He'd never touched troll skin before, but he was almost certain that hers was far too cold, regardless of her species. It had to be shock; he remembered all too well that sensation of freezing cold when he'd first realized that Emmeline was truly dying and there was nothing he could do to save her.

He had to swallow down that memory, hard, before he continued, rubbing her hands gently to impart as much warmth as possible. "You smelled the poison in her mouth just now. That means you would have smelled it in any food or drink you sent her."

"Did anyone taste it first?" Morlokk rumbled.

"You think I'd send our queen a meal I hadn't tasted myself, to be certain of its quality?" To Felix's relief, the implied insult seemed to rouse Mrs. Haglitz a little. Her snort sounded weaker than usual, but her haunted gaze finally refocused on the men before her. "I sent three solid meals to her today, along with a good-sized snack to keep up her strength, since she *will* insist on being so stubborn and not looking after herself."

"Who took them to her?" Felix asked.

She shrugged impatiently, her mossy hands still pliant in his hold. "Krakk, I think? It doesn't matter. None of the kitchen staff would harm her."

Thinking of the cheerful little goblins who'd welcomed him from the beginning, Felix wanted to believe it. All his years at the Estarian court, though, had taught him to ask the question: "Even if they were bribed? There were visitors here only a week ago who might have talked one of them into it."

"With *what?*" Her laugh was sharp-edged as she finally pulled her hands free. "You think *goblins* need human help to get hold of gold or diamonds? With our queen on the throne, we all have rights we'd never even dreamed of in this kingdom. The last thing any of us want is that uncle of hers back on the throne, determined to grind us all back down into what *he* sees as our proper place."

"I believe you." Felix let out a long sigh, sitting back on his heels. This castle wasn't like any court he'd ever known; every servant here knew their queen, and she cared for every one of them. He'd seen her fierce protectiveness for himself.

And yet, *someone* had poisoned her.

Turning his head, he looked up at Morlokk. "How certain are you that every guest who came for Winter's Turning really left?"

A low growl rumbled through the ogre's chest, and his eyes flashed an inhuman gold. In that moment, he looked every bit as dangerous as the caricatures from the warning pamphlets. "*We'll find out.*"

Outside the castle walls, a wild winter storm was raging, whipping snow and lightning into a lethal brew. No crow, no matter how brave, could fly into that night in search of a physician, nor could the queen herself be moved. Two goblins volunteered to go instead, following their own intricate maze of tunnels under the mountain in a quest that might well take a day or more.

The urgent notes they bore for Saskia's allied queens would take even longer to arrive . . . and everyone in Kadaric Castle knew that time was running out.

While Mrs. Haglitz investigated Saskia's laboratory for clues, Morlokk, the crows, and the other goblins searched the castle, hunting for the perpetrator. If they did find the poisoner and learn the type of poison used, they *might* find a remedy for it within Saskia's laboratory . . . but it was difficult for Felix to hold much hope when even Mrs. Haglitz admitted she didn't know at least half of the ingredients Saskia stored there.

It was time to finally take the risk he hadn't even dared to imagine until now.

Fortunately, the others had left the queen lying on the couch of her library—with a soft blanket spread over her shivering body and the fire carefully built nearby—so that Felix could stand guard over her as he continued his own search through the medical texts. That was the official agreement.

Unofficially, he waited until the others had left the room . . . and then he took a deep breath before leaving that standard shelf behind and crossing to the side of the room where all of the late queen's radical manuscripts were stored.

He had never been so conscious of his own beating pulse as he felt now, striding towards the moment of truth.

How much *had* he learned in the last few months? And was there any chance that his childhood examiners could have been wrong when they'd declared him free of magic?

Everyone knew that those exams were infallible—but then, everyone in the Empire also "knew" that trolls and ogres were evil, monstrous creatures. If only they were wrong about this, too . . . then Felix might have one option left after all.

The spell for leeching *all* types of poison was clearly recorded where he remembered it, written in the late queen's elegant script, along with the story of how she'd acquired it in her youth from a solitary and unusual dark wizard in an isolated corner of Kitvaria. She had spent weeks proving herself to the cantankerous old woman, first through patient assistance in cleaning and washing up the wizard's impossibly messy hut, and then by sharing a troll recipe for a magical liniment that would soothe the many aches and pains suffered by that hut's ancient and withered pair of chicken-legs.

At last, the old wizard had rewarded the not-yet-queen with the gift of this astonishing spell . . . which required a strong reservoir of magical power in order to take effect.

On the couch, Saskia let out a low moan of pain. She shifted restlessly under her blanket, and Felix's jaw tightened into rock.

Enough. He might have spent most of his life having the lesson of his own powerlessness ruthlessly ground into him, but he wasn't in Estarion any longer. For months now, he had successfully played the part of a dark wizard.

Now, it was time to act like one.

The spell itself was short and simple enough to memorize. He knew, from close reading of the late queen's primer, that focus and intent were both required. Divine Elva knew, he had all the *intent* that anyone could possibly ask for. The sound of Saskia's increasingly labored breathing grated against his senses like a whip, lashing him on. But when it came to focus . . .

Closing his eyes, he focused all his willpower on finding that quiet center in his mind where he was detached from all sensations and the world could no longer reach him. In his youth, it had helped him to endure the worst and most brutal of punishments. Now, he breathed deeply and evenly until he found himself safely enclosed there once more, far away from the fear and the grief that he felt.

Alone in that space, he began to chant the words of the spell, with the intent behind it ringing through them:

Just heal her. Heal her. Heal her.

He spoke the words of the spell in his head, but he pushed them out through his body, distantly aware of his moving lips and the push of air through his chest. Of course, it was reckless to attempt his first spellcasting in a not-yet-catalogued library of magic—but he knew how much this whole castle loved its queen. He couldn't imagine that anything in this room would lash out at his attempt to heal her.

There *was* heat somewhere nearby—and pain, too—but both of those were distant realities that couldn't touch him now.

He recited the spell again and again. *Heal her. Heal her. Heal . . .*

How many times *had* he cast the spell, now? His focus wavered with the question.

Had it been nine times now, or ten?

Felix slid back into full awareness . . . and stiffened with the impact of his sudden pain and shock. His left ear—! Was it on fire?

Forcing his eyes open, he scrambled upright and found himself on the carpet just beside the couch. *Ah.* He must have knocked the left side of his head against the arm of the couch on his way down. The only real fire in the room was safely contained in the hearth.

It couldn't warm the chill in his chest when he saw Saskia's unaltered expression.

Her eyes were still closed. Her fever hadn't broken.

Felix had failed her.

19

Everything was roiling, whirling darkness—no words, no air, no hope left in the pitch-black sea of feathers that had sucked Saskia down and held her there, drowning—until a faint, golden glow appeared high overhead.

Saskia surged upwards, too desperate even to care what it might be. Something warm and strong caught hold of her fingers and *pulled*— and as feathers began to clear above her, she finally realized exactly where that golden glow had originated.

Divine Elva grinned down at Saskia as She effortlessly pulled her up, on top of the shifting sea of feathers beneath an endless, starry sky. "FANCY SEEING YOU HERE, YOUR MAJESTY." The goddess's shifting form—young/old, small/large—fluctuated with every instant around the shape-memory of Her priestess's face and figure, and it glowed in the darkness like a star, making Saskia's eyes sting.

She refused to rub them or look away. Her heartbeat was a desperate thrum against her chest as she sat perched atop her shifting, impossible seat, braced for the feathers to part once more beneath her and suck her back down to drown at any moment.

All around her, more black feathers stretched to the horizon, without any landmarks in sight. Her castle was nowhere to be found—and as for the people in it, left without her protection . . .

Her fingers clenched around black feathers. "Is this Your doing?" she demanded fiercely. "Have you kidnapped me on behalf of the Estarian Archduke?"

Divine Elva tipped back Her head and laughed, a deep, rolling sound that shook the sea of feathers beneath them. "OH, CHILD. THERE'S VERY LITTLE THAT A GODDESS CAN ACTUALLY *DO* IN THIS MODERN WORLD. HAVEN'T YOU WORKED THAT OUT AFTER ALL THE TIME YOU'VE SPENT IN STUDYING ME, LATELY?"

Curse take it, of course the goddess knew about her research. Had Saskia really imagined that anything could stay secret from an all-knowing being? Fighting down a snarl, she said, "According to my research, you're all-powerful."

"AND ARE YOU ALLOWED TO USE ALL OF *YOUR* POWERS?" the goddess inquired.

"There are limits, even for a queen," Saskia said tightly. "Lines that cannot be crossed, to stay safe. But—"

"ARE THEY TRULY UNCROSSABLE? OR DO YOU HIDE BEHIND THEM? HOW MANY TIMES DID YOU TRY TO PRAY AWAY YOUR OWN POWERS WHEN YOU WERE A GIRL?"

"That's not the point!" Saskia was breathing hard. "I'm not a child anymore."

"NO?" The goddess looked at her with a face that shifted from youth to age again and again. "BUT DO YOU NOT STILL FEEL THAT CHILD'S FEAR?"

Oh, she remembered those frantic, sobbing old prayers far too well. She'd aimed them at every god and goddess she could think of, with a single, desperate message every time: *Just take them away. Take them back! Set me free!*

Her powers had broken her family. They'd turned her into a monster whispered about and feared by everyone.

Back then, she would have given anything to be rid of them.

Now, Saskia said with all the adult calm she could muster, "My uncle used my powers as his excuse to seize the throne. He would have found another reason, though, if he hadn't had them to seize upon."

"VERY WISE." There was a maddeningly indulgent tone to the goddess's words. "BUT DO YOU BELIEVE YOUR OWN WORDS? TRULY?"

"We're not here to chat about my powers. I didn't do any of *this*!" Saskia waved at the expanse of feathers and darkness around them. "Only a goddess could."

"MM..." Divine Elva cocked Her head. "IT IS AN INTERESTING QUESTION, WHAT A GODDESS CAN OR CANNOT DO NOWADAYS. WE MAY NO LONGER ACT DIRECTLY IN THE HUMAN WORLD. WE MAY WATCH. WE MAY WHISPER A DIVINE BREATH OF PER-SUASION FROM TIME TO TIME, IN AID OF THOSE CREATURES WE HOLD MOST DEAR. WE MAY, OCCASIONALLY, DEIGN TO APPEAR IN DREAMS. AND EVERY SO OFTEN, MOST RARELY OF ALL..."

She swept out Her own golden-glowing arm in display, her smile curving wider. "WE MAY ENACT A TINY MIRACLE."

"You mean . . . this?" Saskia's eyebrows furrowed as she looked around once more at the surreal landscape. "Why waste a miracle on me?"

"OH, THIS ISN'T THE MIRACLE. NOT YET." Divine Elva's gaze caught hers and held. "HAVE YOU NOT NOTICED THAT YOU'RE DYING?"

Saskia went still, awareness crashing through her.

When she'd felt herself drowning under that impossible sea of black feathers . . . what *had* she actually been doing, before the goddess had yanked her free for this dreamlike conversation?

Goddesses could appear in dreams, Elva had said. Could They appear in other forms of unconsciousness?

Saskia had felt so unnaturally dizzy and weak in her last memories of the real world of her castle. The past and present had merged around her, the room had disappeared, and then . . .

I was attacked. At home, in her very safest of places, someone had found a way to pierce all of her magical defenses and bring her down without her even recognizing the assault as it happened.

But if that were true, where was she now?

The body she wore now felt as hollow as air the moment she focused upon it. How had she not realized? It was a dream-form with no substance. What was happening to her true body in the world outside?

And if an enemy had somehow reached into her castle once already, what else might they do to everyone left there?

"I have to get back!" she said. "I have to protect—"

"NOW, THAT WOULD TAKE A MIRACLE." Smiling serenely, Divine Elva raised her eyebrows. "DO YOU WISH TO PRAY FOR ONE?"

Saskia gritted her teeth, rage and fear uniting. "First tell me what you'll demand if I do." She might still be confused and hopelessly out of her depth, but she *knew* the goddess wouldn't have bothered with this offer of salvation if She didn't have another purpose in mind. Saskia had never been one of Elva's worshippers. This was no random act of kindness . . . and her months as a queen had taught her to beware of hidden schemes.

Goddesses could whisper persuasion in aid of their favorites, and this goddess had visited Saskia twice now—a singular effort, if She was to be believed.

The first time, at Winter's Turning, She had pointed a finger directly at . . .

"*No!*" Saskia lunged to her feet as that shared memory filled the space between them, eerily mirrored in the goddess's shining eyes. "I will not hurt Fabian. Not for You and not for anyone else. I don't care what he's done to anger your precious Archduke! I will not release him from my protection. If that's a condition of my survival, You might as well just let me die."

She expected divine outrage or disdain. Instead, Elva's lips stretched into what could only be termed a *smirk*. "ALL OF MY CREATURES ARE PRECIOUS," She murmured, as horns and wings and fangs joined the whirl of fluctuating characteristics in Her golden form, "BUT YOU'RE RIGHT: ESTARION'S ARCHDUKE IS IN-DEED DEAR TO ME. I HAVE MANY PLANS FOR HIM."

Saskia eyed Her warily. "I won't allow Fabian to be harmed, no matter what the Archduke wants."

"VERY WELL. I ACCEPT THAT CONDITION." Divine Elva lowered one shining eyelid in a wink. "I SHALL GRANT YOU A MIRACLE OF ONE MINUTE'S LENGTH. I SUGGEST YOU LISTEN TO ADVICE AND USE IT WELL. BUT WHEN YOU ARE FINALLY INTRODUCED TO ES-TARION'S ARCHDUKE? RESTRAIN YOURSELF FROM HARMING HIM, FOR MY SAKE. I PROMISE, YOU WON'T REGRET IT."

Saskia was fairly certain that she *would* regret it if she came face-to-face with that bastard and didn't mete out the treatment he deserved—

But as she opened her mouth to argue, she found herself abruptly surrounded by bright light and freezing cold, lying propped along one of her library couches with Fabian's familiar, masked face just before her.

His hands were clasped beneath his black half-mask as he knelt before her, his lips moving continuously with inaudible prayers ... until a fresh shiver racked Saskia's freezing body, she let out an involuntary huff of air, and his brown eyes flashed open to meet hers.

Felix nearly fell against the couch with the force of his relief. "Your Majesty! Elva be thanked, you're awake—"

"Elva gave me only one minute," Saskia muttered, pushing herself up onto one elbow with what looked like intense effort.

"I beg your pardon?"

As Felix frowned at her, the door to the library burst open. "I've found it," Mrs. Haglitz announced. "It was in a pot of coff—Saskia!"

"Your Majesty." Morlokk's thunderous strides shook the floor in Mrs. Haglitz's wake. "Are you cured?"

"For less than one minute, now." The queen's face was still flushed with fever, and her shadowed dark eyes burned with ferocity. "Divine Elva gave me a deadline and told me to use it by following advice. Are any of you prepared to offer any?"

For one awestruck moment, Felix stared at her in incomprehension . . . and then realization clicked into place. He could have laughed with both relief and despair. *So much for attempting this in private.*

Everyone who held any authority in this castle was here in this room now to serve as an observer if this shattered his disguise—but no matter.

"*I* am ready to advise you," he told her firmly. "You need to cast a particular spell." If anyone in the world could make it work, *she* could. No one else had a greater reservoir of magical power. "Repeat these words after me, and put all of your intent into expelling the poison from your body."

Her dark eyebrows rose sharply as he uttered the word "poison," but she didn't waste any time by asking for clarification.

Her trust was humbling.

As Felix coached her through the words of the short spell, Morlokk and Mrs. Haglitz drew closer and closer around them. The fire in the hearth crackled with heat. The air crackled with magical power.

Queen Saskia spoke the final word of the spell . . .

And then gagged uncontrollably as the contents of her stomach erupted and overwhelmed her.

Felix lunged forward, ignoring the mess showering onto his cloak, to hold and support her shaking shoulders as the heaving waves broke through her.

"It's all right, you're all right, my queen, you're going to be all right now—*Saskia!*"

As the tall clock across the room chimed dolefully, Queen Saskia's eyes abruptly rolled back in her head. She slumped in his arms, still heaving uncontrollably but no longer aware of any of it. As promised, the queen had lost consciousness once more at the end of her single minute . . .

And as Felix caught her for the second time that night, a faint ripple of warm air brushed over his body, making every hair on his arms stand on end . . . like the breath of unimaginable divinity passing over him.

Divine Elva. The goddess truly had interceded. Felix swallowed hard, wonder and gratitude nearly overwhelming him.

"Don't you let her fall!" Mrs. Haglitz rushed up to his side, propping the queen's still-spasming body carefully against the back of the couch. "If she chokes on any of this now, we'll be lost."

"We won't let her choke," Morlokk said grimly, taking his place behind the couch and putting one big hand on Saskia's shoulder. "But will it be enough? If it's been too many hours since she first ingested the poison . . ."

"It was slipped into some coffee she drank," said Mrs. Haglitz. "I found a pot and cup in her laboratory, but I can tell you, they didn't come from *our* kitchen, and I didn't send them to her. There's no way to know when they were delivered."

"That doesn't matter anymore." Felix's own body felt utterly wrung out. The smell of vomit was overwhelming, and the tip of his left ear was still throbbing from his absurd earlier injury . . . but relief and wonder combined to make him feel as if he were floating above it all. "She cast the spell, and it *took.* Even if not all of the poison physically emerges now, the spell will see to all the rest."

He might not have the power to cast it himself, but he *had* learned from his time in this library. He knew how to read and interpret magical spells, and he had felt the force of this one as Saskia cast it.

"You saved her, Sinistro." Tears shone openly in Mrs. Haglitz's eyes as she turned and grasped one of his hands in both of her own. "Without that spell, we would have lost her. *Thank you.* We won't forget this, any of us."

"You have all of our thanks," Morlokk said gravely.

Felix's eyes widened as the majordomo bowed respectfully over the back of the couch. "But I didn't. If the goddess hadn't intervened—if Her Majesty hadn't awoken to cast the spell herself—I *couldn't do it.*" The truth burst out, uncontrollably. "I tried to cast that spell while you were both gone. I didn't have the power to effect it."

Morlokk nodded. "Very few people do have Her Majesty's level of magical power. It takes a strong man to admit to his own weakness in comparison."

"I . . ."

"Enough," said Mrs. Haglitz firmly. On the couch, Saskia had finally finished emptying her stomach; now, the housekeeper stood, wiping her hands briskly on her nightgown. "We've all had enough worries for the night, so you'll accept our gratitude and be done with it. Now, I need to get our girl cleaned up and into bed, and you, Sinistro, are not required for any of that."

"I could—"

"You've done quite enough already." She gave Felix an imperative look, and he slowly and reluctantly rose to his feet. "Her fever's already gone. You told us yourself that she'll be fine. Go and get some rest, so you can sit by her bedside tomorrow and make certain she doesn't overexert herself while she recovers."

"I can do that." Letting out a long sigh, Felix started for the door. There was no Oskar here to flutter after him; every crow was busy now on the hunt for the poisoner, no matter where they might be hiding in this ancient castle full of secrets.

His own disguise hadn't been broken after all. Still, as he looked back at the small gathering around the couch, his deception felt more fragile—and more unforgivable—than ever before.

20

When Saskia awoke the next morning, every muscle in her body clamored in protest. Her parched and aching throat tasted utterly foul. Worse yet, her stomach felt as if someone had reached inside with a flaming scalpel to scrape it clean, leaving raw, bleeding wounds behind.

She finally blinked her heavy eyelids open and found Fabian, of all people, sitting directly beside her bed in a comfortable-looking, unfamiliar wing chair, reading a thick, leather-bound book and making studious notes in his commonplace book with his faithful fountain pen.

Saskia's throat felt as if it had been peeled with a rusty knife as she rasped, "What are you doing here?"

"Your Majesty!" The joyful smile that lit up his face was almost enough to make her forget, for a moment, her own physical misery. Quickly capping his fountain pen, he set everything aside and leaned forward, over her bed with shocking intimacy, to look her up and down.

For once, he wasn't wearing his familiar, shroud-like cloak. Instead, he was clad in an elegant mourning suit of all black that complemented his lean figure beautifully and looked to be made to a high Imperial design. Small jet buttons lined his black silk waistcoat, and close-fitting wool trousers would—she was almost certain—reveal every single inch of those long legs she'd been dreaming about for weeks . . . if only she could raise herself high enough to see them.

Really, it was absurd to lie here unmoving while he gazed down at her with such tender care, as if she were some helpless creature. Pressing her hands against the mattress, Saskia began to push herself up—and let out an involuntary grunt at the effort it took, as if she were fighting to raise a heavy castle rather than her own ordinary self.

"Stop!" Fabian's sweet smile vanished as he put one hand on her closest shoulder, fingers closing gently around its curve. His brown eyes still looked soft with emotion behind the eyeholes of his mask, but his grip was firm. "You mustn't even try to get up yet. You need to lie still and recover for at least a week."

"A *week*? Don't be ridiculous." Scowling, Saskia continued to hold her half-raised position, even as her muscles trembled from the ongoing exertion. "I *hate* lying still."

"Imagine my astonishment," Fabian said wryly. One corner of his lips turned up in a tiny, rueful half-smile.

Oh, that's just not fair. Saskia loved that secret smile. It wasn't right for him to use it against her now, when she was weakened.

Still, he continued inexorably, "Take pity on me if nothing

else. Mrs. Haglitz will have my head if I let you hurt yourself by getting up when she trusted me to keep you resting."

"*Ugh.*" Why in the world had Mrs. Haglitz chosen *him* for that task? He was far too close and too tempting for Saskia's peace of mind, here in her own private bedchamber with that tiny smile still playing across his lips. It made her think of other things she'd like to do to those lips . . .

Until she swallowed over her still-parched throat and felt the horror of the taste in her own mouth fill her senses all over again.

No kissing!

Saskia clamped her lips shut and fell back onto her pillow, hoping he hadn't been able to smell her foul breath from his position.

"Are you thirsty?" Fabian stood, consoling her with—at long last—a proper view of the lower half of his body, clad in those lovely tight black trousers. She wholeheartedly approved of them—and when he turned his back, she didn't even have to pretend not to be ogling him. "I have a jug of water from the kitchen spring just here," he said, innocent and unaware of her shameless appraisal. "I'll ring for more food and drink for you, too."

Saskia accepted the cup of water that he handed her with a rasp of thanks, and she took her first sip as greedily as she could from her awkwardly prone position. Frowning, he bent over her once more.

"If you'll allow me . . ." He reached beneath her to lift her upper half with one arm while he propped more pillows behind her back, then lowered her to rest against them in a perfectly supported position. Every move felt confident and knowledgeable, and the touch of his hands on her aching body felt as gentle as if he thought her made of glass or crystal, something infinitely precious and breakable.

She wasn't. She was a wicked queen, and she couldn't let herself—or anyone else—forget it, no matter how dangerously good it might feel to lie back and let him handle her with care. So, as soon as she finished her cup of water, Saskia cleared her throat and said sharply, "Have you done this before?"

"I beg your pardon?" He'd been in the middle of sitting back down in his chair, but he hesitated at her question. "Done what, exactly?"

"Sitting by sickbeds with invalids." She gestured irritably at the pillows beneath her. "You knew just what to do."

"Ah." He sank the rest of the way down into the wing chair, his face tightening and his voice lowering. "I . . . have had some experience with that, yes."

She didn't need to ask what the outcome had been, that last time. The note of grief was unmistakable.

A truly wicked queen would have probed that wound, no doubt, to prove her own careless power. Saskia said quietly, "I'm sure they were glad to have you there."

"I hope she was," he replied, every bit as quietly. "There was nowhere else I would rather have been."

She? A question hesitated on the tip of Saskia's tongue . . .

But the door opened before she could ask it. Mrs. Haglitz bustled inside with a large, covered tray in her hands, while one of the goblin footmen, Krakk, capered after her with a toothy grin of delight, waving two fistfuls of cutlery in greeting.

"*Here* we go!" Mrs. Haglitz placed the tray on a round side table and carried it all with ease across the room to set the table down between Saskia and Fabian. "I've got a good lot of food here to bolster your strength without hurting your stomach— and as for *you* . . ." She turned her forceful gaze upon Fabian. "See that she eats every bite, and you do the same with yours. You need to keep up your own strength if you're to look after Her Majesty properly!"

"Very well," Fabian said, with apparent meekness—but with another of those slanting, half-hidden smiles. "Thank you."

Saskia's eyebrows rose as she watched their exchange of glances. *Well, that's new.* Fabian had only been living in this castle for a few months, but he had apparently already found a way into Mrs. Haglitz's well-guarded heart—which Mirjana, for all of her charm, never had, even back when Saskia herself had been most moon-eyed over her.

"I don't suppose I have any say in this?" she asked dryly.

Mrs. Haglitz glowered down at her. "Are you insulting my food, young lady?"

Saskia cast up her eyes in dramatic defeat. "As if anyone would ever dare."

"Hmph." Mrs. Haglitz lifted the metal cloche off the tray, and mouthwatering scents immediately came drifting out from the newly revealed bowls and plates, making Saskia give an involuntary sigh of yearning. "*That's* better! Now, it's soup for you, after everything your body's been through. If your spoon's too heavy, make this lad hold it for you, and be certain he does it properly."

Saskia narrowed her eyes at her beloved mentor. "I believe I can hold my own *spoon*, Mrs. Haglitz."

"Hmm. No coffee yet—you'll have to give your stomach time to recover—but I've made you healing tea, and you'll drink all of it."

"Of course I will." Saskia sighed. She'd drunk Mrs. Haglitz's healing tea before and knew its benefits . . . along with its downsides, beginning with its taste. Still, she wasn't a complete fool. If she wanted to return to full strength before the week was up, the last thing she needed was to refuse her medicine.

Although, speaking of coffee . . .

She frowned. "Did someone different make two of the pots of coffee yesterday? It tasted . . . *oh!*" Her weary brain finally put together all of the pieces.

Last night, in that brief, vivid moment when Divine Elva had brought her back from the verge of death . . .

"Was *that* what held the poison?"

"We will not talk about that now!" Mrs. Haglitz slammed down the cloche with a clatter that rang through the room and made even cheeky Krakk lean away from her, wide-eyed and wary. Her eyes sparkled with fury—and something more—as she pointed at Saskia with one sturdy, horn-nailed finger. "*You* are going to focus all of your strength on *getting better* and never scaring us like that again, and we are not going to discuss *anything else* until I've forgotten what it felt like to watch you *dying* in front of me!"

Saskia drew an exasperated breath—but then took in, once more, the sparkle of unfamiliar tears in Mrs. Haglitz's eyes. She nodded. "Very well," she said just as meekly as Fabian had earlier.

Still, the mood felt distinctly subdued as Mrs. Haglitz and Krakk left the room, the little goblin waving a sneaky farewell over his shoulder as he followed the housekeeper.

Saskia returned his wave with one of her own and turned to Fabian as soon as the door fell closed behind them. "Now," she said, "tell me everything."

He didn't immediately answer. Instead, his brows furrowed as he studied her face as if searching for something.

Saskia didn't even try for menace. She only spoke the simple truth. "If you treat me as if I'd lost my wits along with my strength, I will never forgive you."

His eyebrows rose above his mask. "I understand. But do you think you could eat some of your soup while I tell you?"

Relief cascaded through Saskia as the tension flooded out of her. Whatever this sweet, tenuous connection was that shimmered between them—no matter how dangerous it might be— she suddenly realized that it would have hurt even more to lose *that*, now, than anything she'd experienced last night. She took a deep, thankful breath through her aching chest. "I think I can just about manage that."

Accepting the bowl he handed her—*and* the spoon, with a minatory look—she began to take slow, careful bites of the savory broth while he explained the discovery Mrs. Haglitz had made in Saskia's laboratory.

"Of course." Saskia winced, resting her hand with the spoon

against the side table. "I should have known that Mrs. Haglitz would never allow any coffee that tasted like that to be served, no matter the circumstances. I *would* have known, if I'd only stopped to think about it."

"Indeed," Fabian said dryly. "How unforgivable of you not to think of absolutely everything, always. It almost makes you seem . . . human."

Saskia narrowed her eyes, but she couldn't stop her lips from twitching. "How dare you."

"I do beg your pardon." He glanced down at her hand, which still rested on the table. "Would you like me to hold the spoon for you?"

"Ha. I could strike you down at any moment, you know." She firmly scooped the spoon back into the broth by herself and took a long, hot swallow . . .

Exactly as he'd intended her to, no doubt. Fortunately, the taste was so heavenly that she couldn't bring herself to mind his management, just this once. The broth carried a perfect blend of flavors, including the herbs that he had given her the day before—and at that thought, Saskia suddenly paused, instinctively grasping with her free hand at the back of her gown.

No. She wasn't even wearing yesterday's gown anymore, but a colorfully embroidered cotton nightdress. No stalks of herbs itched against her back. Where had her bouquet gone? And—

Curse take it. When her gown had been changed, had Fabian's poem been left out in the open, where he could see it if he only looked in the wrong direction?

Oh, gods. Suddenly, her whole body felt hot.

"Is something wrong?" In the last few months, his dark brown hair had lengthened until it brushed against the fine black wool of his collar. Now, the long, soft-looking strands slid over his face as he leaned forward, as if they were trying to tempt her into brushing them away.

"I'm fine." She curled the fingers of her free hand tightly around her faded patchwork quilt. It was not an impressively royal bed-cover, the sort that really ought to adorn the terrifying Witch Queen of Kitvaria's bed, but it had been far too beloved a point of comfort to give up when she'd finally moved back into this castle—the quilt Mrs. Haglitz had sewn and given to her when she'd finally reached safety.

She'd never expected anyone else to see it here.

It was impossible to look properly haughty or regal while half-lying against a stack of pillows, prickling with embarrass-ment and barely able to lift a spoon, but Saskia forced her gaze to stop darting around the room. If Fabian hadn't yet glimpsed the embarrassing evidence that she'd kept his poem—no, that she'd *cherished* it, carrying it with her—she could at least prevent herself from giving away its location now.

"I am *fine*," she repeated sternly, and she lifted the soup spoon once more, refusing to allow her aching arm to visibly tremble with effort.

"As you say, Your Majesty." Fabian's voice was gently skeptical, but he sat back without an argument, digging his own spoon into the meaty, spicy-smelling ragout that he'd been given as his meal. "So, the hunt for the poisoner is still ongoing. It was thought that every visitor for Winter's Turning was long gone—and Morlokk is certain that all of the official visitors *are*, because he attended them to their carriages—but most of them arrived with large ret-inues of servants and other attendants. Any one of those could have slipped away during the confusion and found a hiding place until the time felt right."

"There are so many hiding places in this castle . . ." Saskia tapped the spoon against her bowl, thinking it through. "They were definitely here yesterday afternoon when they left that pot of coffee outside my door. Was it already snowing hard by then?"

"If they left immediately afterwards, they may have made it out of the castle, but they couldn't have gone far along the mountain pass. The storm hit in the early evening. No one could travel through that."

"It would have been sensible for them, regardless, to wait until the sun went down to make their escape. Otherwise, they would have been spotted by my crows on their daily guard-flights around the mountainside. On the other hand . . . could they have gone underneath the castle, following the goblin tunnels?"

"I'll ask Morlokk if any of the goblins have been sent to comb those yet. The two I know about were on their way to fetch a physician, so they wouldn't have stopped to let us know if they saw any signs of passage there."

"*Physicians.*" Saskia rolled her eyes. "As if I need one of them fussing around me."

Fabian's eyes narrowed, and he set down his spoon with a small but distinctive *clink*, his expression suddenly astonishingly authoritative. "And yet, you *will* allow the physician to inspect you, to be certain that there's nothing more we can do to aid in your recovery. Yes?" His voice was harder than she'd ever heard it.

Too baffled to be annoyed, she frowned at him. "You know just as well as I do that the spell I cast removed the poison. Why bother asking someone else—not even a magic-worker!—what we both know already to be true?"

"Because everyone in this castle needs to know the same." Fabian's voice didn't soften. "Mrs. Haglitz was up all night with you. I've never seen Morlokk so shaken. They both need that reassurance, even if you don't."

Saskia held and matched his gaze . . . and then sighed. "Oh, very well," she muttered.

Even the most wicked and unfeeling of queens wouldn't choose to make Mrs. Haglitz weep again.

"I'll let him poke and prod me," she grumbled, "but in exchange, I want you to *promise* that you'll keep me updated on everything, no matter how much the others may want to shield me from bad news. And—oh, gods." She sagged back against the pillows, letting the spoon slip from her hands onto the tray. "I'm going to have to tell Mirjana about all of this, aren't I?"

"Mm." His lips twitched as his eyelids lowered. "If you do take a day or two to rest beforehand, you could simply explain that you *wished* to speak to her before anyone else, but your cruel staff members didn't allow you to think of any difficult or unpleasant matters in your fragile, invalid state."

"Most amusing." She rolled her eyes at him. "No, you can bring me my speaking box in an hour or so, and I'll deal with her then." There was no use in putting it off much longer. "However . . ."

The bowl of soup was nearly finished. Her stomach still hurt, but it felt warm and full, and a great weight was pulling down on her eyelids.

"Just to make Mrs. Haglitz happy," she said, fighting down a yawn, "I *might* close my eyes for a little while, first."

"Very wise, my queen." Fabian leaned over her to rearrange her pillows, bringing her back to a prone position.

His arm felt warm and firm around her back. His face was calm and intent on his work, but she breathed in his bergamot scent with every moment.

She'd never welcomed anyone like him before into the intimacy of this bedchamber, where all of her deepest weaknesses were laid bare. Somehow, though, it felt utterly right to have him here.

"Fabian," she murmured as her eyes fell closed, "you don't *have* to leave the room while I sleep if you don't wish to."

Warm, familiar fingers brushed against her cheek for the most fleeting and precious of moments. "Don't worry, my queen. I'm not going anywhere."

For her conversation with her First Minister, Saskia chose to be propped up once more against the pillows at as vertical an angle as possible. With Fabian's help, she even managed to array herself in a crimson velvet dressing gown of appropriate magnificence.

"There," he said as he tied the belt with a final flourish. "Now, you look like a perfectly terrifying and bloodthirsty queen ready to cut off anyone's head at the slightest provocation."

"Just so long as I don't fall asleep midexecution," she said dryly. "That might lower the tone just a bit."

"Not at all. It would only make you seem *too*,

too, impressively world-weary," he informed her in a perfectly executed high Imperial drawl.

Saskia only snorted in reply . . . but she was still smiling as he politely withdrew from the room a moment later, and as she steeled herself to open the speaking box in private, she wore the dressing gown like an old-fashioned suit of armor.

Mirjana's face popped up in the mirror almost immediately. "Saskia! I've been wanting to—*oh.*" Her blue eyes narrowed as she leaned closer to her side of the mirror. "What's the matter with you?"

"I thought *I* was meant to be the one with bad manners," Saskia rasped.

"Don't be flippant. You're in bed, not in your office, and I can see for myself how ill you look. Should I send you a physician?"

"Morlokk's summoned one already, but it isn't necessary." Saskia shifted uncomfortably against her pillow as the food she'd eaten earlier made its presence known with a stabbing pain in her wounded stomach. "I only need a few days to recover. There was a . . . small poisoning incident last night."

"A *what?* Saskia, if this is your idea of a joke—"

Saskia gritted her teeth as a new wave of leaden exhaustion poured through her veins, mingling with the pain. "One of the guests *you* talked me into inviting into my home slipped me poison. Believe me, it's the last thing I want to joke about!"

Mirjana's eyes flared wide. A moment later, she parted her lips just enough to say with cold precision, "Tell me *everything.*"

Saskia hadn't been anticipating quite how difficult she would find it to recite the bare facts of what had occurred, no matter how unemotionally she tried to present them. Of course, she had dealt with assassination attempts before. There'd been a time, when the tides of public opinion were first beginning to turn against her uncle—before she'd given in to Mirjana's group of rebels and seized the throne for herself—when Yaroslav had made at least one attempt a month, although poison had never been his chosen weapon until now.

And yet, somehow, it *still* hurt to admit that, yet again, she had foolishly allowed herself to feel safe—that for all that she'd sworn to protect the kingdom against the next attack from the Archduke or her uncle, she hadn't imagined it might actually come in this fashion, sneaking into the comfort and privacy of her own laboratory.

. . . Just as her uncle's first attack had slipped into the heart of a different royal home.

By the time she finished her explanation, exhaustion was a physical force dragging down on her muscles. All she wanted to do was close the box and her eyes together and allow sleep to claim her. However, Saskia had learned, years ago, never to show any weakness in front of her former lover, lest it be held over her in future arguments. So, she held her eyes firmly open and her chin raised as Mirjana spent a moment in silent consideration.

"I have a few different ideas," her First Minister said at last. "Nobles who may miss the old regime more than they claim—or who were hoping for more personal benefits from our new one."

Saskia snorted, trying not to let discomfort show on her face as her stomach gave another painful twist. "You think, from now on, I ought to bribe my guests *not* to poison me?"

"Don't be naive," Mirjana said impatiently. "There's a constant flow of bribery between *every* successful government and its highest aristocracy. The only question is how to manage the outliers with so many wolves circling at the moment, hunting for any signs of discontent. You'll need to move to the capital yourself as soon as you've fully recovered, both to show off your strength to the world *and* to remind your nobles that you are one of us, even if your style is different from the norm. Start to hold open evenings at the palace twice a week, honor a chosen few by attending their functions, listen to complaints, offer favors, force yourself to smile . . ."

"I hired you to do all of those things for me!" Saskia could hear the petulance in her own voice, but with pain spiking through her weary body, she couldn't summon the strength to hold back the words. "You swore, that final time you begged me to take the throne, that you would handle all of the public-facing charm. You said I'd never have to worry about any of it!"

"Oh, *Saskia*. I said whatever I had to say back then to save the kingdom. Even you must have known better in your heart! I've been trying for months, now, to spur you into finally accepting the role that you were born for—and just look at the result of your refusals." Mirjana waved expressively towards Saskia's side of the mirror, her cheeks flushed with emotion. "One of the highest nobles in the land just tried to murder you!"

"And you believe that's my fault." Saskia closed her eyes as renewed pain jabbed through her stomach. With all her might, she kept her expression unmoved, forcing down the pitiful whimper that wanted to emerge from her aching throat. When she finally opened her eyes again, her voice was steady. "Tell me, Mirjana. Do you think my parents were to blame for *their* murders, too?"

"Saskia—"

Saskia cut her off. "You know perfectly well that the same man was behind both attacks, no matter whom he happened to use as his go-between this time."

Mirjana grimaced, sitting back. "Your parents were progressives, and I truly admire them for their principles. But your uncle built his support base by playing upon real fears within some of the most powerful families in this kingdom. If you want to push forward your own reforms—the ones we *agree* on, the ones we've always wanted—you will have to convince our people that those reforms, and you, are not a threat to their comfortable way of life."

Oh, this was Winter's Turning all over again, along with a dozen other arguments beforehand, the same debate returning in endless cycles without any resolution . . . but this time, Saskia didn't have the physical energy for a screaming argument. More than that: as she took a painful breath, she felt the warmth and softness of the dressing gown around her shoulders like a re-minder of an entirely different kind of strength.

Breathing slowly and deliberately, she took the time to gather her thoughts and control her voice.

She said at last, "Mirjana, I appointed you my First Minister because I agreed with your ideas for the kingdom *and* I respect your particular skills. I've hoped that you would come to respect my skills, too. But if the truth is that you'll only ever respect my *birth*—if all of your plans from the beginning have relied on the assumption that you would eventually talk me into giving up all of my focus on magic to become a polished and inoffensive figure-head, ready to smile and wave from your side—then we have both made serious mistakes."

"What are you trying to say?" Mirjana frowned, tilting her head. "You know, you really don't look well. Perhaps we should discuss all of this another time."

"Perhaps," Saskia agreed, "but I need you to think hard about the future in the meantime. If you can't work with me as I am, I will genuinely regret that, but I will accept it . . . along with your resignation."

Mirjana's head jerked back as if she'd been slapped. "You know I've only ever tried to help and guide you! From the very beginning—"

"I know that's what you intended," Saskia said wearily, "but I am telling you now that I will *never* choose to hide who I am for the sake of imagined safety. Like it or not, we both know I'm the only ruler who can hold Kitvaria against my uncle at this point—because of my magic every bit as much as my birth. So, you'll have to decide for yourself whether it's worth continuing to serve as my First Minister even with the understanding that I'll never become the queen you always wanted."

"The queen I . . . wait." Mirjana's gaze sharpened. "Are you saying all of this because of your *librarian?*" She bit off the final word like a curse. "Whatever he may have told you about me and about our private conversation at Winter's Turning—"

"He said nothing, but now you and I are most certainly finished for today. Good-bye, Mirjana."

Saskia closed the lid of the box as gently as she could and surrendered, at long last, to sleep.

There were multiple wakings through the day and night, as Saskia's recovering body alternated demands for soothing liquids, pain relief, and rest. Still, when she awoke late the next morning, the unmistakable sound of a fountain pen scratching against paper made her lips instinctively curve. She chose to focus on that soft, familiar sound rather than on any of the myriad physical complaints that had awoken with her—and she already knew what she would see when she opened her eyes: Fabian sitting once more by her bed, as he had for almost all of her prior wakings, taking industrious notes on yet another book.

. . . Except he wasn't. This time, his usual pile of library books, awaiting categorization, was being entirely ignored as he frowned down at his own commonplace book, which was balanced on his casually crossed legs. He didn't even notice her eyes opening; all of his attention was keenly focused on whatever literary challenge had led to such passionate bursts of writing—interspersed with so much crossing out.

As he slashed a line through his latest discarded attempt, he blew out a frustrated breath. The column of air was strong enough to lift one of the locks of thick brown hair that had slipped onto his cheek. At the sight, Saskia felt her heart squeeze tight with helpless affection.

"Are you writing more poetry?"

At the sound of her rasped question, he startled, ink spattering across his page. Then he relaxed and gave her a rueful smile beneath his half-mask. "I beg your pardon. Did I wake you by muttering to myself?"

"Not at all." She shifted awkwardly against her pillows, trying to find her way into a comfortable position after sliding downwards sometime in the course of her long nap.

Without a word, he set down his pen and commonplace book and leaned over the bed to help her back into place, his arms warm and firm. As he carefully adjusted the pillows behind her, she breathed in his bergamot fragrance and curled her fingers against her palms to stop them from reaching out towards the irresistible warmth that emanated from his figure. His form-fitting wool jacket was so dangerously, touchably close . . .

"I like seeing you without your cloak," she murmured before she could think better of it.

Fabian's body stilled, but his face turned down towards her, eyebrows raised and brown eyes warm and questioning.

Saskia swallowed. Her whole body was aching, although the worst of her stomach pains had subsided; her throat still felt prickly and half-parched. And yet, as his body hovered over hers . . .

His shoulders rose and fell with a quiet sigh. Then he gently lowered her the rest of the way onto her pillows and sat back in his own chair.

Just as well. None of her logical reasons to avoid more intemperate kissing had altered in the last two days . . . but still, Saskia couldn't help feeling a foolish stab of disappointment.

It all came from how natural Fabian looked in that comfortable wing chair set so close beside her bed; how carefully he touched her aching body and how he made her feel safe falling asleep with him nearby.

She was a pitiful excuse for a terrifying, magical queen, and she needed to shift her thoughts to bloodshed immediately.

She cleared her throat, ready to begin.

At the same moment, Fabian looked up, met her gaze, and asked, "Would you like me to write more poetry for you?"

Saskia's mouth fell open, every gear in her brain lurching to a halt at the shock of such reckless vulnerability.

A sharp knock sounded on the door, immediately followed by Morlokk's entrance. "Your Majesty, we've found your poisoner."

"Oh, thank the gods." *Bloodshed it is!* With deep relief, she turned to a far safer topic of conversation. "Who is it?"

"He was posing as a footman for one of your guests, the Countess Markovic."

"Who?" Saskia frowned, wracking her memory, but her librarian reacted as if stung.

"Did you say *Markovic?*"

Startled, Saskia glanced at Fabian. "Do you know her?"

"We've met." He grimaced. "I wouldn't say I know the lady, but she is certainly . . . persistent."

Oh, Saskia really would be happy to execute the woman if the discomfort in Fabian's expression implied what she thought it might about that past encounter—and the word "persistent" was enough to finally unlock her own memory of grasping fingers, strong perfume, and insistent, purred demands for rare secrets to gossip about.

The idea of those soft hands ever grasping *Fabian* . . .

"She won't have the chance to bother you ever again," Saskia said through her teeth. "Where did you find her lackey hiding, Morlokk?"

"Actually, it was the goblins who found him," said Morlokk. "He'd attempted to take refuge in their tunnels beneath the castle when the storm prevented him from taking a safer route." The majordomo's upper lip lifted in a sneer. "Needless to say, he was unable to navigate the tunnels unassisted."

"Of course." She snorted. "Bring him in."

"Ah . . . ?" Morlokk looked meaningfully at the crumpled nightgown she still wore under her faded patchwork quilt.

Saskia sighed. "Fabian, would you please hand me my dressing gown? And lay that black velvet throw across the bed?"

She couldn't possibly hold up the heavy crown of bones right now—but she practiced her haughtiest and most disdainful expression to keep her emotions under control while Fabian spread the warm velvet across her legs and then helped her into the magnificent crimson dressing gown, tying its belt around her waist with care.

He looked up through his eyelashes and caught her gaze as he tied the belt's knot. "You *deserve* poetry," he whispered, too quietly for Morlokk to overhear.

Then, out of sight of the doorway, he traced the tip of one long forefinger in a tantalizingly light line over her dressing gown, just above the belt.

Saskia's breath stopped in her throat. The trail of heat he'd left across her skin tingled almost unbearably as she stared at him. She couldn't look away from his brown eyes, only inches away from hers, so beautiful and so familiar—and now, for the first time she could remember, lit up with an unmistakable spark of mischief.

He was *teasing* her!

She wanted to launch herself into his arms.

She wanted to pull him under the covers.

She didn't have the physical strength to do either . . .

But the sound of footsteps coming down the hallway made Fabian rise and step back from the bed, his head respectfully lowered—and that damnable, secret half-smile that she loved tugging once more at the left corner of his mouth.

Oh, curse it! She'd work out how to resist this new, seductively playful side of her librarian later.

Saskia stiffened her shoulders, readied her magic, and prepared to meet her would-be murderer.

22

Felix lost all urge to smile as a smirking, sharp-eyed man in footman's uniform, his knees and elbows covered in dirt, strolled into the room with perfect ease ahead of three uncharacteristically stone-faced goblins.

The poisoner's silvering eyebrows rose appreciatively as he took in the sight of Queen Saskia, pale but glorious in crimson and black velvet, sitting upright with the help of the pillows on her bed. "Now, *there's* a sight I never expected to see."

Felix's teeth set together. In the corner of his vision, he glimpsed Morlokk stiffening—but the queen herself responded with none of the icy disdain that he expected.

Instead, her dark eyes widened until she looked haunted. "I know you," she breathed. "Was it . . . Kosar? Your face . . ."

"Oh, yes. We met a time or two in your youth, Your Majesty." The man's smirk deepened. "Your uncle often found me useful for one purpose or another."

Felix could easily imagine what sort of purposes a ruffian such as this might have served for an amoral king . . . but from the look on Saskia's face, they might have been even worse than he guessed.

His own back twinged with the memory of old wounds as he tightened every muscle, forcing himself to stand still and make his face expressionless. He'd given up, years ago, on defending himself, but it would be all too easy to fight for Saskia now . . .

And it would be the least helpful thing that he could do, if he truly wanted to support her.

Before his eyes, she regained her own self-control, nostrils flaring as her eyelids drooped and shock transformed into regal disdain. "What reward did my uncle promise you this time, for poisoning me?"

"Not enough, I can tell you that." Shrugging, Kosar stuck his hands in his pockets as casually as if he were chatting with an old friend. "That's Yaroslav—always stingy when it comes to everyone's needs but his own. Now that he's got less funds for his own luxuries, he's turned even more miserly with his dirty work—but if he thinks *that's* a way to buy true loyalty . . ." He let his words trail off, dangling an all too obvious lure.

Felix needn't have worried. Saskia's voice was as cold as ice. "And how much did the Countess Markovic know of your plans?"

"Ha!" Kosar snorted, rocking back on his heels. "You think either of us was fool enough to share any details with that gossip? She was more than happy to take the lure and sneak a spy into your castle, to stay in your uncle's favor, feel important, and play both sides of the game—but she wouldn't risk her own life for his any more than I would."

The queen's eyebrows arched, with chilling effect. "And yet, you already have."

"But here's the thing." He leaned forward confidingly, hands still hidden in his pockets. "You were always a clever girl, even when you were a child. Too clever to stay under your uncle's control for long—and now that you've got me, you can take control of the game for good."

Saskia's eyebrows rose even higher, but she didn't say a word.

Kosar took her silence as an invitation, sauntering forward. Morlokk's wordless snarl halted him a foot away from the bottom of the bed, but it didn't halt his eager spill of words. "I know *all* of your uncle's secrets. You, of all people, understand how many decades I've been working for him, taking on all the jobs he doesn't want anyone to know about! I can walk back through his open door and slip the same poison into *his* drink without him thinking twice about it. Or I can arrange for you to do it yourself, if you'd prefer that satisfaction!"

"Intriguing." Saskia's head tilted. "And what would stop you from doing exactly the same to me, a decade later?"

"Easy." He grinned. "Don't make your uncle's mistake. I'll do everything you ask and never balk, no matter how dirty my hands may get—and in return, all I need is an employer who's clever enough to value me properly. Based on what I saw in the walls of those tunnels, you've got access to more than enough gems to afford what I'm worth—and as long as you keep passing those payments on, I'll be your man forever."

"So simple?" Saskia murmured. "I'm afraid there's one slight problem with your plans."

"Oh?" His eyes narrowed, his hands digging deeper into his pockets. "If you want to haggle about my price . . ."

She spoke over him, her words precise. "Unlike my uncle, I will never—*ever*—hire a man so devoid of any conscience that he will happily take on the cruelest of tasks . . . and I'll never allow you to hurt anyone else, either."

To any observer who didn't know her, the slow rise of her hands would have looked like pure theatre, intentionally drawing out the agony of anticipation for her helpless victim.

Felix, though, had spent every waking minute of his past two days at Saskia's bedside, alert to every subtle sign of the pain and exhaustion she fought so valiantly to hide. He knew that those particular creases at the corners of her eyes signaled intense internal effort. How painful was it for her to summon up magic in her current state?

All of her attention had to be devoted to that challenge—so the moment that Kosar began to pull his hands from his pockets, Felix flung himself forward.

He would always defer to his queen's authority, but he *would not* allow anyone to take advantage of her temporary vulnerability.

Sadly, he still had no martial training whatsoever, as his brother-in-law had always been ready to remind him. Still, Felix barreled into Kosar hard enough to knock the poisoner off-balance. Kosar stumbled, grunting with surprise, and Felix grappled with him, fighting to bind the other man's arms to his sides.

Kosar was shorter but bulkier, stronger, and—undeniably—a far better fighter. Felix gritted his teeth through the impact of an elbow against his gut and the slam of Kosar's hard head against his cheekbone. He knew how to withstand pain. He wouldn't let go while the other man still held any possible weapons.

"Fabian!" Saskia's voice was hoarse with something that sounded like panic. "What are you doing? Get away from him!"

"*Not*," Felix gritted, "*until . . .*"

"Allow me." Morlokk's giant fist closed around Kosar's right hand with implacable force.

As Felix heard the gut-churning, crackling sound of small bones breaking, he released his own grip and stepped back, panting. Kosar crumpled to his knees, and sparkling silver powder showered out of his broken hand onto the floor. With a hiss of pained frustration, he let his head fall forward. "Shit. Should've known . . . pay wasn't worth it . . . this time round."

"Nothing you did for my uncle was *ever* acceptable." Saskia's face was chalk white, and her dark eyes burned with rage. "But you will regret this task most of all."

"Fine. Go on and kill me, you and your monsters together!" He laughed weakly as the goblins clustered behind him, snarling, and Morlokk loomed over him with silent menace. "Just like your uncle always said you were after all, eh?"

Felix's jaw clenched, but he didn't move forward. This was Saskia's battle; he wouldn't speak for her.

She looked directly at him, though, ignoring the other man's taunt. "There's blood on your face. How badly are you hurt?"

Felix blinked, taken aback. His face was certainly hurting; his cheekbone and jaw both throbbed where the other man's head had slammed into them, and there were various other aches and pains he hadn't paid much attention to, but . . .

He lifted one hand to his cheek, feeling for any telltale dampness, and shrugged. "It's nothing," he said sincerely. The blood came from a minor nosebleed, along with a cut on the inside of his lip. They were laughably minor injuries compared to the danger *she* had risked from that silver powder, whatever nightmarish concoction had formed its base. If Kosar had managed to fling it at Saskia . . .

"It is *not* nothing," the queen said with cold precision. "It is the last mistake my uncle will ever make." Finally turning her attention back to her poisoner, she said, "As for you, I will *not* be killing you now. Unlike my uncle, I am willing to take good advice." Her gaze slipped swiftly towards Felix and then back again. "This time, I'd rather choose a more . . . effective punishment."

Her hands were already raised. She brought them down with as much force as if she were pressing a heavy weight into place . . .

And the kneeling poisoner became a venomous green viper, hissing and swirling frantically on the carpeted floor.

Morlokk stooped to grip the furious snake behind its head, holding it calmly in the air before him as its body wriggled uselessly and its tongue flicked out again and again. "Shall I dispose of this vermin for you, Your Majesty?"

"I'd prefer you to have it shipped." Saskia was breathing hard, but her voice held firm. "I'd like it to be delivered to the Countess Markovic with the message that she should learn a valuable lesson by viewing her accomplice's new state. From now on, she can spread as much gossip as she likes about *exactly* what will happen to anyone who ever dares to attack me or mine. She'll have to spread it from abroad, though, because all of her properties and bank accounts are to be confiscated by the state, effective immediately. She will be escorted to the border to ensure she does not bring any valuables with her."

Sagging back against her pillows, Saskia said, "She'll have to hope my uncle is more loyal in his exile than she ever was herself."

"A fitting punishment." Felix shook his head with rueful appreciation as Morlokk carried out the viper, followed by the jeering goblins. "Your uncle will have to raise his rate of pay to attract any more willing villains from now on."

"He won't have the chance." Saskia's gaze returned to his blood-dampened face, and her expression hardened. "I didn't kill my uncle when I last had the chance. In a moment of weakness, I let him go—but I won't make that mistake again. It's time to finally listen to Lorelei and Ailana and go on the attack—against him *and* the villain who's given him all of his shelter and support for years, now."

"Ah . . ." Felix braced himself. "You don't mean . . . ?"

"My neighbor, the Archduke Felix Augustus von Estarion," said the Queen of Kitvaria with loathing. "I put this moment off as long as possible. I did my best to avoid any more open war! But when his protected, beloved pet sent an assassin into my home and hurt *you*, he broke the bonds of my patience."

"But . . ." Words slipped from Felix's grip as he shook his head, overwhelmed by the surreality of the moment. "Don't, I beg you. Not for my sake—I would *never!*—believe me, if you only understood . . ."

"No more arguments." Saskia's eyes closed as her chest rose and fell. "Not anymore." Her voice was thready with exhaustion, but Felix could hear the unbending resolution underneath. "I need to rest, and I need to recover. But then, it will finally be time for me to end the Archduke."

By the time the Queens of Villainy held their own meeting at her bedside three days later, Saskia had reached the most maddening stage of her recovery. The burning tedium of staying still was *so much* harder to bear than any lingering physical malaise. If it weren't for Fabian and Mrs. Haglitz's joint insistence, she would have been up and out of bed at least half a dozen times by now.

For once, the sight of Lorelei's over-the-top rainbow portal shimmering into place brought nothing but relief. At least these two could be counted on not to coddle her or worry overmuch about her safety. She'd had to ban Fabian from uttering a single word more about the Archduke *or* her plans for vengeance until she was entirely recovered. Still, she'd only half-solved the problem; he might no longer be voicing his concern, but she could see the tension pinching his bruised face more and more, and she knew he hadn't forgotten the matter.

Whatever the Archduke had done to Fabian in the past, the bastard must have transformed himself into an unbeatable foe in Fabian's usually orderly mind. It was unendurable to imagine that kind of trauma for her sweet librarian—so she simply wouldn't endure it a moment longer than necessary.

Saskia might not be capable of writing poetry to express her most vulnerable and uncontrollable feelings, but she could *absolutely* act upon them with vengeful pleasure. So, the moment she regained full energy, she would take firm steps to remove Fabian's nightmare from the world, whether or not that irritated any lurking goddesses. It was the least that she could do, after all the care he'd shown her . . . and she knew exactly who would help her.

"Saskia, darling!" Fresh flowers—lush, perfumed, and abundant—showered over her bed as Lorelei burst out of the shimmering portal. "How are you recovering? Was it utterly dreadful? The last time I was poisoned, I remember I had to sleep for days and days . . . well, once I'd dealt with the culprit, of course."

"It was a pleasure to hear of how you dealt with your own pest, Saskia." Ailana stepped out of the portal with calm composure, lifting her long, ice-blue skirts above the rainbow shimmer.

For once, neither of them had brought along their riding gryphons, for which Saskia was thankful. With the addition of a second wing chair for this meeting, her once-private bedroom had become far too cluttered to withstand any of the gryphons' battles for dominance. Fortunately, Morlokk had thought ahead when it came to their regal owners' more subtle rivalry and had arranged the wing chairs on either side of her bed, each of them equally close to her, each with a side table loaded with delicious food and drink, *and* each with an equally good line of sight towards the bedroom door. It only took a single exchange of raised eyebrows for her two visitors to silently agree upon their seats.

As Lorelei threw herself down onto her own wing chair, she scooped up a pastry covered in powdered sugar and bit into it with enthusiasm. "Oh, yes, Ailana told me what you'd done, but frankly, I could hardly believe it. That was so very cunning of you, darling! And so *diplomatic.* I thought for certain you'd choose the classic destroy-everything-in-a-red-rage option, for the most villainous effect."

"I do keep telling you," Ailana said mildly, "menace can work every bit as well when it's understated." Carefully arranging her skirts, she sank down onto the other wing chair, where Fabian usually sat. "Saskia's choice sent a far more powerful message . . . and given that she's finally invited us here of her own accord, I expect she isn't done with her vengeance yet. Am I right?"

There was never any point in trying to surprise the calculating Queen of Nornne. "Of course you are," Saskia said on a rueful sigh.

Really, it was a pity that Ailana hadn't been born to rule Saskia's kingdom. Ailana was exactly the sort of queen Mirjana would have preferred to serve and, no doubt, wed; between the two of them, they could have easily outwitted and outshone any rival contenders at diplomacy, fashion, and more.

Personally, Saskia's own preferences ran irresistibly towards a perilously gentle heart, clever hands, a poet's soul, and that secret smile that felt like a victory every time she caused it . . .

But now was not the time to be distracted by such frivolities. Instead, she would indulge her affections in a far more practical way. "We all know my uncle was behind my attack—and he won't stop until he loses his most powerful supporter."

"Oh, goodie!" Bouncing in her seat, Lorelei clapped hard enough to send powdered sugar flying through the air. "We've finally talked you into joining with us against the Empire."

Ailana tapped one finger on the wooden side table, ignoring her own pastries and coffee. "None of us can afford to launch an outright attack without clear external provocation . . . but Saskia, if my spies are right, Emperor Otto is very close to breaking the leash of his cautious high priest and launching an attack upon your border. You will be entirely justified in launching a counter-attack . . . and we can both be ready to join you. We simply need to work out the details."

"You know . . ." Lorelei's eyes slitted, like a playful cat contemplating new mischief. "We could ask for more help with our planning. Saskia, why don't you call in that delicious librarian of yours? If he really is a dark wizard, it would be foolish not to take advantage of his power, wouldn't it? And besides—"

"*No*," Saskia said with all the menace she could summon as she met Lorelei's sly gaze. "We are *not* involving Fabian in any of this." Dark wizard or no, she knew his tender heart too well. The last thing she would ever do was draw him into any brutal battles—or worry him sick over her own welfare.

"But Saskia, darling . . ."

"Enough." Saskia pushed herself up higher in her bed to remove any impression of softness. She might not yet be fully recovered, but she was still a queen in her own right. "I don't care what scheme you're planning, Lorelei. Whatever's circling your mind, I don't want to hear another word about my librarian, or this plan is off. Do you understand?"

For a moment, a spark that looked like frustration—or was that real anger?—flashed across Lorelei's face. Then she lowered her long, glitter-dusted eyelashes and pouted dramatically, and the fleeting impression passed. "Oh, very well. Go ahead and spoil my fun! I'll just take care of my own lovely schemes by myself, as usual."

"In the meantime . . ." Ailana cleared her throat as she reached for her waiting pot of coffee. "Shall we get on with our rather more important plans to stop the Empire's expansion across our continent?"

"Yes, please." Saskia took a long sip of her own coffee—which she was finally allowed to drink as of that very morning, thank every god and goddess for the blessing—and squared her shoulders in her dressing gown. "It's time to fight back."

23

By the time another week had passed, Felix knew he wasn't only marking the days until his queen's full recovery. He was counting down the moments until his own farewell.

Three months ago, he had fled to Kadaric Castle because there was nowhere else to go. He'd been prepared to meet his death or, at best, a wary half-imprisonment, fed and housed as a political pawn but kept under heavy guard.

At the time, he hadn't even been able to imagine any better outcome. Now, he knew with bittersweet clarity *exactly* how much better his life could be when he was given fulfilling work, an almost-family, and a thrillingly powerful and soft-hearted wicked queen to adore . . . so, despite the guilt that burned through his gut, he savored every moment that passed as he waited to give it all up.

Perhaps Saskia would decide against executing Estarion's Archduke once he told her who he truly was. However, whether she chose to let him go or made him her political prisoner, he knew that nothing would ever be the same between them once she learned the truth of his deception.

He had never meant it to be a betrayal, but with every hour that he spent by her side, helping her while away the days of her enforced bed rest, his pretense felt increasingly unforgivable.

He would give anything to be able to discard his own past as thoroughly as he'd discarded the all-enveloping cloak ruined on the night of Saskia's poisoning . . . but from the moment Felix had been born, he'd been the living symbol of his principality. The more time he spent outside Estarion, the more clearly he saw just how deeply he'd been tainted by its political actions, all of them taken under his name.

No, he couldn't have stopped the Count at the time—but now that he was free, he had a voice and a responsibility to use it if he ever hoped to make amends.

Today, barring any sudden turnarounds, Saskia would finally be allowed out of bed by Mrs. Haglitz. Tonight, at long last, he would flout her ban on the subject of the Archduke and tell her everything.

First, though, there was to be a celebration.

Garlands of ivy had been pinned along the curving walls of the tower staircase in honor of Snowfest, a troll midwinter holiday. As Felix stepped into the first of the maze of third-story rooms that led towards Saskia's bedchamber, he found Krakk pinning up even more garlands over a large fireplace, while the other goblins added pine branches, small carved wooden figures, and winter berries to the room's decorations.

Krakk grinned and waved with his free hand when he spotted Felix and the crow who accompanied him. "Queen's up!" he croaked, his voice muffled by the pile of pins that he held in his mouth. "Back in her laboratory. Won't be seeing her again until tonight, no doubt!"

"No doubt," Felix echoed, shaking his head with rueful commiseration.

Truly, it was a wonder that they had all managed to keep her resting for so long. He wouldn't be surprised if she'd leapt out of bed before dawn even arrived that morning, sticking more to the letter than the spirit of Mrs. Haglitz's decree . . . but by now, at least, he knew the housekeeper well enough to know that more than one servant would be stopping at the laboratory to keep a careful watch on Saskia throughout the day. If she showed any signs of lagging, Mrs. Haglitz would swoop down to cart her back to bed, like it or not . . .

And in the meantime, this gave him the chance to make his own preparations for tonight's festivities.

The day passed all too quickly as he raced to write out as clearly as possible all of the organization he'd managed of the library thus far. He surely wouldn't be allowed back into it again, after tonight; the least he could do was to leave a helpful summation for whichever dark wizard Saskia hired to complete the job.

. . . Only *please* let it be a better option than the last blowhard who'd attempted to take Felix's place! He winced at that thought as he rose, reluctantly, from the table in answer to Oskar's urgent squawks of reminder about the passing time and the snowy darkness outside the library windows. Pausing, he ran one hand in a last, lingering stroke over the pile of books that still sat unsorted beside his final notes.

There was so much more left to be done here! It all deserved the utmost care and loving attention . . .

But from now on, he would have no say in any of it.

Taking a deep breath, Felix scooped up the pile of carefully wrapped gifts from the corner of the table and set off, following Oskar's excited, flapping path, for his final night of warmth and safety.

The sound of enthusiastic, croaking song reached him first from the big second-story parlor that Mrs. Haglitz had directed him to join for the castle's private celebration of Snowfest, an entirely new holiday to him. From the sound of thumping feet that accompanied the goblins' singing, Felix guessed there might be dancing as well as gift-giving involved. The sound of many voices joined in laughter—including Saskia's, warm, throaty, and reassuringly strong—made his own steps quicken as he passed through the final drafty rooms that led him towards the parlor door.

Warmth billowed out to meet him as he opened it—warmth, light, color, and sound joyously mingling together to repel the winter cold and dark. Felix felt all his exhaustion fall away as he stepped into the parlor with its blazing fireplace, brightly lit candelabras, garland-bedecked furnishings, wrapped gifts piled around a large pine log and three colorfully painted rocks . . . and, most of all, the family at the heart of this castle, all gathered together to share the joy.

The goblins didn't halt their singing, but they waved to him while they continued their festive, stomping dance in the center of the room, interspersed with laughter over the hilarity of it all. Saskia sat on the couch beyond, clapping for them with unmistakable affection and delight, while Morlokk and Mrs. Haglitz rested contentedly in big, comfortable chairs on either side of the couch. Saskia's crows and bats lined the high shelves of the walnut cabinets that stood against the walls, and Cook bustled back and forth, laying out a glorious long table of food with her human arms while her smoothly scaled lower body swept across the floor. Her twin pet snakes wove their heads in happy circles above her shoulders, hissing in time with the goblins' song.

Near the corner full of gifts, set upon a side table over a

miniature, portable stove engraved with mysterious etchings, was a steaming—and magically self-swirling—pot of thick, creamy liquid that smelled deliciously of cinnamon, nutmeg, orange peel, and the deepest, darkest chocolate. Only two mugs were set out beside it—but as Cook was the only one in the room without a mug already in her hand, Felix knew that one of those mugs must be intended for him.

His chest squeezed with bittersweet appreciation as he filled his cup with the steaming drink. Every moment of this shared celebration was a stolen gift—but he couldn't bear to refuse any of it. Not yet.

How many years had it been since his last family holiday? The former Archduke and Archduchess of Estarion had been rigidly proper and formal in all of their public celebrations. Still, when Felix strained his memory, he could recall the glorious feeling of those few, precious evenings in his early childhood when his nanny would bring him to the family parlor and he and his parents would, at long last, enjoy an evening of private celebration, just the three of them together.

Those memories were terribly faint, more traces and hints than any solid visions—the echo of his father's deep laugh, for once unguarded; the rustle of silk against the floor as his mother shocked him by getting down onto her hands and the immaculate knees of her elegant gown to play with whatever set of trains or wooden soldiers that young Felix had been gifted— but the *feeling* of those evenings still remained, buried deep inside him.

He'd never thought to experience it again. As he turned away from the side table, clasping the heat of his filled mug in both hands, he found Queen Saskia looking over her shoulder at him, her lips curved into a mysterious smile and her dark eyes alight with a heat that shot through him . . .

And Felix realized that this, tonight, was already even *better* than any of those half-remembered evenings in his past.

"Well, come on over, boy!" Mrs. Haglitz summoned him towards the half-circle of seats with an impatient gesture as the goblins finished their song and clashed their mugs together. For once, the housekeeper didn't even snap at the mess being made. "We've all been waiting for you!"

"You have?" Felix crossed the room to join them, but hesitated by their half-circle, looking for another empty chair to match Morlokk's and Mrs. Haglitz's seats. Cook, of course, would rest upon her own comfortable coils once she was ready—and Oskar, already flown to join his flock, was no help in this search.

"Here." Saskia patted the velvet cushion just beside her on the deep-blue couch. "I've saved your place."

Gods, yes. Every instinct in his body urged him to lunge forward and take what he was offered—but Felix hadn't allowed himself a single romantic gesture since her announcement about the Archduke a week earlier. He might have been rash enough to indulge in wistful, impractical dreams until that sobering moment of truth, but it had been a turning point for him. No matter how tempting the offer, he would *not* willingly give her any added reasons to hate him when he told her the truth tonight.

So he said, "You should lie down, Your Majesty, to conserve energy. I'll find myself a chair—"

"Don't be absurd." She rolled her eyes. "You've all kept me resting far longer than necessary already."

"But—"

"I wouldn't waste your breath in arguing, Sinistro," Morlokk rumbled with unhidden amusement.

"Otherwise, she'll get up and dance a jig just to prove she can," Mrs. Haglitz added tartly, "and for all our girl's gifts, I can tell you right now, you do *not* want to see her try to dance!"

"*Ahh!*" Saskia gasped in mock outrage—and with her family's warm laughter surrounding them, Felix gave up and sat down on the couch beside her, keeping a careful six inches of distance.

He took a long, luxuriant sip of the creamy, flavorful hot

chocolate, but it couldn't diminish his awareness of her lithe fig-ure beside him as she took off her satin slippers and drew up her legs to curl comfortably across her own cushion of the couch, rest-ing one elbow on the padded arm. The hem of her flame-colored gown drifted across the seat to brush against his trousered leg, while her stockinged toes rested tantalizingly beside it.

Felix drew a deep, slow breath between his teeth, suddenly in-tensely aware of the lack of any concealment, now that he'd given up his old black cloak . . . and then he fixed his mind firmly on her family all around them.

Discreetly lowering his cup and crossing his legs, he turned away from Saskia's too-magnetic presence. "I am sorry to have kept you all waiting," he said to Mrs. Haglitz. "There were a few things I had to finish up in the library before I could leave it."

"Of course there were." Mrs. Haglitz snorted, lifting her cup to toast him and Saskia together. "You and her make a perfect pair. If it were up to either one of you, you'd never stop for a mo-ment's break!"

Felix couldn't help the wistful twinge in his chest at her first words, but he found a smile at the end. "I am glad to have stopped for this," he said, "and, Cook?" He raised his voice, shifting in his seat to address her as she moved around the long table behind them with her twin snakes' eager supervision. "This hot chocolate is *delicious*."

"Now stop fussing around with your art, for the Moon-Mother's sake!" Mrs. Haglitz added. "It all looks more than beautiful enough, and you know it. Let's settle down for presents!"

Cook gave in with a gusty sigh, and the goblins scurried for the pile of wrapped gifts by the pine log and rocks, laughing and jostling each other as they raced to each scoop up the most in their small, strong arms.

As Felix turned to watch, his gaze crossed Saskia's. She hadn't turned to follow the path of the goblins. Instead, she'd been watching him . . . and the focused intensity of her gaze made his mouth go dry.

Until today, he'd spent almost every waking hour of the past week by her side. Again and again, he'd seen her lapse into silence, eyes narrowed in brooding contemplation as she worked out some inner dilemma. Naturally, he'd assumed that it must have to do with her simmering plans of revenge—so every time she'd lapsed into that sort of silence, his gut had twisted even tighter with the guilt of his secret.

Tonight, though, her expression was finally unclouded . . . and full of hot determination. A scorching wave of awareness swept across his skin as she bit down on her lush lower lip, holding his gaze a helpless captive.

Had she solved her dilemma by deciding on *him*, now, tonight—just when he was about to give up everything?

Felix could have fallen to his knees in gratitude or tipped back his head in despair at the sheer impossibility of it all. Before he could do either, a large, heavy parcel landed on his lap with a *thump* that startled him free at last.

Swallowing hard, he looked down at the present on his lap as the sounds and sensations of the room around him suddenly rushed back in.

"From us!" Krakk croaked delightedly. "From all of us!" Bouncing up and down on his spindly legs, he gestured towards the other goblins, all of whom were busy distributing their other parcels around the room.

"I . . . thank you." Overwhelmed with conflicting emotions, Felix had to take a long, steadying breath before he could begin to unwrap the many sheets of baking paper the goblins had used to cover their gift. Inside the final layer was a solid wooden chest; when he opened its lid, he found five cheerfully grinning, carved wooden replicas of the five goblins he'd come to know, each one with an identifying mark.

It was a whole world away from any of the polished, diplomatic gifts he'd been presented with at countless glittering events as the Archduke of Estarion . . . and it meant a thousand times more than any of them.

"*Thank* you," he repeated as he turned Krakk's own wooden replica in his hands, giving it the slow and careful appreciation it deserved. "It is truly remarkable work. I love it."

If he did have to flee the castle tonight, he would at least be able to carry these visible reminders of friendship with him . . .

And the gift-giving was far from over.

Over the past few weeks, Felix had worked hard to create small, bound books for each of the goblins with the types of adventure stories that he knew they all preferred, writing them as the brave and clever heroes of each piece. Their cries of delight at that discovery, now, were welcome affirmations that he had done well.

For Morlokk, Felix had ordered a case of the finest port, and he savored the appreciative lift of the ogre's right eyebrow when Morlokk took in the label on that bottle. Felix had chosen a fine silk shawl in shades of emerald green and blue for Mrs. Haglitz. He was glad to see how well it complemented her own green skin when she arranged it over her existing layers—and gladder still to see her stroking one gnarled hand over it a few minutes later, visibly luxuriating in its softness.

For Cook, he'd chosen a gorgeously perfumed skin cream from the Empire to rub into her shimmering scales, which too often dried and cracked in this cold winter weather. And for Saskia . . .

"Oh, no. You open your gift first," she told him, waving off the parcel that he'd offered. "I've had to wait for *weeks* to see your reaction! You can't expect me to wait any longer after all that torture."

"I beg your pardon?" A half-laugh of surprise escaped him. "I'm fairly certain you've had more important things on your mind, these past few weeks."

"Just *open* it," she commanded, steely-eyed and formidable . . . and he had to bite down hard on his lower lip to hide exactly how much he enjoyed obeying that tone of command, from her.

This gift had been wrapped, not in baking paper, but in colorful, elegantly gilded paper that must have been imported from Kitvaria's capital city, judging by the quality. The expensive ribbons that sealed it, though, were knotted with big, impatient knots . . . which made him treat them with even more care.

This queen hadn't relied on anyone else to choose or wrap her gifts.

When the final knot fell away under his fingers, Felix opened the folds of the paper to reveal a small, rectangular case that looked about the right size and dimensions for . . . *oh!*

His fingers stilled. Surely . . .

"Well, don't sit around staring at it all night, boy. *Open* it!" Mrs. Haglitz demanded—and Felix realized that the attention of everyone in the room was fixed eagerly upon him.

Holding his breath, he opened the velvet-inlaid wooden case. A new fountain pen did indeed lie inside—but it wasn't made of any of the materials in the collection he'd had to leave behind in Estarion when he'd fled. *This* pen shone silver in the fire-and candle-light, and when he slipped the cap free with painstaking care, the nib itself glowed gold rather than steel.

"*Ahhh!*" The sigh he let out was very nearly obscene; he caught himself, flushing, but too late. The room had already erupted into laughter, warm and affectionate.

"Now, *that's* what I've been waiting for," Saskia said.

"But . . . how?" Wonderingly, Felix tilted the pen back and forth, taking in every angle of the extraordinary nib. "Where did you even find such a pen? I've never seen its like."

"Ahem." Morlokk cleared his throat. "It is a new design, not yet released to the general public. An artisan in the capital designed it on Her Majesty's commission."

Tucked across and beside Felix's lap were thoughtful, personal gifts from every member of this household. Now, as he felt their group delight wrap around him, emotions rose chokingly in his throat.

At the archducal court, he'd learned to always express himself in the most diplomatic fashion possible. Now, he couldn't find any words at all.

Smiling, Saskia lifted the gift he'd given her, which she had saved for last, and pulled aside the knotted ribbons. A scant moment later, she had removed all of the carefully folded wrapping paper and was staring, open-mouthed, at the thick, bound volume in her lap.

The cover of the book was made of gold-tooled leather of the finest quality; when she opened the front cover, she exposed the deep-blue endpaper, decorated with golden stars.

The title page, printed in an elegant and easily readable typeface, read:

A New Approach to Wizardry, from First Principles Onwards
By Her Majesty, Ana, the Queen of Kitvaria

"The printer stands ready to print as many commercial copies as you desire, to spread your mother's work and research across the continent," Felix said, "but only if you so wish. This copy is permanent, and should last for centuries in your library. You'll never have to fear it being lost again."

Saskia's fingers tightened around the corners of the book as her eyelashes lowered.

When she looked up again, her face was drawn into sharp—almost desperate—lines, and her voice sounded pinched and thin. "Everyone, this has been the finest Snowfest that I can recall. I truly appreciate every one of you, and I hope you'll all stay and celebrate in comfort. But, Fabian?"

Rising to her feet, she looked down at him with eyes that

blazed with fierce emotion, only barely controlled. "I require *you* to attend me elsewhere, *urgently*, for a private conversation. It cannot wait another moment."

Felix's chest twisted as he searched her expression. Had he guessed wrong? Was she offended rather than pleased with her gift? If he'd somehow hurt her . . .

She waved one hand impatiently, gesturing him upwards. "Don't worry about bringing any of your belongings, Sinistro— you can come back for all of them later."

"As you wish." Squaring his shoulders, Felix rose to his feet, leaving behind his gathered gifts—and leaving behind, as well, all of the safety, trust, and precious sense of belonging that he had found in Kadaric Castle across the past few months. "The truth is, I have an urgent matter to discuss with you, too."

As soon as they were alone, it would be time. He couldn't keep his secret any longer.

24

Saskia could barely contain herself as she led the way through the maze of dimly lit, second-story rooms. A wildfire had been set loose inside her body in that parlor, growing more and more out of control with every moment that had passed since it burst through her last remaining protective shields and left them in smoldering ashes.

Yaroslav had referred to her so many times as a monster, a slave to her own unnatural powers. When Saskia was young, her desperation to prove him wrong had been the impetus for all of her years of laboratory work, forcing her to perfect her self-control as she honed her powers into that close, sharp focus. That same binding fear had stopped her, too, from killing him when she could have in their final confrontation, in case that act might prove his point about her.

She'd already taken a first step away from those smothering bindings when she'd announced herself a wicked queen, without apology, and then refused to change her presentation despite Mirjana's urgings. But over the past week of steady, affectionate intimacy with a man who'd never asked her to change, she'd finally begun to wonder: what if she let go of those fears at a deeper, far more vulnerable level? Could she trust any lover to see her true self and *not* try to shape her into something more palatable?

More, could she trust herself to care for *them*, despite every insult she'd ever believed about herself?

Fabian had been so careful not to pressure her with any added steps of that courtship in her recovery. He was far too gentle and principled to put her in such a potentially difficult situation.

Saskia was neither gentle nor principled when it came to those she cared most ferociously about—and the gift he'd given her tonight had burst through the last of her own lingering restraints. She flung open the door to her room and lit every candle inside with a flick of her fingers as she swept inside. Fabian entered after her, his eyebrows rising above his mask—and another flick of her fingers sent the door slamming shut behind him.

"The answer," Saskia said through gritted teeth, "is *yes*."

"I . . . beg your pardon?"

There was *still* a full foot of distance between them. It was unbearable. How much longer would she have to wait? Saskia pointed imperiously at the cabinet nearby. "Look in the top drawer."

"Very well." Moving cautiously, he pulled it open . . . then stilled, as he looked down at the poem and the bouquet inside. His tall, lean body formed an exquisite arch that made her fingers ache.

She curled them into her palms, fighting to hold herself back. "You gave me those, asking a question," she said. "My answer is yes."

"Oh, gods." He tilted his head back, closing his eyes as if in pain.

Cold humiliation sliced through all of Saskia's heat, and she fell a step back. "Have you changed your mind since then? Do you not want me anymore?"

Perhaps all that intimate time he'd spent caring for her had changed *both* of their opinions on the matter. Had witnessing her vulnerability taken away all of the appeal she'd held for him? Or . . .

"Never." Fabian left one hand on the drawer as if for balance—or to hold himself back—as he turned to look at her, his brown eyes haunted. "I will *never* change my mind about you. How could I? You have my entire heart."

Saskia's mouth fell open.

His mouth curved gently as she gaped at him. "I adore you," he said softly. "I'm hopelessly in love with you, Saskia. Didn't you know that by now?"

She shook her head, wordless. She might have thought . . . perhaps she'd hoped . . . but to actually *hear* him, of all people, say such a shocking thing out loud, so simply and openly, without any prevarications?

Fabian drew a deep breath, his fingers visibly tightening around the drawer as his smile fell away. "If all that mattered were my feelings, I would be on my knees before you right now, worshipping you in every way you could imagine. I would devote the rest of my life to proving *exactly* how desperate I am for you, body and soul. You would never be left any reason to doubt it."

Saskia had to bite her lip to hold back a whimper. She had to speak. She had to tell him—had to offer up her own feelings, in return. He deserved no less, after his own bravery.

She tried to speak, to answer his declaration in kind. She *couldn't.* A knot was rising in her throat, almost choking her.

... And a niggling sense of warning was rising within her, too—more pronounced with every word. *"If all that mattered were my feelings . . ."*

"But you don't know everything about me," said Fabian. "There are things I haven't told you . . . haven't dared." He squeezed his eyes shut. "I don't think you will ever forgive me when—"

"Are you married?" The words burst out from Saskia's lips before she could call them back. "Promised to someone else?"

It would be wrong to kill anyone who kept him from her. *Too* wrong, even for her.

And yet, if he had been forced into a match against his will and had come here running from that trap . . .

"No!" His eyes flashed open. "Not anymore. Not since . . . my wife died, some time ago."

"Ohhh." Saskia let out a shuddering breath of relief. "That is, I'm sorry. I truly am sorry for your loss." No wonder he'd been so familiar with the workings of a sickbed.

"Thank you. But she's not—that isn't what I was referring to." He shook his head, pressing his lips together for a moment before speaking again. "Emmeline would never try to hold me back from finding happiness. She was the truest of friends to me, always."

"I'm glad." Saskia would never wish him anything but kindness in his life. "In that case . . ." She took a prowling step closer.

"Wait!" He put up his free hand. "Before anything else, you need to know . . ." He paused, breathing hard, as his gaze flicked up and down her figure and his face tightened with what looked like excruciating pain. "I can't allow you—you don't know who I really am. Who I was born to be, like it or not. If you did know, you would hate me. You *will* hate me, in a minute. So—"

Oh, for darkness' sake. "Fabian," said Saskia firmly, "do you honestly imagine that we would be here now if I didn't know exactly who you are?" He opened his mouth to argue, but she waved one impatient hand to cut him off. "I'm not talking about which family you happened to be born into, or who the people around you told you to be. I'm talking about *you*, the man I've known and worked beside for months. Do you think I haven't seen you and paid attention?"

Keeping her right hand raised for silence, she counted off her points. "I've seen a man who treats every single creature he meets with unfailing respect and kindness, regardless of species or rank. I've seen a man who treats my library *and* me with a gentleness and care that *neither* of us . . . gah!"

She had to break off to swallow down emotion. He started forward, frowning with concern, but she held him off with one raised hand. "No. I have to say this, first: I *see* you, Fabian. I saw you in the poem that you wrote, too." She shook her head, helpless in the face of that memory, and pushed her left hand against her chest, where it ached. "It *pierced* me."

"Forgive me." He winced. "I shouldn't have—"

"Oh yes, you should," she said fiercely. "You don't have to hide your true feelings from me, *ever*. Do you have any idea what it's meant to me to see more and more of the real you, these past few months?" She gestured at the delectably formfitting outfit that he wore, unshielded by any cloak, and the skin of his face exposed below the half-mask. "I don't know what your name used to be, what you came here running from, or who made you feel this way about yourself. But I know *you*, and you never have to fear that I would turn my back on you, no matter what terrible secrets you disclosed."

His shuddering breath sounded almost like a moan. "Gods help me, I can't put this off any longer. Saskia, I am the—"

"*No.*" She spoke over him. "*I'm* going to prove something first."

Unlike her librarian, she couldn't express herself in poetry or flowery words, but this one thing, she *could* do.

Stepping closer, she held his gaze in hers. "Answer me honestly, right now. Do you actually *want* to tell me whatever truth is haunting you before I launch into ravishment? Or are you only doing this because your conscience demands it? I can tell you now that it won't change *my* desires."

His jaw set, impenetrably bound by the ethics that ruled him. "Of *course* I'd rather just be ravished by you," he gritted. "You must *know* that. But I would never forgive myself if I didn't tell you first—"

"Only if you had the choice." Saskia's lips curved into a predatory smile, and his eyes widened, his breath shortening as she stalked even closer. "But you've forgotten something, haven't you, Fabian? I'm a wicked queen, and everyone knows it. Unlike you, I don't *care* about right and wrong."

His lean cheeks hollowed with the effect of her words. Her smile deepened as she leaned up to whisper in his ear, bracing herself with one hand on his tall shoulder and the other on his warm chest. "I'm going to take this burden from you. You would never be unethical enough to make this choice . . . so you don't have to." She lifted her hand from his chest to his lips and *focused*.

"There." Stepping back, she grinned up at him with all the deviousness in her heart . . . which beat for him. "Now you can safely abandon yourself to pleasure and know that it's not your fault."

He opened his mouth to speak.

All that emerged was a silent puff of air.

Saskia cocked one eyebrow, delight fizzing through her as his eyes widened with realization. "Of course," she murmured, "you are free to turn around and walk out the door right now if you don't actually *want* this to happen—*but* . . ."

Narrowing her eyes, she gave his chest an admonitory tap. "If pretending you don't want this would be a *lie*, then what happens next in this room will be *my* choice instead."

Holding his gaze, she licked her upper lip with slow, unhidden purpose. ". . . And *I* choose for you to stay and let me have my way with you."

Divine Elva, forgive me. Felix couldn't breathe.

He ought to turn around and walk away now, for her sake . . . shouldn't he? On the other hand . . .

Saskia's face glowed with mischief and wicked purpose as she cocked her head to give his whole body a leisurely, up and down consideration, taking the time to survey all of her options before beginning her feast. Every inch of his body tingled with the heat of her examination.

Tugging her bottom lip between her teeth, she frowned . . . and then, with a firm nod, she made her decision and reached for the top button of his silk waistcoat.

Clearly, Felix was shamefully devoid of morals, because there was no magic in the world that could have forced him to walk away from her now. As her clever fingers slipped every one of the small jet buttons loose, every light brush of contact through layers of silk and cotton lit hot sparks against his chest and stomach.

He reached out, breathing hard—

And she stepped back with a warning tsk that made his hands fall away immediately. "None of that! This is all *my* doing, remember. I'm having my wicked way with you. You're merely my innocent victim."

Felix would have laughed in raw disbelief at that idea—there was *nothing* innocent about anything he felt now!—but the sound stopped in his throat, sealed by her magic as his movements had been halted by her words . . . and at the joint effect of both interdictions, a hard shudder rippled through his body.

It was almost too good, *too* intense for him to bear.

All he could do was stand and silently endure whatever pleasure she chose to give him—and somehow, that made each sensation even more overwhelming as she returned, humming in satisfaction, to the task of carefully unbuttoning his waistcoat and the lower buttons of his jacket, too.

She peeled off that black wool jacket first, running her hands over his arms and back as she freed him. Was it her magic that rippled across his skin in her wake, leaving his breath ragged? Or was that just the natural effect of *her*, mapping his body as if she owned it?

She did. Gods help him, she absolutely did.

Felix didn't deserve any of this pleasure, and he knew it. Still, he pressed his eyes shut and surrendered to the exquisite torture as she pressed herself against him from behind, her soft breasts flattening against his back, clever fingers unknotting his cravat from behind. He would have groaned if he could have made a sound—but he let her move his arms exactly as she liked to remove his waistcoat and toss it aside. It landed on the floor behind them with a soft thump that made his breath catch in his throat . . .

And then she was tugging his long-sleeved cotton dress shirt over his head, and he bent his knees eagerly to help her in her task.

It was only when he heard her sudden gasp of horror that he remembered what he should have thought of first.

Oh, no. Felix spun around, already holding his hands out in placation.

Just as he had feared, his mischievous seductress was nowhere to be found. Power charged the air around them, and Saskia's dark eyes burned with rage in her chalk-white face. "*Who did that to you?*"

Felix bit back a sigh. At least the long, raised scars left by old whippings were limited to his back—but he could see her ferocious gaze cataloguing every other kind of telltale scar that lingered on the skin of his chest and arms. The Count and his lackeys had always taken care not to leave any marks that could be glimpsed by the public at large—but to Emmeline, of course, they had never been a secret, and Felix had never had any other lovers.

How could he not have expected the effect this sight would have upon his protective queen?

Ignoring her earlier prohibition, Felix took hold of her shoulders and tipped his forehead to meet hers. Holding her irate gaze, he shook his head in a gentle but firm rebuttal.

She scowled even more fiercely. "I should give you back your voice right now, so I can make you tell me—"

He shook his head again, even more firmly. This was no time to raise old nightmares. Even if this was to be their only night together, he couldn't bear for the Count to taint it in the same way that he'd shadowed so much else in Felix's life.

Leaning down, Felix captured her lips in a kiss so sweet and drugging, he was nearly swaying on his feet with the sheer intoxication of her taste by the time she finally pulled back.

"Oh, very well." Saskia's eyes were heavy-lidded, her cheeks covered in a hectic flush, as she clung to his bare shoulders with warm, possessive hands. "We can forget about it for now, but I won't let you get away without telling me the whole of it later. Whoever did that to you *will* come to rue the day, I swear it!"

When Felix had first arrived at this castle, he would never have dared to contradict Kitvaria's notorious witch queen in a threat. Now, he openly rolled his eyes at her—and her lips quirked in response.

"Oh, but have I forgotten what I was meant to be doing to my poor, helpless victim? *Do* forgive me," she purred. "Now, let me see. What shall I do next? I think I'll leave you your mask, just this once. Which means . . ."

She sank to her knees before him. *Ohhhh.* His breath shortened in his throat. Then she unbuttoned the placket of his woolen trousers, and he swallowed convulsively.

"Ah, yes." Setting him free, she ran her tongue over her lips in a manner so openly lascivious, it made his whole body tighten in response. "I always have enjoyed a good experiment . . ."

Divine Elva, preserve me. As everyone knew, the Queen of Kitvaria took *all* of her experiments seriously. Within minutes, Felix's fists were tightly clenched with the effort of standing still, and he was panting so hard, it was nearly painful.

He couldn't let himself come yet . . . no, he *wouldn't*, not without her . . . *oh, gods!*

He could have sobbed with relief when she finally sat back, her eyes bright with satisfaction and her lips scandalously wet and swollen. "In a hurry?" she inquired innocently.

She truly *was* wicked, after all! Narrowing his eyes at her, Felix un-fisted his hands to grasp her upper arms and yank her upright in a single move.

She let out a full-throated laugh of delight at the move. "Well, then. What are you waiting for?"

Together, they tumbled onto the bed in a hungry, playful knot of interlocking arms and legs and hot, devouring kisses. Felix un-pinned her upswept hair with shaking fingers. It fell around her body to shield them both in a heavy black shower as she pushed him onto his back and crawled on top with predatory grace.

Kneeling triumphantly above him, her bodice tugged out of place and her drawers flung aside, she grinned down at him. "Admit it," she said breathlessly. "You're all mine."

Had that ever been in doubt? Felix knew his heart was in his gaze as he reached between their bodies. She tipped her head back on a raw groan, shifting against his seeking, learning fingers and rewarding every successful new discovery on his part with gasps that felt better than any other gift he had ever been given.

When she finally let out a cry of shocked glory, her eyes snapped open, glowing with the power of all of the wild magic within her. "*Now*," she gasped—and batted his hand aside to sink irrevocably over him.

She was heat and magic and power in his arms. He had never

in his life felt so free or so exhilarated as he did now, moving with her, fighting with all his might to postpone that final moment of catharsis . . .

Until he finally gave in to it with a silent shout of exhilaration and pure gratitude.

Saskia collapsed, still rippling around him, and he wrapped his arms tightly around her warm, still-clothed figure, overwhelmed by emotions even more powerful than the pleasure that still wracked his body.

Peace and pleasure and wonderment and love . . .

Laughing ruefully, she finally reached up to stroke aside their mingled hair where it had fallen over her face. With another flick of one finger, she released the spell that had silenced his voice. Her own voice was a low, sleepy drawl. "I hope you didn't mind *too* terribly much being my helpless vic—"

Her voice cut off as she stiffened in his arms. Then she pushed herself up and pulled back more of his hair to wholly uncover his left ear. "What is *that?*" she demanded, her voice sharp and accusing.

Felix blinked up at her, baffled. "What do you mean?"

She reached out—then stopped an inch short of his ear, her face contorting in repulsion, as if she couldn't bear to even touch it. "*That.*"

Tensing, he followed the direction of her pointing finger with his own left hand . . . and then relaxed as he felt the familiar shape of his own single earring, the sealed golden circlet that had enclosed the tip of that ear ever since he was a child, on his parents' command. "Oh! Of course." He let out a relieved huff of air. "I suppose you never saw that behind my haircut before. Do you not care for it?"

"*Care* for it?" She stared at him in what looked like disbelief. Then she swung herself off his naked body, yanking up her bodice and smoothing down her skirt, leaving him cold and uncovered on the bed. "How could *you?*" she demanded. "What kind of dark wizard would *ever* willingly wear an abomination like that?"

"An . . . abomination?" he repeated blankly.

She stared back at him with just as much confusion. "How can you not know? That earring is a magical suppressant. With that sealed in your ear, you could never access your own magic. How could any dark wizard not understand and hate that?"

Felix gaped at her for a long, silent moment.

There was too much in her words for him to take in all at once. His mind was whirling with impossible ideas and long-buried memories, all seeking a whole new frame of reference. There was no solid ground left that he could hang on to, nothing he could say or . . .

No. There was one thing he *could* do—and like it or not, it was long past time to do it.

Taking a deep breath, Felix lifted his head from the pillow to untie the soft laces of his half-mask. Then, under the full force of Saskia's shocked gaze, he took off the mask to reveal, at long last, his full face . . . just as it had been painted in so many portraits and circulated around the continent for years.

"This," he said in resignation, "is what I was trying to tell you."

25

For a moment, Saskia could only stare. Of course, she already knew most of Fabian's features—those soft brown eyes, the clean line of his jaw, the sensitive curve of his mouth—but as she took them in anew, the rest of his features, finally revealed, added themselves to the puzzle . . . along with the vicious magical suppressant that had been bound in his left ear this whole time.

"Oh, darkness!" She lurched backwards, nausea rising within her.

She knew that face.

How many times had she thought those

dreamy, beautiful poet's features were wasted on such a villain?

"You're the fucking *Archduke of Estarion!*"

He flinched, but he didn't drop her gaze. "Felix," he said quietly. "Not quite Fabian."

She waved that off with an impatient slash of one hand. "The *Archduke.*"

Gods, all these months, when the other Queens of Villainy had been trying so hard to work out where he'd gone, and she'd left it to her sweet, innocent librarian to carry out her side of the hunt . . .

"You've played me for a fool." The realization came out on a whisper. "Have you been laughing at me all along?"

"No. Never!" He pushed himself up, dark hair falling over his face. "Saskia . . ."

"Was this your plan all along?" It hurt even to force the words through her lips. "Your forces couldn't defeat my wall of magic, so you planted yourself as a spy to find another way in?"

"I would *never* wish to hurt you. Think, Saskia." His voice was as gentle as ever, but his eyes looked haunted. "You said it yourself—it's not about the families we're born into, or who we're told we have to be. Think about me, the man you've known for months. The one you told me about, only minutes ago!"

"I know the *Archduke of Estarion.*" Gods, she was going to be sick. "He sent gold flooding into my uncle's coffers for decades. He paid for my uncle's assassins to hunt me!"

. . . Her uncle, whom she'd trusted, too. She'd thought *he* loved her and her family when she was a child.

How could she have been so unforgivably stupid as to make the same mistake twice?

"No, the Archduke *didn't,*" Felix said urgently. "It was done under my name, but not by my choice. Saskia, you have to believe me. I had nothing to do with any of that!"

She laughed, a harsh, pained sound. "Oh, are you going to hide behind a wall of advisors and pretend all the blame rests with them?"

He closed his eyes, his face tightening as he drew a shuddering breath. "When I first arrived, I meant to fling myself upon your mercy. I came here for sanctuary."

"*What?*" Another disbelieving laugh might have escaped, but it felt too perilously close to a sob. She wrapped her arms tightly around her chest, holding everything in.

This was why she couldn't let herself be weak and trust new people. This was what happened whenever she did.

"I was going to offer myself as your hostage against the Empire, to save my life." He opened his eyes, his expression weary. "You asked who gave me my scars? That would be the Chief Minister of Estarion—my father-in-law—Count von Hertzendorff, along with various lackeys of his and also his son, the current high general. I've been under their full control ever since the Count was appointed my guardian fifteen years ago. I was never allowed anywhere near politics from then on, never educated in anything but poetry and languages . . . and once my wife died, they began to plot my death. You were the only escape I could think of—the only person who'd ever successfully stood against them."

She had. She would again. And she had sworn to herself, only minutes ago, to kill whoever had left those scars. And yet . . .

How could she possibly know what was true? Warring instincts made it impossible to think. Curse it, if only the other Queens of Villainy were here to help analyze this conversation! Though, actually, no.

Gods, no! If they found out just how badly she'd been fooled . . .

"*Ohhh.*" Her eyes narrowed. Someone else *had* known, hadn't They?

That damned smirk Divine Elva had given her, when She had asked Saskia not to harm the Archduke . . . and the way She'd pointed him out to Saskia at Winter's Turning!

As Saskia's mouth dropped open in outrage, the Archduke—Felix—continued. "I don't even know how I managed to escape. I should have been caught a dozen times along the way! But everyone simply bowed me past, and no one asked any difficult questions, even when I finally arrived here. I still don't understand it, but . . ."

"I do," Saskia said grimly.

She well remembered Divine Elva's list of the powers a goddess could wield in the world. "WE MAY WHISPER A DIVINE BREATH OF PERSUASION FROM TIME TO TIME, IN AID . . ."

"*Someone* had plans for you," Saskia snarled, "but She didn't bother to share them—or ask my permission first."

"I beg your pardon?" Felix blinked.

A rap sounded on the door, making Saskia startle. "Your Majesty?" Morlokk's voice sounded through the thick wood. "Forgive me for the interruption, but you have a guest."

"Oh, for . . . !" Saskia had to squeeze her eyes shut to hold back a curse. At last she managed to call back through the door, "Send them to a spare bedroom for the night, please! I'll deal with whoever it is tomorrow, but for now, I'm far too busy—"

"That's not possible, I'm afraid." Morlokk's voice sounded pained. "It is your First Minister, you see. She says she absolutely cannot wait—and she's bearing urgent news about your wall."

Oh, gods! That wall was all that held out the Empire. If something had happened to it . . .

Saskia flicked a desperate glance between Fabian—*Felix*, damn it—and the closed door.

"I understand," he said quietly. "See to your kingdom first. We can talk afterwards."

"We *will* talk," she said firmly, "so stay *right here.* Don't go anywhere! And don't speak a word of this to anyone else until we've finished our conversation."

He was still naked in her bed. For one excruciating moment, she couldn't help sweeping her gaze across him, her body flushing with too-vivid memories. If there was any chance at all that he was telling the truth, that he hadn't been deceiving her about everything after all . . .

Stop. She had to shut down all of that—the pain, the betrayal, and, most dangerous of all, that single thread of shimmering, desperate hope. She couldn't possibly hold her own against Mirjana with a clouded head.

"*Stay,*" she repeated, and stalked out of the room to take on the world.

Felix was on his feet less than a minute later, scrambling to collect his scattered clothing. He couldn't stay still—not after everything that had happened.

Not after seeing the agony on Saskia's face when she'd realized exactly who he was, remembering everything done to her in his name.

"Are you going to hide behind a wall of advisors and pretend all the blame rests with them?"

He *refused* to spend a minute longer than necessary wearing the earring that had given everything away . . . and raised a whole host of new, world-tilting questions.

His fingers shook too badly to knot his cravat; he finally flung it aside, giving up on the whole endeavor and leaving his neck bare. He would have left behind the mask, as well, but he hesitated with his right hand on the door handle, remembering Saskia's second order: *"Don't speak a word of this to anyone else . . ."*

He owed her the respect of following that command—and she deserved to choose how to break this news to his fellow staff members. So Felix gritted his teeth, stalked back to the bed, and fought to retie the slippery laces at the back of the mask. By the time he finally threw open the bedroom door, shock and panic had combined so deeply that he felt nearly numb, untethered from his body. He had to press one hand against the wall of the stone staircase to keep himself grounded as he hurried down the long, winding stairs to the underground kitchen, and he still tripped on his way into the room.

For once, the vast space stood empty, with the Snowfest

celebration still going on upstairs without him. His wild gaze darted between different hulking stoves and counters.

He had hoped to find an obvious tool, but even in his current state, he wasn't reckless enough to try slicing through that golden earring with any of the heavy carving knives that he saw.

He was rummaging through random drawers in a frantic search when he heard a quiet, surprised croak. ". . . Sinistro?"

Gods, what must he look like, crouched like a thief in the kitchen? Sighing, Felix swung around and found Krakk standing behind him, bulbous eyes wide.

"I'm looking for something that can cut through gold," he said wearily. "You don't have any idea where to look, do you?"

"Ha!" Krakk snorted with open disdain, and Felix belatedly remembered Mrs. Haglitz's words from the night of Saskia's poisoning: *"You think goblins need human help to get hold of gold or diamonds?"*

"You, *wait*." Krakk pulled open a nearby cabinet door to reveal a deep, dark opening behind it. A moment later, he was gone, closing the door behind him to vanish into the depths of the mountain.

This time, Felix had no choice but to follow that command. He braced his hands on the marble countertop and forced himself to slow his breathing and keep his feet planted firmly in place as the endless seconds and minutes ticked by in silence, carrying too many vivid memories with them.

Saskia rising above him, her face fierce in climax . . .

Saskia lurching away from him in pain and horror . . .

No! He would only focus on one thing now.

". . . A magical suppressant. With that sealed in your ear, you could never access your own magic."

What magic could it have been intended to suppress? No one in his family had been magical; he couldn't have inherited it. And his examiners had all cleared him in the standard childhood exam. Imperial law was clear and unbending: no matter what rank in society a child's family might hold, from the lowest to the highest, they would *all* lose their children to a school of Gilded Wizardry the very moment those children were revealed to hold even the tiniest sparks of magic.

On the other hand, if he had worn that magic-suppressing earring when they'd tested him . . .

How old had he been when his parents had ordered it to be implanted? The truth was, he couldn't remember ever *not* having worn it. They'd always been so firm that it could never be removed or revealed to anyone else . . . and the Count had been so uncharacteristically indulgent in allowing him to keep it just so long as it remained carefully hidden behind his hair.

Had *all* of Felix's supposed protectors known about his magical abilities?

The cabinet door creaked open behind him, and Felix spun around just in time to see Krakk step out of the darkness, carrying an intimidating-looking tool with two handles and a set of sharp metal teeth.

"*Thank* you," Felix said on a sigh. "I'll just borrow those long enough to find a mirror and—"

"No, Sinistro." Krakk shook his head indulgently. "Krakk will do it."

"But—"

The goblin looked at him with pity. "Safest this way."

"Ah . . . you may be right." Felix's hands weren't entirely steady, even now—and he had to admit that it *would* feel better to do this with a friend, even if that friendship might not last the night.

Sinking to his knees and ducking his head, he drew back his hair and tucked it behind his left ear. "It's this earring, you see? It was welded together, so I can't remove it without breaking it."

"Pah." Krakk snorted. "*Humans.* Can't see five paces ahead in the dark."

"I can't argue with that." Felix closed his eyes, the better to *not* see those sharp metal teeth as they approached his ear.

Luckily, Krakk proved as adept with this tool as he had been in carving the detailed wooden figurine he'd gifted Felix for Snowfest. Felix felt only a whisper of cold behind his ear as the metal teeth fastened around the slim golden hoop . . .

And then they closed with a *crunch!* that sent a jolt through his whole body. His vision turned black, his mind a sudden void.

"Careful!" One small, strong hand propped him up as Felix blinked back to awareness a moment later. "Now." Krakk peered into his eyes. "Better take a minute," the goblin advised. "Breathe deep, drink water. Back soon."

He left again through the cabinet door, presumably to return the tool, and Felix followed the advice, taking a deep breath through roiling nausea. The earring still sat in his ear, but he could already feel the shifting balance in his body now that its circle had been broken. Once he was steady enough to pull the hoop out . . .

"Ah, *here* you are!" Rainbows shimmered through the air, and gauzy skirts in shades of red and gold appeared before his eyes. "Oh, dear, are you not feeling well? Perhaps you celebrated to-night's news a bit too much?" Queen Lorelei of Balravia batted sparkling eyelashes down at him as flirtatiously as ever, but her blue eyes were hard, and her grin looked nearly manic. "I'm afraid I can't offer you any time to recover. You see, our dear Saskia is *so* very protective of her people, even when they're not so loyal to her—and with events moving so quickly, now, she hasn't left me any choice but to take charge of the situation myself."

"I—what?" Head and stomach both spinning, Felix blinked up at her in bafflement from his kneeling position. "Your Majesty . . . ?"

"Shh, Your Highness." The hand she closed around his shoul-der was warm and soft. "There will be plenty of time for conver-sation once the two of us are back home in Balravia. I'm going to find *such* good uses for you!"

Rainbow shimmers closed around them, and Kadaric Castle—the first true home Felix had known in years—fell away as the fae queen took him captive.

26

We have . . . how long, exactly?" Saskia asked numbly.

This was the moment to be swift and decisive, she knew, but it was almost impossible to think through the realization that tolled inexorably within her: *Everything is falling apart.*

Fabian—*her* Fabian!—was the Archduke she'd hated and feared for most of her life. And now . . .

"Perhaps twelve hours at the most." Mirjana looked more haggard than Saskia had ever seen her. Sitting huddled on the couch across the room, she was still wrapped tightly in her travel cloak, despite the warm fire that burned in the hearth of the first-story parlor. Judging by the unhidden shadows beneath her eyes, for once she hadn't bothered with any cosmetics—or any sleep—before launching into what must have been a desperately uncomfortable carriage journey through the snowy mountain terrain. "We only have that long because the Imperial Corps of Gilded Wizards won't travel on iron railways and Estarion's General von Hertzendorff refuses to start the fight without them. Even the Emperor's high general knows better than to attempt your wall without their aid."

"The Emperor's high general . . . yes, of course." *That* would be Gerard de Moireul, the officer who was known across the continent—in honor of his victories and his famously golden hair, as well as his supposed virtue—as *the Golden Beacon* . . . and who was the object of Lorelei's repeated scorn every time he came up in conversation. "How many troops is he bringing in support of Estarion?"

"Too many for us to fight off on our own, even if we can somehow assemble all of our troops in time. The news has gone out to your generals, but in this weather . . ." Mirjana glanced meaningfully at the flakes of snow that clung to the closest high, dark window.

"Troll warriors aren't bothered by the snow." Saskia spoke with only half of her attention; her mind was already racing ahead, forming and discarding plans. Clearly, her first order of business must be to pass the news of this upcoming battle to Lorelei and Ailana, but when it came to her own troops . . .

"Human soldiers aren't impervious to it, though. And as none of our neighbors is a committed enough ally to stand by our sides once those mages break your wall . . ." Mirjana jerked to her feet in a sudden, uncharacteristically graceless moment that brought Saskia's attention swinging back to her. Holding Saskia's gaze, she took a ragged breath and then lowered herself, slowly and deliberately, to her knees on the rich red carpet and bowed her head low. "Forgive me, Your Majesty. I have failed you."

Saskia gaped down at her, dumbstruck.

Mirjana was always confident, always certain in her judgements—but now, her voice weakened with despair. "It was my sworn duty to ensure Kitvaria's safety in this new world order which I persuaded you into. Yet as your First Minister, after all these months, I've formed no alliances solid enough to hold us safe against the Empire's looming threat. And, more than that . . ."

She took another gasping breath, then forced herself onwards with what looked like agonized determination. "You were right. Even your *librarian*, of all people, was right about me! Any decent First Minister would have swayed you by now into using the one great asset we had—your hand in marriage—to cement a strong alliance. I, though . . . I was so blinded by my own personal hopes and plans, I never even paused to question what might be better for our nation, or grant you the respect of believing what you'd said when you first walked away from me—*no*." She bit herself off with a snap and lifted her head to face Saskia, her eyes bleak. "I have no excuse. My resignation is yours, should you wish it."

"Mirjana," Saskia began . . . and then stopped. Her head was whirling.

Even years ago, when they'd been at their most intimate, she had never been allowed to witness this kind of vulnerability from the other woman. Had Mirjana ever willingly taken blame for *anything* in their lives or their relationship before?

"No." Saskia shook her head firmly as she moved forward, reaching out to take her former lover's hand and pull Mirjana to her feet, to face her as an equal. "*No*. You cannot take all the blame. We've done this together—and if we'd both been more open with each other, you would already know that Kitvaria has indeed formed solid alliances. Ailana of Nornne and Lorelei of Balravia are only waiting for my call to stand with us against the Empire."

"But . . . wait, not *them*?" Mirjana shook her head frantically. "Those two may have made you all the promises in the world, but you must know you can't rely on them! You've seen how they behave even in the highest of gatherings. They blatantly flaunt their disregard for social rules! Neither of them cares whom they make into an enemy—"

"But they *do* care for the security of their nations," Saskia said. "That's why they reached out to me to form an alliance—and they've proven their loyalty already. Don't you remember the impact of their display at Winter's Turning? We have them to thank for the fact that none of our neighbors dared allow Estarion's troops to use their land as a passageway to invade."

"But . . . well, I suppose that *could* have been the reason. But all the same . . ." Mirjana stepped forward, one hand held out in supplication. "Saskia, I know I've made mistakes, but you must believe me on this: if you publicly commit yourself to those women now, for good, there will be *no chance* of ever convincing the continent that you are a safe and respectable ruler, the kind the Emperor would never dare to harm for the sake of his own reputation."

"Then I'll choose to be a wild and dangerous ruler instead and prove why he should *never* try again." Saskia bared her teeth in a fierce grin, gathering magic around her. She could feel her crows assembling in the castle above, pulling themselves away from the last of the festivities (and the last scraps of scavenged food) in answer to her call. With a *push*, she urged them all towards the library. She would meet them there soon—but first, she had more than one thing to do.

"Rest," she told Mirjana, "for an hour or two, at least, and eat something substantial, too. I'll contact Lorelei and Ailana, and I'll reach out to our generals. There's nothing needed from you in the meantime, and you'll want to have all of your wits about you once we make our move."

Mirjana grimaced. "I *would* prefer to put myself together first, it's true." She started to turn away, then hesitated. "That is . . . if you truly aren't asking for my resignation, after all?"

For the first time in years, Saskia reached out to put one hand on Mirjana's shoulder. All the sparks that she'd once felt were long gone, but the potential for something real and valuable finally shimmered in the air between them. "We're both learning how to play our new roles," she said. "Can *you* bear to give up on making me respectable, if we win this battle and you stay?"

The small, wry curve of Mirjana's lips was pained . . . but also the most sincere smile Saskia had seen from her in ages. "I thought respectability would keep our people safe," she said. "But if you are right and your new alliance saves us . . . then, yes. For the sake of Kitvaria's survival, I can learn to bear—and support—a bit of intentional wickedness as well."

Saskia left Mirjana to ring the bell for Mrs. Haglitz as she strode out the door. She was hurrying towards the closest staircase, ready to contact her fellow queens, when a single crow came shooting out from the stairwell that led to the kitchen, squawking urgently.

"Oskar?" She paused, caught by the panic in the crow's tone. "Why aren't you with the others? . . . Oh." She let out her breath in a heavy sigh. "Of course." Fabian—*Felix*—would still be waiting in her bed with the door closed. No doubt Oskar, as his familiar, must be feeling all of his emotions and be desperate to reach him.

But with this kind of panic as a reaction . . . Saskia bit her lip. Of all possible moments, this had to be the worst time to allow herself sentimentality.

Still. Even the most devious of dark wizards couldn't hide his true emotions from a familiar. If Oskar felt that deep an anguish, it couldn't have been put on as a mere disguise. Felix must be genuinely *miserable*—not simply disappointed that a clever plan had failed.

And if that was the case . . .

"Arggh!" With a groan of frustration, Saskia changed her direction, heading for the staircase that led most directly to her own chamber.

She wasn't postponing the defense of her kingdom; she was being *strategic*. How could she not include the Archduke of Estarion himself in her calculations?

Felix had told her, hadn't he, that his initial plan was to offer himself to her as a hostage against Estarion and the Empire as a whole? Saskia's teeth clenched at the very idea as she swept up her skirts and hurried up the sloping stone steps, ignoring Oskar's cawing attempts to lead her elsewhere.

She might be a wicked queen, but she wasn't an actual *monster*, no matter what her uncle or the rest of the continent might think. The idea that she would ever actually hurt that man, after everything they had shared together in the last few months, not to mention tonight . . . ! Even aside from her promise to Divine Elva, Felix had *saved her life* when that poisoner had attacked. So . . .

Wait. She thudded to a halt, catching herself on the closest curving wall.

In all the chaos and emotion of the last hour, that point hadn't occurred to her before. Why *had* he saved her life, if he'd been here to undermine her? The Archduke of Estarion had supported her uncle's assassins for years.

It hadn't been a move calculated to earn her trust; he'd known she trusted him long beforehand. More than that, no one would have blamed him if she had died from that poison. Morlokk and Mrs. Haglitz had both been adamant in their retellings of the event: Saskia would have had no hope of survival without him. She would have lost her life in her own library if it hadn't been for his extraordinary efforts in finding the spell that could heal her.

She'd felt for herself the depth of his care as she'd recovered. None of that made any logical sense at all . . . unless she remembered those terrible scars on his back and let herself *believe*. And if she actually believed everything he had told her . . .

Or if she believed what she'd said herself, earlier tonight, about the gentle, kind-hearted man she'd come to know and—*oh, gods, no*—to love, just as he'd said he loved her . . . and if he'd actually *meant* it . . . !

A hiccupping sob burst from Saskia's throat. Horrified, she clapped one hand to her mouth.

Was this what vulnerability felt like, as an adult? Darkness above, this was terrifying! *Unbearable.* She couldn't—

Oskar's desperate caws finally broke through her daze.

"Of course," she said thickly, "you're right. There's no time for nonsense." Swallowing hard, she dashed her hands across her cheeks.

She wouldn't be able to hide all evidence of tears—but then, what point was there in erecting a mask now? Felix had already seen into her heart for months.

Scooping her skirts back up, she hurried the rest of the way up the stairs to the closed door to her room, preparing herself for her own moment of truth. She would open the door and say to him . . .

She would be brave and say . . .

Oskar's anguished screech hurt her chest. She pushed the door open, allowing him to fly in first, and then stopped.

Her rumpled bed was empty.

Felix was nowhere to be seen.

Saskia was still standing, open-mouthed, a full minute later when she finally realized that Oskar hadn't given up. After a quick, exploratory stop at the empty bed, where the disordered sheets and quilt were a raw reminder of its earlier passionate use, he'd flown back, over her shoulder, to the corridor outside and was still calling for her to follow.

Clearly, he wanted to search the castle.

Unfortunately, she knew better. "There's no point," she told the crow softly. "He's left us. You see? He's run away."

It was a sensible move. She was the wicked Witch Queen of Kitvaria, after all. When he'd tried to reveal his heart to her, she had refused to believe him. She'd even accused him of being a spy, conspiring against her. Anyone would have advised him to run from her as fast and as far as he could, lest she wreak her revenge in some horrifically gruesome manner.

Saskia had worked hard to build her reputation, and she was proud of it . . . but somehow, she'd still held out hope that he would know her better.

"*Never mind.*" She whispered the words to herself like a spell to bind her broken heart. There was no time left to give in to devastation.

She had a kingdom to save. She had allies to summon. She could feel all her heartbreak later, in the bleak future that suddenly stretched out before her, devoid of poetry and flirtation, unbending support, and kisses more intoxicating than wine.

Saskia didn't need gentleness in her life, anyway. She never had.

Lifting her chin, she started in the direction of her study, her back straight and brittle.

Before she could even take the first turn, running footsteps hurtled towards her from the opposite direction. "Queen! *Queen!*" Krakk burst into view, panting, his green cheeks flushed nearly brown with overwhelming emotion. "Sinistro—"

"Is gone," Saskia finished for him. "I'm aware. He was perfectly free to leave, so—"

"No!" he shouted, shaking his head wildly. "Not left. *Taken.*"

"*What?*" Suddenly, all the rest of Saskia's crows were flying towards her, leaving the library behind to prepare for battle. Metal clanging filled the air as the sconces on the walls around her rattled with her fury. "Who would *dare* invade my castle and—"

"Rainbows, Queen!" Krakk fell to his knees as he blurted, "Rainbows everywhere. All that was left behind after *she* came for him."

Oh, Divine Elva . . . Ice-cold fear flooded Saskia's veins with her realization.

"Lorelei," she whispered.

Lorelei knew who Felix really was. *That* was what had lain behind all of her hints and urgings across the last few months!

What was it, exactly, that she'd said at their last meeting when Saskia had shut her down on that topic? *"I'll just take care of my own lovely schemes by myself . . ."*

"No!" Saskia turned, not towards her study after all, but towards her laboratory, where all of her most desperate weapons were waiting.

"Tell the others not to worry," she said over her shoulder. "I'll be back soon."

She had less than twelve hours to save her kingdom—but first, she had to save her librarian from her most dangerously unpredictable ally.

27

Now, then!" Queen Lorelei said brightly. "This should be *much* more comfortable."

Felix was on his knees once more, where he'd landed on a thick pink carpet when he'd fallen through the fae queen's portal. Just before him rose a large four-poster bed with delicate, gauzy curtains held back by chains of scented roses. It all seemed surprisingly luxuriant for either a prison cell or a torture chamber—but as he looked up at the infamous Siren of Balravia sprawling casually on the bed above him, kicking up one small, bare foot behind her back as she grinned down at him, he had to swallow down thick, choking dread.

His head was still whirling from the combined effects of the trip and the breaking of his earring, but he was sickeningly aware that he was in more immediate danger now than ever before.

"You know, until tonight, I've never had an Archduke of my own to play with," Lorelei said idly. "Princes, certainly. And counts, well . . . pfft!" She gave a delicate snort. "I can hardly sneeze without one of *them* falling over! They're no challenge at all. But as for you, Your Highness . . ." Her eyes narrowed, catlike, as she peered at him more closely. "I expect no one lower than the Emperor himself has ever dared say 'boo!' to you before."

At that, Felix almost choked out a bitter laugh . . . but the reminder was a gift. He stiffened his spine, breathing deeply.

He *had* endured physical punishment before. He could manage it again . . . and if he knew his own queen, she would be here soon to stop it.

Unless she really has given up on you forever . . .

No. He quashed that creeping fear.

Whether or not Saskia ever allowed him back into her bed or her heart, he knew one truth for certain. She would *never* let any member of her staff—no matter how traitorous—be kidnapped from her castle without her permission. Even if she planned to turn him into a worm herself, she would rescue him from Lorelei first. All he had to do was endure until then.

"Oh, *interesting.*" Lorelei's tone lowered to a purr. "You're less afraid now than you were before I said that. Are you someone who actually *enjoys* a bit of punishment?"

Setting his teeth together, Felix didn't answer. Still, she let out a delighted laugh. "Not from me, eh? Ooh, this *is* fun. I've been dying for a proper conversation with you for months now! If only Saskia weren't so stubborn, we could have cleared this all up ages ago . . . but you and your little friends in the capital haven't left us time to dance around it anymore."

Propping her pointed chin on her hands, she gazed down at him with gleaming blue eyes. "You *were* cutting it awfully fine, weren't you? If you'd only crept away a few hours earlier, you could have escaped *and* met up with your troops in time to inspire all of them."

"*My* troops?" With a sudden cold chill, Felix remembered the message from Morlokk that had taken Saskia from him. No doubt Lorelei had her own sources for urgent international news. "Is this to do with Kitvaria's magical wall? Everyone knows Estarion's troops can't get through it. The high general gave up on that months ago."

"Of course. Isn't that why you weaseled your way in? To find another avenue of attack, in case dear Yaroslav's heartfelt pleas didn't work on your little emperor?" She batted her eyelashes coquettishly. "Do tell me, Archduke. Were you planning to seduce Saskia all along? Or was breaking her heart a mere bonus?"

Felix's hands knotted by his sides. "I would never harm Queen Saskia. *Ever.*"

"Hmm." Her sparkling eyelashes lowered to hide her eyes. "Well, we'll spend *plenty* of time talking about that later. Really, you should have listened better at Winter's Turning. If you had, you would know that it's *never* wise to play unpleasant games with my friends."

Her words struck painfully close to home. "I told Queen Saskia the truth tonight," Felix said quietly. "She knows everything."

"Hmm. And yet there you were, wandering freely around her castle when I found you, still wearing your adorable little disguise. So, I wonder . . . are you lying to me now? Or did you somehow persuade her to forgive you?" Lorelei's upper lip curled as her voice hardened. "Everyone thinks our Saskia is so fierce, but *you* know exactly how soft her heart is, don't you? I imagine you acted terribly apologetic when you made your grand confession. Did you weep and give her big, soulful eyes? I'm afraid you won't find me so easy to persuade. As anyone on the continent can tell you, I'm completely heartless."

That had certainly been the message of all the songs and stories about Queen Lorelei from the moment she'd sentenced her first lover to death . . . but Felix didn't allow his expression to alter at her threat.

Instead, he said, "What did you mean about my troops? Have they found a way through the wall?"

"Had you actually *not* had the glorious news yet? Did they make their move before ensuring you were safe?" Lorelei's grin was a vicious slash. "Oh, dear. Poor little Felix. All your lovely allies left you in the lurch and at my mercy."

"But what *happened*?" Felix demanded.

"What else?" She gave a graceful shrug. "After all these months of circling round the problem, Emperor Otto finally cut his leash. The Imperial high priest, who's preached peace and diplomacy for years, was arrested this morning for corruption and high treason. In other words, he wouldn't allow Otto to bribe him into nodding along with any plans for expansion . . . and nowadays, in the Serafin Empire, that apparently counts as treason. Luckily, his successor shouldn't share that difficulty."

Lorelei smirked, playing with one of the long, golden curls that cascaded over her shoulders. "You see, Otto's appointed his own sister, Princess Clothilde, to be the new Imperial high priestess, guaranteed to give divine approval to any plan he suggests. So, less than an hour after the former high priest's arrest, Otto ordered the *Golden Beacon*"—her nostrils flared with distaste—"to march his legions to Kitvaria in support of Estarion's Archduke, with a full corps of Gilded Wizards to clear their way."

"Elva preserve us!" Felix jerked to his feet, looking wildly around the small, perfumed bedroom. "What are you doing here? You must help Saskia. Now!"

"Oh, she knows all about *that* part of the situation, I'm sure." Lorelei's voice was sickly sweet as Felix strode to the bedroom door and rattled the handle with all his might, to no avail. "Darling Saskia was busy meeting with her First Minister when I arrived.

She'll be calling for me and Ailana to join her soon enough—but you and I both know that Saskia is too soft to defend herself the only way she should, with the Archduke of Estarion in her grasp and the Serafin Empire hammering on her doorstep. So . . ."

Her smile deepened as he turned back to face her. "It's simply up to her friends to do it for her. Think of it as a helpful intervention."

Felix let out a heavy sigh, his right hand still resting on the immovable door handle. "You don't understand the truth of this. I'm not on the Emperor's side, I swear to you. I'm not even the man you think I am."

"And I'm sure you made that case to Saskia . . . but unlike her, darling, I couldn't care less." Lorelei's voice turned brisk as she rolled upwards into a sitting position. "As far as *I'm* concerned, you're no more than a pawn that I can use to protect my friend—so, if you have even half the wits you've displayed in the last few months of your pretense, you'll avoid irritating me now with any more pleas for pity. Otherwise, I might decide that the best way to prove you're in our keeping is to start cutting off body parts to send to your Chief Minister as evidence."

Felix bit back a groan. "You'll be playing directly into his hands if you do."

The Count would be utterly delighted by the news of Felix's murder at another party's hands—*especially* if it gave him the excuse to send even more troops into Kitvaria and make himself, in the eyes of every loyal citizen, the official avenger of Estarion's tragically lost Archduke.

Ignoring Felix's words, Lorelei murmured, "I just need to check one final, tiny detail before I go . . . aha!" A teasing gust of cool air, like a wild spring breeze, suddenly blew through the room and lifted the long hair away from Felix's left ear. Lorelei clapped in delight. "And we're done! *Do* enjoy your stay."

Rainbow shimmers erupted around her on the bed, and she

disappeared through a portal that snapped shut behind her before Felix could even lunge forward.

Taunting rainbow sparkles shimmered across the bedcovers as he raised one hand to his exposed left ear . . . and felt the golden earring still hanging there, the break in its hoop hidden from view.

Of course. That earring was how Lorelei had worked out the truth—and it was all his fault. Felix had thought himself so clever, the first time they'd met, when he'd revealed that unregal ornamentation to her . . . but just as Saskia had earlier tonight, Lorelei must have realized on first sight of the magical suppressant that he couldn't possibly be a working dark wizard after all.

"I'm such a fool." He slumped against the door. Tipping his head back against the unyielding wood, he let his eyes fall shut. As he breathed in the smothering, overwhelming scent of roses, despair rose within him . . .

And then his eyes snapped open. *Wait.*

In the whirl of sickness, confusion, and fear that had overwhelmed his last half hour, he hadn't yet had any chance to attempt the next part of the experiment he had begun when he'd gone looking for a tool to cut through that golden hoop.

Lorelei still didn't know it was broken. *That* was why she'd felt safe leaving him trapped here.

But if the earring had been implanted for a purpose, no matter how impossible that might still seem . . .

Remembering his body's reaction to the break, Felix braced himself against the door. Then he pulled out the earring with one decisive tug.

This time, his vision didn't go black. Instead, it seemed to *explode.* The intensity of the colors all around him made him stagger as a rush of tingling awareness roared through his body.

Every shade of color in the room was suddenly five times more vibrant. Every scent was stronger. And, tingling and roiling beneath his skin . . .

Was that actual *magic?* It tingled in the same way Saskia's magic had whenever that had brushed against him in the past—but this time, it felt almost like another, sixth sense or an added source of energy. Something he could actually make use of, if only he knew how . . .

And fortunately, he *did.*

Incredibly, locked within the fae queen's prison, Felix felt his lips stretch into a wide, disbelieving grin.

He wasn't just a pawn after all. Not for Lorelei, the Count, or anyone else. Not anymore, and *never again.*

After a lifetime of brutally enforced helplessness, he held actual power—*magical* power of his own—and better yet, he had spent the last few months studying the fundamentals of magic in the Witch Queen of Kitvaria's own personal library, with the helpful guidance of her mother's textbook. That primer had taught him everything he needed to know in order to harness his inborn power, using spells that built on the classical structures he had studied throughout his childhood.

Oh, the Count must have thought he was crushing Felix's chances at future rule by having him learn nothing but classical poetry and languages, but now . . .

Felix shook his head, a half-laugh of wonderment falling from his lips.

He couldn't have had a better basis for learning how to analyze *and create* new spells of his own.

Felix had given up, years ago, on making any difference to his nation or his empire. But now, in the depths of his captivity, he saw the truth at last.

He had never been truly weak at all. He had only been tricked and tortured into thinking so.

Now, it was time to save himself and become the Archduke he should have been from the beginning.

28

Saskia might not know how to magically find an Archduke she'd never met, but she knew exactly how to find her lover.

With all of her crows hovering anxiously around her, bags of supplies knotted into her belt, and enchanted combs pinned into her thickly plaited hair, she stood in her bedroom before an open drawer and held Felix's poem in her hands.

"Shot through with glory . . ."

Mine, she thought with all of her magical might and certainty. Then she closed her eyes and *leapt,* with an exertion that drew on every resource she had.

Eyes closed, she hurtled through elements and space in a wild storm of magic that swept her across mountains and cities and countries in a shrieking, furious whirl. Frigid winds whipped past her skin. Branches snapped against her hair. Feathers brushed against her neck, and fae voices screamed and giggled at unnerving pitches, grating against every nerve. She set her teeth through it all and kept her focus on the link that pulled her forward.

All she cared about was the end of the magical line she'd cast, that soul still alive and pulsing with emotion, closer and closer until finally . . .

"Ahhh!" She rebounded with a physical *snap* that sent her flying, helpless and out of control, passing through walls without connection until she landed exactly where the laid trap had sent her.

The fae queen's throne room.

Saskia forced herself, with agonizing effort, to twist just before her final fall so that she didn't drop onto her hands and knees. Instead, she landed on her feet, panting and furious, on a pink-and-silver marbled floor, just in front of a delicately wrought silver throne sculpted to look as if it had been formed from twining roots and branches. The beautifully crafted floor-to-ceiling windows on every side of the octagonal room showed nothing but pitch blackness outside, but golden fae lights danced below the ceiling, casting a warm glow through the mostly empty chamber.

Mostly empty . . . but not quite. Lorelei was sprawled across the cushioned seat with her half-bare legs casually crossed over one branching silver arm. "Saskia, darling!" she caroled. "How delightful to have you pay me a visit. Why, I think this is the first time you've ever decided to drop by without an invitation!"

"You know why I'm here," Saskia said flatly. "Give him back. *Now.*" She was still short on breath, but she didn't need it for this.

She wasn't a wizard, to rely on spoken spells. *She* translated her power through her body and the physical supplies that she had already infused with deadly magic.

Lorelei's eyes glinted gold at the challenge. "But why are you in such a rush? We haven't even shared a cup of tea yet, to catch up. We have so much news to share! For instance . . ."

Tipping her head to the side, she widened her eyes in exaggerated shock. "Did you know that the elusive Archduke of Estarion has finally been found, after all our months of searching? I've taken him captive myself! Aren't you delighted? Ailana will be here any moment now, so we can decide on the best purpose for him together, as allies. Still, I don't mind chatting about the matter with you in private, first."

"As *allies?* You betrayed our alliance," Saskia gritted. "Sneaking into *my* castle and kidnapping *my* staff without a single word—"

"Oh, darling, that is unfair. I used *so many* words to warn you that he couldn't be trusted! Don't you even remember all of our conversations?" Pouting, Lorelei pushed herself upright on her throne, golden curls falling over her eyes. She blew them out of the way with an impatient huff of air as she frowned at Saskia. "I *said* you really ought to find out more about him. And I tried to show you, that night in your library—"

"I'm not here to play your games, Lorelei. I never have been." Saskia set her teeth together against her own surging temper, which wanted her to send that dainty silver throne flying and smash all of the pretty glass windows on the way.

Think of Felix. Whenever he'd stood by her side in the past, she'd felt his calming presence like a cooling salve, gifting her control. She could find that calm center again now, for his sake.

"Listen to *me,*" she said, with all of the steady calmness she could summon. "I want our alliance to continue and grow stronger. I never want to be your enemy. But I will *burn this palace to the ground* if you don't give him back to me now . . . and if you've harmed a single hair on his head, I *will* destroy you."

Lorelei's eyes widened as her lips formed a silent, startled-looking "O."

Then the hoarse cry of a gryphon sounded in the night outside.

"There, now!" Lorelei relaxed back into the seat of her throne, smiling. "Here's Ailana. *She'll* help you see sense."

Darkness take it. Saskia could just about imagine defeating Lorelei on her own. Taking on both of the other Queens of Villainy at once, though?

Divine Elva, if You truly care for Felix's safety, You'd better lend me Your aid now. It wasn't quite a prayer, more a demand . . .

But Saskia could swear she heard the faint echo of a goddess's throaty laughter in response.

It wasn't reassuring.

Ailana strode into the room a moment later, peeling off long woolen gloves as her heeled boots clicked against the marble. Crystals of snow clung to her thick winter cloak and hat. Her cool, analytical gaze swung between the other two queens.

"I believe we have only eleven hours until Saskia's wall is due to be demolished. Is there a reason you two are wasting time posturing like cats instead of working the plan we all agreed on?"

"I have a *better* plan," Lorelei said smugly, just as Saskia snapped, "Lorelei kidnapped my librarian instead."

"Oh, for . . . !" Cold swept through the room as Ailana shut her eyes and inhaled deeply through her nose. Then her eyes flashed open, newly silvered with frost. Ice shot across the floor in a crackling rush that made Lorelei's throne rattle and Saskia's feet skid as she fought to keep her balance. "Are we all children?" the Queen of Nornne demanded. "Or can we possibly set aside a *minor disagreement* until—"

"It is not minor to me," Saskia snarled. Darkness, if she even gestured too hard, she'd fall over! She'd have to deal with Ailana's ice before she attempted any attack. Otherwise . . .

"It's a major coup," Lorelei said firmly, and the ice around her throne melted in an instant. The scent of summer, hot and lush with flowering blossoms, floated from her dainty figure like a challenge as she leveled her blue gaze at Ailana, ignoring Saskia completely. "This is the lever we've sought for months. Ailana, the Archduke of Estarion is in our hands at last."

"Finally!" Ailana's shoulders relaxed. "Did Saskia track him down?"

"Oh, no, Saskia's been harboring him all this time," Lorelei began in an intimate, gossipy tone, "but she didn't even realize it until—"

"*Saskia*," said Saskia through her teeth, "never gave you permission to steal him from *my own home* without warning, betraying the trust in our alliance." She turned her hard, meaningful glare at Ailana. "If you care at all about maintaining that alliance, you will agree to release him to me before we speak more about the matter."

The pouch of silversand in her belt would deal with Ailana's ice, at least for a few minutes. Then, if she swept out with her own magic to attack Lorelei, while she used her other supplies to hold off Ailana for as long as possible . . .

"I don't understand." Ailana's elegant brows drew together over her silvered brown eyes. "Are you saying that the Archduke of Estarion was hiding somewhere in your castle until Lorelei seized him? You're angry over the breach of territory?" Shaking her head, she turned to Lorelei. "That *was* thoughtless. Why, in the names of all the gods, would you do that without warning Saskia?"

"Because he'd already seduced her by then!" Lorelei snapped. "Do you think *I* can't tell when a clever woman's been made stupid by a cunning man?" She lifted her pointed chin, glaring at both of them. "No matter what either of you may think, I care about my friends and alliances. I wasn't about to stand back and let him make a game out of you!"

"He never did. *You're* the one—"

"Wait. *Wait*, both of you." Ailana's mouth dropped open for a long, silent moment of revelation as the other two queens glowered furiously at each other. "By Idrin's heart," she finally breathed. "Do you mean to say that Saskia's *librarian* was the Archduke all along?"

"Yes!" Lorelei crowed. "*Now* do you see?"

"It's true," Saskia admitted. "But, Ailana, I swear . . ."

"Oh, thank goodness." The ice queen's shoulders slumped as she gave a small, satisfied smile. "Well, that's all right, then!"

The other two queens stared at her. She shrugged, as if the answer should have been obvious to all. "That man has been head over heels for Saskia for months! Clearly, whatever his plan may be, he isn't plotting against her."

Breath whooshed out of Saskia's tight chest with such force that she staggered on the slick, iced floor. Lorelei shot to her feet, face flushing, but Saskia spoke before the fae queen could. "Felix was held prisoner and brutalized for years by Count von Hertzendorff. I've seen his scars myself. He's never had any control over Estarion's policies. He fled to Kitvaria to offer himself as a hostage in exchange for personal protection, but due to a misunderstanding *and* an intervention from Divine Elva Herself . . ."

"I cannot believe you've both been fooled!" Lorelei spat. "If you knew what I do about men—!"

"I've never been able to slip any of my spies into the Archduke's personal household," Ailana mused. She tapped one long, brown finger against the embroidered sleeve of her floor-length woolen cloak. "They always said the Count rotated that staff on a surprisingly frequent basis—no servant was allowed to stay for long. I'd assumed that was due to secret irascibility on the Archduke's part, but if von Hertzendorff wanted to keep the Archduke under his control and unable to make any helpful outside contacts . . ."

"How can you be so calm about this?" Lorelei cried. "Oh, I know he's got Saskia fooled, but *you* don't even care for men in your bed! So you can't possibly have been softened by his eyes or his manners."

"But I know something that you don't." Ailana gave her a faint, wintry smile. "I've seen them together several times now, Lorelei. I've watched his gaze follow her and seen the depth of that yearning, the way his body leans towards her like his personal sun . . . and unlike you, I've always known for a fact that true love does exist. That's why *I* take such care to guard my heart against it, while you recklessly risk yours again and again."

Lorelei's eyes flared wide . . . and then she clamped her lips shut, slamming herself back down onto the seat of her throne and crossing her arms tightly. The scent of rotten vegetation filled the air.

Saskia ignored the sickly stench. "So, we're agreed? Felix will be released immediately and—"

An explosion of magic rocked the throne room, cutting off her urgent words and sending her sliding on the ice. She flung out one hand to catch herself with a focused burst of her own power . . .

And a tall, masked figure landed just before her, making her skin tingle with the lingering force of his spell.

"Thank the gods!" Saskia flung herself forward into his arms without a second thought, barely even aware of the ice disappearing all around them at Ailana's wordless command.

Felix's arms were warm and firm as he pulled her close with a groan of pure relief. "It worked. I can hardly believe it!"

She eased back just enough to examine his face with ferocious care, patting his unmasked skin with hands that trembled uncontrollably. "You're unhurt? She didn't—?"

"I am *fine*," Felix assured her, eyes shining behind his mask. "More than fine, if you've actually forgiven me."

"You're *mine*," Saskia said fiercely, "forever. You know that! I only needed a moment to think everything through."

"So did I," Felix said. "Saskia . . ." Lifting one hand, he drew back his long hair to reveal a small hole at the tip of his left ear, where the cruel magical suppressant had been bound. "Because of you, I'm finally free."

"Not only me," she said. "You cast that spell yourself just now, didn't you?" Pride rose within her as she curled one hand around the nape of his neck, beneath his soft, curling hair. "Of course you did. I knew I'd hired the right dark wizard for my castle."

Behind her, Lorelei snorted loudly, but Saskia ignored the interruption. She tilted her head away from Felix but remained possessively tucked against him as she met Ailana's gaze. "We will not be using *anyone* as a political lever," she said in a tone that defied any challenge. "We three will defeat the Golden Beacon and his Gilded Mages together. Just let me quickly take Felix back to safety, and then—"

"No." It was Felix, not either of the other queens, who spoke. He shook his head at her in emphasis when Saskia jerked back to face him. "My queen, I first came to you in search of protection. I love that you want to give it to me now. But I've been thinking, since we last talked."

He gave a pained sigh. "My parents must have bound me with that earring for my own protection all those years ago, so I would never have to face the consequences of my power. But I think I know why Divine Elva gave that magic to me in the first place, when no one in my family's history had ever shared it."

Saskia frowned. "Whatever plans She may have concocted for you over the years, you aren't required to follow them. I've told Her, and I'll tell you, too—"

"I was the first royal heir born to Estarion after it joined the Empire," Felix said implacably. "After *my father* agreed to institute harsh Imperial law, remove every magical child from Estarion's families, and banish Elva's other, wilder children—the trolls, the hags, the goblins—from their borders."

Darkness take it. She knew that tone in his voice.

"It's not your fault," she began anyway.

"But it is my responsibility."

"*Ugh,*" Lorelei groaned. "Now *I'm* even starting to like him. This is dreadful! Can we please go kill somebody?"

"We should make haste," Ailana said calmly, "but I believe we can still take a moment to amend our plans."

"Thank you." Saskia felt Felix's chest rise and fall against her with his breath, but his voice was as firm and confident as if he were discussing his favorite pens and inks instead of upcoming warfare. "As Archduke of Estarion, I would be honored to join your alliance."

29

It was a bright, cold, and snow-covered late morning when the Archduke of Estarion returned to his homeland at last. It had taken nearly the full eleven hours to shift every element of the alliance's revised strategy into place. Even the three most powerful magical queens on the continent couldn't move armies without significant time and effort. However, between Ailana's spy network and Lorelei's fae portals, their final group was ready to land at just the right moment on Estarian snow.

They weren't there to fight the assembled ranks of soldiers or even the Emperor's top corps

of Gilded Mages. They were there to attend the theatrical performance that was guaranteed to come first.

After all, the breaking of the witch queen's infamous wall—
and the expansion of the Serafin Empire in the name of aiding
Kitvaria's former king Yaroslav, who would then agree to be re-
titled an Archduke—could hardly be wasted on the soldiers and
mages who were necessary participants. No, this news would
need to be broadcast across the continent for the glory of Estarion and the Emperor himself. *That* required an assemblage of
international journalists, all ready to memorialize the moment
and record the kind of carefully scripted speeches that Felix had
memorized and delivered countless times across his life.

Until now, he'd never written his own script. But as snow
crunched beneath his feet with the force of his portal-shifted
landing and all three Queens of Villainy and Saskia's First Minister surrounded him, he drew in a breath of icy air and prepared
himself for something far more intimidating:

His first sight in months of his former in-laws.

Count von Hertzendorff stood on the raised and ornamented
dais that had been carefully placed before the wall of shimmering
air to address the journalists in their gathered wooden seats. His
moustache bristled as his voice rolled across them with the same
aggressive authority he'd used to rule the archduchy ever since
he'd first arrived in Felix's life.

". . . And our Archduke will *never* stand for wickedness and
depravity to rule unhindered. Always will Estarion nobly stand
with our friends, as our Archduke bids us—and we gladly obey!"

Of course, the Count's voice could never reach all the ranks
of uniformed soldiers that spread in shocking, overwhelming
numbers across the snowy fields and slopes beyond, nor even the
small white-and-gold-cloaked group of Gilded Mages who stood
in a hooded cluster. However, the political image—witnessed
now and recorded by every journalist—would speak for itself

as he stood shoulder-to-shoulder, dress swords gleaming, with Saskia's uncle, the lean, hungry-looking former king of Kitvaria, who wore Divine Elva's symbol alongside various other medals to signify his status as an official paladin. Behind them stood the Count's looming son, Radomir, High General of Estarion, and also a tall, broad-shouldered, blond general in uniform who could only be the famous Golden Beacon.

Only the Golden Beacon's keen amber gaze moved as he stood, implacable and unemotional, at military rest behind the Count . . . until, with a finger-flick of warning to the others, Lorelei popped the bubble of the portal that had held them invisible upon their first arrival.

"Well, isn't this perfectly delightful!" As rainbow sparkles shimmered with the closing of the portal, Lorelei cast a flock of fluttering white butterflies, unbothered by the wintry weather, from her upflung hands into the air above to form the shape of a flag of peace. Then she twirled in place, barefoot and sparkling with mischief, on the patch of snow between the journalists and the dais . . .

And for just an instant, Felix saw the Golden Beacon physically twitch in an uncontrollable reaction.

"What the—? Soldiers!" the Count shouted as the assembled journalists shifted in their seats, clearly torn between panic and professional interest. "Mages! We're under attack! The witch queen and her allies—"

"Are standing beneath a white flag of peace," Mirjana said coolly as she stepped forward to face him, standing between the stage and Felix's cloaked and masked figure. "As am I. You do remember my father's diplomatic visit to your court, don't you? So you must be aware that, as First Minister of Kitvaria, I am capable of civilized behavior."

"Traitress!" Yaroslav snarled. Swinging around, Saskia's uncle grabbed hold of the Golden Beacon's impeccable blue uniform.

"Do something! Use your men and those mages to kill them all. Now!"

The Golden Beacon's blond eyebrows rose, chillingly, and the gathered soldiers and mages remained unmoving, awaiting his command. "Under a flag of peace?"

"And in front of *journalists*?" Radomir muttered, not quite quietly enough. "Shut up, you fool."

"Oh, I know my niece." Releasing the general, Yaroslav swung around to point a furiously trembling finger at Saskia, who stood silent and watchful on the snow beside Ailana, swathed in a deep-purple cloak that rippled with the force of the magical power gathered around her. The crown of bones sat firmly atop her head, her chin was raised, and her face wore an expression of unmistakable disdain that made the last of Felix's own nerves finally drop away. As his queen gazed up at the man who had murdered her parents and done his worst to crush her in every way, there was no mistaking the contempt she felt.

Still, Yaroslav spat, "She's a monster. Violent. Uncontrollable! If *she's* pretending to be here on a peaceful mission, it's a trick. None of us can trust her for a moment!"

"*I* do." Felix stepped forward between Mirjana and Lorelei, untying the ribbons that had held his half-mask to his face until this moment. "And it was publicly stated just now that Estarion will gladly do my bidding."

Pushing back the hood of his dark cloak, he dropped the half-mask to the snow, revealing the famous face that had been painted again and again over the years . . . and the murmuring mass of confused noise erupted into utter chaos. Every one of the journalists surged to their feet from their chairs, shouting and baying like a pack of hounds set loose on a hunt. Only Ailana's swift and efficient erection of a sliver-thin fence of ice stopped the journalists from flooding over their group, regardless of consequence.

There was chaos on the dais above, too, as the Golden Beacon started forward with sudden, sharp interest and Radomir grabbed the Count's arm for a swift, whispered consultation.

"Why, there you are at last, my boy!" As Count von Hertz-endorff straightened, his eyes held a hard, menacing light that sent an added chill through Felix's bones. Felix knew exactly what that look signified—but the Count's voice was warm and avuncular as he spoke for the benefit of everyone else. "Thank Elva, you've returned to us at last. We were horrified to learn that you'd been kidnapped by the terrible witch queen—"

"Kidnapped?" The Golden Beacon's voice rapped out, deep and commanding. "What's this? I was sent to support the Arch-duke in his aid for an ally in trouble. Why was His Majesty not informed that the Archduke himself had gone missing?"

"Kitvaria *is* Estarion's ally," Felix said, pitching his voice to carry for the crowd as he'd been taught, "but the false king Yaro-slav never will be."

"Clearly, the witch queen has cast you under an evil spell." The Count's voice was clipped. "Radomir—"

"I've got this. Come along, *little brother*." Barely masking his sneer, Estarion's high general loped down the stairs from the dais, his voice pitched to unconvincing affability. "No matter what that woman may have done to you, you're not in danger any-more. We'll get you safely to a physician who can bring you back to yourself in *quiet*, with nobody else to disturb you."

Snow crunched behind Felix as Saskia shifted forward.

Felix put one hand behind his back to stop her. "Not this time," he murmured as he watched the bigger, stronger man approach. Radomir had carelessly, happily brutalized him all across their shared lives. Now, Estarion's high general reached out with one muscled arm to grab him like a recalcitrant pet, as he'd done so painfully often before—and Felix whispered the spell that he'd spent hours preparing for this moment.

Radomir's body flew through the air with such force that he hit the edge of the dais and collapsed, unconscious.

There! Exhilaration mingled with relief as Felix let out a silent sigh. For years, his power had been locked away and kept secret from him—but now, everything was different.

He would never be helpless again.

"So much for a flag of peace!" Yaroslav shouted. "Now you all see what my niece is capable of. Soldiers—"

"Even under a flag of peace, I am allowed to defend myself." Felix met the Count's gaze on the dais and, for the first time in fifteen years, he felt no fear. *"Finally."*

Saskia hadn't stood so close to her uncle since she'd escaped his clutches at the age of fourteen, terrified and running for her life. She'd expected to feel rage when she saw him again today. She had *never* expected to feel delight . . .

But as Saskia watched her gentle, softspoken lover take on Yaroslav and every other pompous bastard on that stage—speaking up for *her*, the most hated and feared witch on the continent!—warmth filled her chest until she could barely even feel the chill of the wintry air around her or the snow beneath her boots.

When she'd first hired this quiet, careful man as her librarian, she had never guessed at the true strength that lay within him, even beyond his untapped magical power. Now, as she compared his steady moral clarity to her uncle's spitting fury, how could she feel anything but fierce pride and delight in the man she loved?

Even the journalists who pressed hungrily against Ailana's translucent fence couldn't diminish Saskia's mood. She had been burned too badly by the headlines of her childhood to allow any of those news-rakers into her presence since her assumption of the Kitvarian throne, but she could see and admire how naturally her lover aimed his words at them. Even Mirjana let out a soft sigh of appreciation as Felix angled himself to be heard and seen by every frantically scribbling reporter, his voice resonant.

"I fled to Kitvaria to save my life—and Queen Saskia, despite every vicious, untrue rumor spread over the years by her murderous uncle, graciously agreed to shelter me from the villain who stands here onstage now, usurping my voice and my role as he has done for well over a decade."

"She's obviously bewitched him!" snarled the Count. "None of these are his words. General de Moireul, you must see—"

But Felix had already shrugged off his cloak and turned his back to the reporters who were his most avid audience.

They were all watching as he lifted his shirt to reveal the telltale scars that had driven Saskia to homicidal fury on first sight. "These," he said calmly, "as all of you can see, are far too old to have been left by any but the so-called *protector* who held me prisoner for years."

He turned in place, pale but composed, to reveal the same damning truth to the men gathered onstage as reporters screamed question after intrusive question. Saskia's teeth clenched at the onslaught, but Felix ignored them all as he turned once more to the stage, lifting his chin with regal hauteur.

"General de Moireul," he said, "as Archduke of Estarion, I authorize you to take control of my principality's army as it's marched back to Estaviel City. General and Chief Minister von Hertzendorff are both to be taken prisoner and held there until they stand trial for high treason."

"You *pathetic weakling!*" Spit flew from his Chief Minister's mouth as he bellowed the words from the edge of the platform. "You've never been fit for anything but ink and poetry. *I'm* the only one who's strong enough to rule. Soldiers—rise up now and *seize him,* for the sake of Estarion and glory!"

Saskia braced herself for battle . . .

But the first rank of soldiers on the snowy field nearby sank to their knees in a unified show of respect for Felix, laying their weapons aside. More and more followed afterwards, in a rippling wave across the field.

For the last decade and a half, Saskia had cursed the insidious way the Archduke's noble profile and virtues had been extolled around the continent, under the propagandist control of Count von Hertzendorff. Now, her lips curved into a smirk of pure satisfaction at the final result.

"Ohhhh." Mirjana stepped back to murmur into Saskia's ear, "I officially withdraw every objection. He *will* make a perfect partner for you after all."

Saskia snorted. "You're just happy to finally be working with a royal who's willing to smile for the public."

Mirjana rolled her eyes, but she didn't argue. The two of them stood together in unusual amity, with Ailana on Saskia's left, as the Golden Beacon lifted one hand to shield his eyes against the low winter sun and looked out into the crowd of kneeling soldiers.

"Lieutenant General." He nodded briskly as he identified an officer. "Take control of the prisoners, if you please."

"Gladly, sir. Your Highness!" The man leapt to his feet and gave two respectful salutes, first to the Golden Beacon and then to Felix . . . who nodded in return with all the grace to be expected of an elegant Imperial Archduke.

Gods, she couldn't wait to get him back into bed! Saskia had to clench her fingers to hold herself back as he watched his lifelong abusers taken prisoner with perfect composure.

She knew *exactly* what that mask looked like when it broke . . . and the prospect of having that astonishing combination of courage, kindness, and passion by her side for the rest of both of their lives was more intoxicating than any magic.

"You did say it would be a good diplomatic move for Kitvaria if I wed another ruler," she murmured thoughtfully.

Mirjana gave a quick, sharp nod. "I do give excellent advice . . . though I didn't anticipate this particular alliance."

"*Enough!*" Saskia's uncle Yaroslav threw himself forward as the Count, still bellowing with outrage, was marched off the stage under guard of multiple soldiers. Slamming one open palm against the Golden Beacon's closest broad shoulder, Yaroslav snapped, "This is *more* than enough. Your emperor sent you here to fulfil Divine Elva's will as communicated through *me*, her paladin, so I could reclaim my rightful throne. Now, are you going to *do your job* or . . . ?"

"Oh, Uncle." Saskia couldn't hold back a derisive crack of laughter as she finally stepped forward to speak. "Your friends may have bribed a weak-minded priest into giving you that trinket on your coat, but you do *not* serve Divine Elva's will. Who do you think sent me the Archduke in the first place?"

"Wha—*what?*" He stared at her blankly for an instant before he recovered himself. "*Heresy!* Did everyone hear her? As a paladin of Divine Elva—"

"Unlike you," Saskia informed him, "I have actually met Her. I wouldn't recommend that you steal Her voice."

"Regardless." The Golden Beacon cleared his throat as he stood indomitably in place on the raised platform, unmoved by Yaroslav's physical or verbal blows. "I was, in fact, sent to support the Archduke of Estarion with my forces and the corps of Gilded Wizards under my command. Therefore, if the Archduke himself would care to command me now . . . ?"

"Estarion thanks you for your service." Felix walked unhurriedly up the wooden steps to take his own place at the front of the stage. He aimed his next words at the breathless crowd. "I ask only that you return to the capital with the excellent news of Estarion's new friendship and solidarity with Kitvaria, Balravia, and Nornne. Their rulers may be known as the so-called Queens of Villainy, but they have proved to be loyal and true."

The general's glinting blond eyebrows rose as his gaze shifted to sweep across the three queens . . . and then landed, for a long, enigmatic moment, on Lorelei's figure.

She wiggled her fingers at him tauntingly, sending sparkles

through the air. "*What* a shame not to be able to trounce you today. Never mind, darling! We can play again soon, I am sure."

Again? Saskia raised her eyebrows at Ailana. The Queen of Nornne's shoulders lifted in a discreet shrug. Apparently, even the ice queen didn't know all of Lorelei's secrets.

A touch even lighter than falling snow brushed against the nape of Saskia's neck. Then a goddess's voice shouted inside her head: "NOW!"

Saskia spun around, her heart thundering with the divine impact . . .

Just as her uncle yanked his dress sword from his belt and lunged directly at Felix. "She *won't* win against me. Not again!"

The last time she'd glimpsed her uncle across a battlefield, Saskia had frozen in panic, every scathing name he'd ever called her ringing in her ears. He'd been swept away by his guards before she could recall herself to fight.

This time, she saw his sword slice towards Felix's unarmored figure, just as another sword had sliced into her parents' bodies nineteen years ago—and she did not hesitate.

Power exploded through the air, compressing and then exploding with a sonic *boom* that sent onlookers staggering and clapping hands to their ears all across the field.

The sword fell to the platform with a clatter, just beside Felix's feet . . .

And a small, greyish white slug oozed helplessly on the wooden platform beside it, leaving nothing but slime in its wake.

Saskia walked up the wooden steps of the platform with her head held high and took Felix's hand as he gave her a low, respectful bow. Standing by his side a moment later, with his fingers warmly twined through hers, she looked out at the crowd of scribbling journalists and, for once, felt pride instead of mortification.

"My uncle lied about *almost* everything," she told them all with the full knowledge that her words would be repeated across the continent. "I am not a monster. My power is fully under my control, and I will never use it against anyone who hasn't attacked my people first. But he was right about one thing: I *am* powerful beyond your wildest fears, and no one—including the Serafin Emperor—should ever forget that again."

As Felix squeezed her hand in his, she looked out across the crowd and saw her fellow Queens of Villainy raising their hands in enthusiastic applause. It was such a satisfying moment that Saskia decided not to even bother stepping on her uncle afterwards.

He wasn't worth the effort anymore.

30

Once all of the reporters had finally scattered to file their reports, the snowy fields were taken over by preparations for the gathered armies and Gilded Mages to depart. Felix knew it was time to make his own next move, but before he could decide how to begin, the Emperor's high general drew him aside by the wooden dais.

It was a perfectly strategic position, within view of all of their allies, but far enough from everyone to avoid being overheard.

"If we might speak a moment in private, Your Highness . . ."

"Of course." Felix fixed a courteous smile on his face. Internally, though, he braced for danger.

Like everyone else in the Empire, he'd been hearing stories about the Golden Beacon for years. The man was near godlike in his luck on the battlefield, chaste and devout, devoted to justice above all else, *and* adored by his troops. When those elements were combined with General de Moireul's curling blond hair, square jawline, unusual amber eyes, and impressive physique, it was no wonder he'd become a figure of near-mythic status in the last few years.

Felix knew full well how propaganda worked—but he also knew that no man, regardless of luck and looks, could have risen to the highest rank in the Imperial army in only thirty years, from a childhood of family notoriety and disgrace, without a powerful drive and a formidably intelligent mind.

"May I offer you lodgings in Estaviel City for the night?" Felix met the other man's gaze directly, his own message unhidden. *I have nothing to hide. Not anymore.* "I would be happy to order a feast in your honor."

"With regret, I cannot accept that invitation. In fact . . ." Clasping his hands behind his back, the Golden Beacon cleared his throat, his brows lowering. "I hope to offer *you* something instead. A warning."

"Ah." Felix's spine stiffened, but he kept his expression unmoved, mindful of every onlooker.

"Quite." The Golden Beacon's broad, uniformed chest rose and fell with a silent sigh. "Your Highness, it has been my honor and my pleasure to follow your commands today. I hope you understand that I have no personal urge to question any of them. And yet . . ."

The rich, overwhelming scent of roses suddenly flooded the wintry air as the Queen of Balravia slipped into place between them, smiling winsomely. "Why, hello! Are you two having a perfectly lovely conversation? I do hope you aren't threatening my darling Felix, Gerard. Saskia wouldn't care for that at *all*, and you know I always look out for my friends." She slid a sidelong glance at Felix. "I may owe this one a bit of extra protection, too, after . . . well, a certain misunderstanding."

"You owe me nothing." Felix inclined his head in a wary but respectful nod. "I understand you were acting to defend your friend."

"Regardless." She narrowed her eyes up at the Golden Beacon and a tinge of rot crept through the lush scent of roses. "I wouldn't advise trying any underhanded tactics, dear, while I'm here as a witness. I know *all* your tricks."

"As it happens, I am currently attempting to assist His Highness." The Golden Beacon's face had been set in impassive lines since Lorelei's arrival, and his words were entirely uninflected.

"How adorable that you think you can!" Lorelei batted her eyelashes. "*Do* tell. What exactly will you be teaching him today? How to be a good little soldier and never think for himself? The easiest way to become Otto's favorite lapdog?"

The Golden Beacon did not respond . . . but Felix glimpsed a twitch at the corner of his closest eyelid.

"Is anything amiss?" Ailana's voice was calm, but her gaze shifted warily from Lorelei to the looming general as she stepped up to join them.

"Oh, no, not anymore." Lorelei smiled sunnily. "*I'm* here now to keep Saskia's consort safe from any more bullying. The so-called Golden Beacon may think he can flex his reputation and threaten all sorts of nonsense, but—"

"*Who* is threatening Felix?" The crackling force of Saskia's magic lit sparks against his skin as she stalked to his side.

Felix's lips curved in helpless adoration as he turned to take her hand in his. "No one," he assured her softly. "They wouldn't dare, after the display you put on earlier. Have I thanked you yet for saving my life?"

"You certainly didn't get any help from the *famous soldier* onstage with you." Lorelei tutted. "If it hadn't been for Saskia stepping in . . ."

"Ahem." The Golden Beacon cleared his throat, his eyelids once more under control. "I deeply regret that I wasn't swift enough to defend you myself, Your Highness. However, I would like to make up for that error by offering a word of advice now." His gaze rested on Felix's face, avoiding Lorelei's mistrustful glare. "I would advise you to find a second residence outside Estarion."

"I beg your pardon?" Felix's eyebrows rose.

Beside him, Saskia stiffened dangerously, but Lorelei let out a triumphant crow.

"See? Threats! I knew it." She shook her head pityingly at the Golden Beacon. "You just cannot help yourself on a battlefield, can you?"

"Let's allow General de Moireul to finish speaking," Ailana murmured. "Personally, I'd quite like to know what he's trying to say."

"Thank you, Your Majesty." The general gave her a grave nod before turning the weight of his attention back to Felix. "As I told you before, I myself have neither the legal right nor any personal impulse to question your authority in Estarion. But there is one authority who rises above us both."

". . . The Emperor." Felix let out his breath in a sigh. "Of course." He might not have been educated to understand every nuance of political devolution and governance amongst the Empire's conjoined archduchies, but even he knew who stood at the powerful center of that web.

"I am more than happy to follow your orders now," said the Golden Beacon, "but once I return to the capital with my troops, I will be required to make a personal report to His Majesty." He cleared his throat. "Needless to say, I cannot speak for his reaction, nor for any decisions he may take."

"I understand." Felix swallowed hard. *Elva forgive me.*

He might have been gifted with magic by the goddess in order to stand for the families of other magical children and wild magical creatures in Estarion, but even he couldn't openly flout the Emperor's commands without being imprisoned—or executed—for treason. Then another, more amenable aristocrat would be elevated by the Emperor to take his place, and life would become even worse for everyone affected.

Ailana said, "Naturally, the Emperor will be pleased to learn that no battle was necessary today, after all, as the request for his military aid was made under false pretenses."

"Mmm," said the Golden Beacon, with careful neutrality.

"Ha!" Lorelei sniffed. "I expect *he'll* be raging around his throne room, kicking around all of his toys for days. This was the best excuse he'd found to invade another kingdom, and we've ruined it for him."

"Regardless." Ailana turned her cool focus upon Felix. "There are many ways to enact change, and not all of them include public speeches before a crowd. Many can be handled effectively behind the scenes, merely by ensuring that the right people are in charge of certain practices . . . and well aware that they need no longer pursue them so aggressively. In fact, they can make quite a show of following Imperial orders with surprisingly little substance behind it—which would *not* give the Emperor any public excuse to supplant a popular and beloved ruler."

"But that isn't enough," Felix said bleakly. "Not nearly enough for everyone who's being harmed by those cruel policies."

"Not *yet*," Ailana said firmly. "But we all know this battle has merely been postponed—which gives us time to gather more resources. In the meantime, once you choose your new Chief Minister and cabinet, I see no reason why you shouldn't primarily reside with your consort in her kingdom and simply make joint visits of state to Estarion, to maintain your connection and popularity with your people."

"Oh, no. I couldn't ask that." Felix was already shaking his head as he turned to Saskia. "I would *never* expect you to leave your home and your work for my sake. I know—"

"*I* know how much easier the Emperor would find his expansion plans if he could quietly arrange your assassination and replace you with one of his toadies." Saskia's grip on his hand tightened as she scowled at him ferociously, every inch the terrifying witch queen. "Don't ask me to stay behind when you're walking into danger!"

Frowning, Felix didn't answer. Of course he would prefer her to be with him, but if it would make her miserable . . .

She sighed heavily as her scowl fell away. "For darkness' sake. I've already had to promise Mirjana I'll attend at least three or four public events in Kitvaria every year from now on. Are you planning to abandon me to endure *those* horrors alone?"

"Never," Felix promised. "I'll be by your side whenever you want me."

"Then let me do the same," she said with urgent, unmistakable sincerity. "Let us protect one another."

How could he ever refuse that request? Felix raised her hand to his lips and exulted in the leap of hot, prickling, magical energy between them. "*Always*," he promised.

He had finally discovered his own strength across the months he had worked in her castle—and he would always support her just as she supported him.

"Ahem." The Golden Beacon cleared his throat. "In the meantime, my troops have had a hard march across the Empire in the last two days. It would be irresponsible of me to push them too quickly for our return." He paused, pointedly, before finishing. "I fully expect not to arrive in the capital, to make my report, for at least three days."

"*Hmm.*" Lorelei's eyes narrowed as she made that ominous humming noise.

Felix probably should have felt concern at that sound—but he was too relieved by the other man's words to worry overmuch about the fae queen's schemes. Three days would give Felix time to travel to Estaviel City with Saskia and speak with all of the members of his official cabinet at last, to decide which one to appoint his new Chief Minister and plan together how to work against Imperial policies behind the scenes.

He and Saskia would return to Kadaric Castle and the home and family they shared well before the Emperor could let loose his fury.

"I thank you for your advice," Felix said to the Emperor's high general with true respect. "I will remember it."

"And I you." The general bowed deeply before turning and striding away to his troops without another word.

"Hmmph." Lorelei's nostrils flared as she watched him leave. "Don't worry any of your heads about *him*. No matter how menacing he may seem, I'll take care of that little problem for you."

"Ah . . ." Felix began.

"I *told* you," she said, "I look out for my friends, whether they want me to or not! I make up for my mistakes, too." The look she gave Saskia was surprisingly apologetic.

"Lorelei," Ailana began warily, "whatever you may be thinking . . ."

It was too late. Rainbow sparkles had already appeared, shimmering around the fae queen. An instant later, she was gone, leaving melting colors on the snow and a sudden extra chill to the air.

Ailana let out a hissing sigh of frustration.

But Felix's attention was caught by a different queen as Saskia wrapped her arms around his shoulders in front of everyone. "Have I mentioned to you yet that you're my official consort?" she murmured.

"Did you need to?" He tipped his head forward to meet hers in a moment of perfect intimacy in the midst of the bustling, snowy field, letting her crown of bones press firmly against his hair. "I've been yours for months now, and you know it."

"*Everyone* will know it once they read the newspapers." She smiled up at him with open possession. "The civilized Archduke of Estarion has been enchanted and corrupted by the wicked witch queen, and she's never going to let him go."

"Never?" he whispered hopefully.

"*Never*," she repeated, "because you've enchanted me, too."

At her words, the power he'd never known he had rose irresistibly within him. Felix felt it meet and tangle with hers, forming something new and astonishing together, as their lips met in a kiss that promised passion and purpose, tenderness and care, and a future more magical than he could ever have imagined.

EPILOGUE

Kadaric Castle

Three nights later, Saskia was lying wrapped up with her lover under her familiar quilt, her cheek resting securely against his warm chest and dancing golden lights flickering like stars in the darkness around them, when a sudden, urgent alarm sounded from the small mirror-box that she had created in her last meeting with Ailana.

"Ugh!" Groaning, she forced herself up from the comfort of the bed and the even deeper comfort of Felix's arms.

As much as Saskia might value her privacy,

even she had to admit that if the Queens of Villainy were to maintain their alliance against an increasingly dangerous emperor, they would need to be able to get in touch immediately, from now on, for any crisis.

Felix sat up in bed as she left, extinguishing the golden lights that he had cast for them earlier with a murmured counterspell that warmed her with pride. As far as the rest of the world was concerned, based on the newspaper reports, that magical counterattack on Estarion's high general must have been cast by her—but the two of them both knew the truth.

As always, her lover was ready to take on a new challenge. Now that they were safely home, he was turning his keen attention to learning and practicing the magic that he'd studied as her librarian for months, in preparation for the next time they were called upon to do battle.

He stayed back now, giving her space, but she could feel his watchful concern like an embrace as she yanked her crimson dressing gown around her naked body and then pulled open the mirror-box to reveal the lovely face of Nornne's ice queen.

"Ailana?" Saskia swept away the thick locks of hair that had fallen over her own face in the last half hour. "What's amiss? Is there news from the Emperor's meeting with the Golden Beacon?"

The expectation of that meeting had guided the schedule of their whirlwind trip to Estaviel City and, this afternoon, their thankful return to Kadaric Castle. She and Felix had been greeted with worried lectures and delicious pastries from Mrs. Haglitz, calm words of welcome from a visibly relieved Morlokk, cawing and shrieking delight from Oskar, and half a dozen new stories about experiences they'd missed from Krakk and the other goblins.

Still, her awareness of that upcoming event had been a thrumming source of anxiety all day long.

"Not . . . exactly." Ailana's face looked uncharacteristically pinched with tension. "Have you heard from Lorelei at all in the last few days?"

Saskia frowned. "Not a word. Why? Should I have?" In the whirlwind of meetings and travel, it hadn't even occurred to her to expect any such communication.

"I had hoped—well, never mind." Ailana released a heavy breath. "The Emperor and the Golden Beacon did *not* meet today after all."

"Why not?" It was Felix who spoke, stepping up to lean over Saskia's shoulder. "Has some other crisis erupted on a different border?"

"According to official reports," said Ailana, "the Golden Beacon has ordered his troops to take a long rest before the Ferian mountain pass. However, according to my spies, there is good reason to believe that no one has actually *seen* the Golden Beacon himself in at least two days."

"So, what do you—? *Oh.*" Saskia sucked in a breath, turning to meet Felix's widening eyes. "You don't think . . . ?"

"Exactly," Ailana said tightly. "No one—including any of my spies—has caught any sight of Lorelei, either."

"Elva preserve us," Felix murmured.

But as Saskia knew, there were some things a goddess couldn't control. The incorrigible fae queen was undoubtedly among them.

"It *could* be only a coincidence," she said, without any real hope.

"Perhaps." Ailana grimaced. "Do let me know if you hear from her?"

"Of course." Gently closing the lid of the box, Saskia looked up at her consort and let out a weary sigh. "I suppose I ought to start casting for her now—but if she's using her own magic to hide herself, it won't be easy."

"I'll help you," Felix promised, "but not yet. You've done more than enough for today. Let yourself have a full night's sleep first. We'll work together on it tomorrow morning."

The Witch Queen of Kitvaria had never believed that she needed any tenderness or care in her life . . .

But as she closed her eyes five minutes later to fall asleep in the warm curve of Felix's arms, she couldn't help sending up her first true prayer to Divine Elva.

Thank You. Thank You. Thank You.

Two nights earlier, in a private hunting lodge in an enchanted woodland deep within Balravia, shielded with ancient fae magic from even the most powerful of prying eyes . . .

Tedious, unimaginative people always threw around words like "reckless" or "foolhardy" when confronted with Lorelei of Balravia's most brilliant schemes and lightning-swift instincts. Naturally, she'd never allowed their disapproval to bother her for an instant.

But as she looked down now, through the darkness, at the infuriatingly beautiful figure of the Empire's beloved Golden Beacon, cast under an enchanted sleep and chained with ropes of twining ivy to his prison bed, Lorelei found herself wondering, for the first time, whether she might have finally gone too far.

Acknowledgments

Thank you so much to my fearless beta readers, who read through every chapter of this manuscript and cheered me on as I was drafting it: Jenn Reese, Deva Fagan, and Ying Lee, you are all AMAZING.

Thank you to Patrick Samphire and Justina Robson for helpful critiques of my book and trilogy proposals, and thank you again to Patrick for cheerfully taking on extra childcare and housecare when I needed to go on a writing retreat to get my head around the second half of this novel. I love you so much!

Thank you to Molly Ker Hawn for believing in this project from the beginning and being the best possible agent and friend in every way.

Thank you to Monique Patterson for believing in this novel, and to Erika Tsang for thoughtful edits that helped *so* much. Thank you to Erin Wilcox for thoughtful and truly helpful copyediting, Megan Kiddoo for careful and perceptive production editing, Ariana Carpentieri and Jennifer McClelland-Smith for marketing, Alexis Saarela for publicity, and Tessa Villanueva for guiding me so patiently through the process.

Thanks so much to Aliette de Bodard for reading early scenes and helping me out with the perfect surname for the Golden

Beacon, and to all the members of my private Slack and Discord groups who've supported me in so many ways as I wrote this.

Thank you to everyone on social media who helped me build the perfect writing soundtrack for this novel! (If you'd like to listen to it now, you can find the link on my website: stephanieburgis .com. Just click on "Wooing the Witch Queen" there!)

Thank you so much to every single member of my Patreon (patreon.com/stephanieburgis). I have so much fun with our monthly book clubs, patron Q&A sessions, Discord hangouts, and more! Your support has made *such* a difference to my writing life.

And to every reader who enjoyed this book: thank you so much for reading! Do sign up to my newsletter to get advance sneak peeks at Book 2 and more: www.stephanieburgis.com/newsletter.

Turn the page for a sneak peek at the next book
in the Queens of Villainy series

Enchanting the Fae Queen

Available Winter 2026

Copyright © 2026 by Stephanie Burgis Samphire

Even the most brutal of tortures could never force Gerard de Moireul to admit it, but the shameful truth was that it wasn't unusual for him to dream of Balravia's queen. After all, the woman had haunted his waking life for seven years.

She was an incorrigible *menace*.

The rest of the Empire might delight in salacious stories and songs of the countless lovers she had publicly discarded—or even executed—in the course of her scandalous reign, but he could only *wish* more of her time was spent that way. Instead, she seemed to take delight in tormenting him, specifically and untiringly, for no logical reason that he had ever been able to fathom . . . and not only when they met face-to-face, which happened far too often for his peace of mind.

If he marched his troops to a carefully planned battle only to find that the other side had somehow mysteriously vanished into thin air, he was certain to find her telltale fragrance taunting him from his pillowcase when he returned to his private quarters afterwards.

Whenever Emperor Otto held a grand new ceremony to award him with another hard-won medal of achievement, rather than taking pride in the Imperial affirmation, Gerard found himself bracing and holding his breath throughout, only waiting for an impossible catastrophe to hit. Once, a sharp-thorned rosebush erupted beneath him just as he was lowering himself onto what *had* been a plain wooden chair only a moment before. On a different occasion, the sudden stench of rotten fruits overwhelmed his senses just as he was drawing a deep breath to deliver a meticulously crafted diplomatic speech to the assembled company. Only the most rigorous, lifelong training in self-control had saved him from collapsing into a sneezing, choking fit that would have made him the laughingstock of every newspaper report.

Of course, there was never any evidence left behind to prove the culprit to any outside observer, much less to provoke the kind of official Imperial reaction that could only too easily crush her small kingdom . . .

But most maddeningly of all, Queen Lorelei always made certain to leave a calling card just for him, whether she conveyed it through the lush scent of fresh roses or via a shimmer of dancing, rainbow-colored sparkles that melted as soon as he'd spotted them.

What was she even trying to provoke?

Obviously, it was a useless effort on her part. He knew his duty well, and his goals were set in stone. He would never allow such absurd teasing to distract him. Still, he found himself turning the question of her motives over and over in his thoughts at night . . . and then dreaming horrifyingly intense, shocking scenarios where he pinned her down on his bed to *force* her to finally answer all of his questions, while she laughed shamelessly up at him and then . . .

No. He would not remember those dreams. Even Gerard couldn't exert control over his own subconscious while he slept, but he *could* resist lingering over those reprehensible fantasies in the light of day.

And yet, it wasn't a surprise when he awoke in pitch darkness, aching with unforgivable heat, once again.

Only yesterday, he'd come face-to-face with the fae queen on a snowy battlefield where she'd stood, barefoot and reckless, allied with two other powerful, independent queens in open defiance of the Empire. It had taken all of Gerard's diplomatic efforts, combined with those of Estarion's surprisingly pacifistic Archduke and the icily calculating Queen of Nornne, to prevent a war that none of them wanted . . . and Lorelei's impudent provocations had come dangerously close to evoking a reaction that Gerard couldn't possibly afford.

It was no wonder she'd invaded his dreams again afterwards.

This time, mimicking real life, he'd dreamed that he was sleeping on the thin cot in the small, plain tent he always used for marching with his troops. When the decadent, unmistakable scent of her perfume had awakened his dream-self, he'd stiffened, his eyes snapping open . . . and found the notorious Siren of Balravia smiling mischievously down at him, lit in the darkness of his tent by a circle of golden fae lights that danced around them both, closing the two of them into a warm, intimate circle.

"Shh, darling." She tipped one palm to scatter shimmering gold dust across the exposed skin of his face and throat before he could rise. "There's no need for you to wake or worry now. I'm taking care of absolutely *everything*."

Even his dream-self knew that was patently absurd. Between the troops he commanded, the dangerously changeable emperor he served, the perilously shifting tides of politics, and the endless weight of his family legacy, Gerard *always* had to worry. It was his responsibility and the choice that he had made and . . . and . . .

And yet . . . somehow . . .

As the gold dust settled and melted into his skin, warm, irresistible lassitude overcame him, and he found his eyes falling inexorably shut. Lorelei's small, soft fingertips stroked lightly across his cheek, leaving tingling trails of sensation in their wake, and despite everything, his rational objections sank too deep to be rediscovered.

It was only a dream, after all. No one could blame him for that. Only a dream . . .

And he reminded himself of that, again and again, for several agonizing moments after he woke, lying spread-eagled and panting, still imagining that aggravating scent of roses and burning with a heat he refused to identify.

Enough! His mind still fogged with sleep, Gerard set his teeth together and turned to roll out of bed for his usual, punishing round of morning calisthenics. They were designed specifically to expel all such distracting nonsense from his head . . .

But the moment he tried to move, he found himself tethered by strangely soft—yet implacable—chains that fastened across his chest, his arms, and his ankles to hold him firmly in place, splayed out across a wide, soft mattress.

Was he still dreaming after all? This wasn't his thin, hard traveling cot. And how could the air ever feel so luxuriantly warm in the middle of a snowy mountain pass?

Gods above. He sucked in a sharp breath through his teeth as the outrageous truth finally hit him.

No wonder he could still smell roses!

"*Lorelei.*" It was a snarl of disbelieving fury—and the most uncontrolled outburst he'd allowed himself in decades.

Rainbow sparkles erupted in the darkness before him as swiftly as if he had uttered an invitation.

"Finally!" The Queen of Balravia burst out of one of her fiendishly unstoppable fae portals, clothed in a low-cut, gauzy gold concoction and beaming triumphantly. As she emerged, the blanketing darkness lifted from the room around them to reveal a large, airy bedchamber wallpapered in shades of green and lit by midday sunlight. There must have been a window somewhere to allow in all of that light, but the full force of Gerard's attention was fixed on the fae queen's deceptively lovely face as she clasped her hands under her pointed chin and regarded him from the floor beyond his prison-bed, her gold-flecked blue eyes glinting with mischief. "I thought you'd never wake up, sleepyhead. I've been waiting for *ages!*"

He would not lose control and bellow, no matter the provocation. But it took all of the willpower he'd learned across his lifetime to keep his voice steady and uninflected. "That, Your Majesty, would be because when you kidnapped me from my tent in the middle of a full Imperial army encampment, you laid an illicit sleeping spell upon me. The number of international laws you have just flagrantly broken—"

"Oh, that was just a tiny little enchantment, not a *spell*. Honestly!" Rolling her eyes, she flicked one dimpled hand in dismissal. "If *that* was all that was keeping you asleep, you would have woken up hours ago, as I'd expected. No, I think you must have been utterly exhausted, poor thing. You do work yourself terribly hard, don't you, running around every day and trying to satisfy all of Otto's absurd demands? Really, you ought to be thanking me right now for whisking you away on this lovely vacation."

"*Vacation*," Gerard repeated flatly. Incredulity mingled with righteous outrage—a reaction that had become intimately familiar across the past seven years of their acquaintance.

Was she actually trying to drive him into madness? Had that been her deeper plan for him all along?

As she glided towards him, the shimmering golden fabric of her gown brushed softly against the sides of the bed, and he found himself intensely, unavoidably aware of his own position, splayed across the silken covers of the mattress and bound by impossible chains of flowers. He'd already felt their magical implacability; he wouldn't humiliate himself by fighting against them now and failing under her delighted gaze.

Thank all the gods that it had been too cold in his tent last night to sleep unclothed. He was still missing his polished boots, vest, cravat, and uniform coat, but at least his chest and outstretched arms were fully covered by a long-sleeved cotton shirt, and his legs were sheathed in woolen trousers.

There was no actual, practical possibility that he could feel the heat of her lingering gaze through those layers.

But there was one certain truth he'd understood about the Siren of Balravia from the moment of their first meeting: she excelled at throwing her opponents off their guard. So Gerard used decades of experience to separate himself, now, from the weaker impulses of his body and gaze up at her with the unaffected shield he'd perfected long ago. "I do wonder, Your Majesty: What do your good friends and allies, the Queens of Nornne and Kitvaria, think of this supposed vacation you've arranged without my permission? Did they agree to it as a sensible political decision?"

Queen Lorelei didn't flinch, of course. Her own shields were far too polished for that—and despite what the rest of the continent might imagine, Gerard had understood for years that she was far more dangerously clever and less emotionally driven than she wished her enemies to realize. He had been teaching himself her tells for years, though, so he savored the brief flicker of her sparkling eyelashes despite the condescending curl of her lips an instant later. "My dear general," she purred, "I know you're on vacation, but surely you haven't already forgotten the rules of successful political alliances? We Queens of Villainy would hardly have chosen to band together in the first place if we couldn't trust each other to keep the details of our private meetings *private*."

Aha. "I take it you haven't told them what you're up to, then." He cocked a single eyebrow in rebuke. "I would have thought you owed them more loyalty than to leave them wrong-footed when the Empire responds with force to this direct attack upon its highest military leader. Both of your allies were witnessed at your side only yesterday by a multitude of reporters as well as my own troops. They will both share in the blame, and the Emperor's response to all three nations, when he hears the news of my abduction at your hands—"

"Why do you think I bothered to steal you in the first place, darling?" Her voice was light, but her eyes glittered with rare temper—another victory for him to mark on their personal battlefield. "You may have a terribly pretty face, but I hardly need to kidnap my playthings, you know. They offer themselves to me on a regular basis without any effort on my part."

That, he didn't doubt—and there was no good reason for hot irritation to flare through him at the reminder. So, he ignored that irrational reaction to focus on the unlikely clue she'd tossed him. "You actually *want* the Empire to attack? You can't possibly think Balravia would survive that invasion—not with both of its allies busy repelling simultaneous attacks on their own lands." If she had any idea just how hard he'd been fighting to temper the Emperor's increasingly disturbing ambitions in that direction . . .

"Not *yet*." Her eyelashes lowered as a wicked smile played at her lips. "Don't worry, darling, I'm not quite so careless as you seem to imagine. I *can* glamour your handwriting, you know— and set a very convincing scene. According to your note, you're trusting your officers to maintain your privacy and allow no one else into your tent . . . while you secretly pursue an urgent quest elsewhere for the sake of the Empire. By the time little Otto finally realizes you're gone—much less who was bold enough to take you—it'll be far too late."

"Too late?" A wave of foreboding rolled through Gerard's bound body as he looked up at that wicked grin. "For what, exactly?"

"Seven years ago," said the fae queen, "you set me a challenge. By the end of our visit, General de Moireul, I plan to finally win it."

ABOUT THE AUTHOR

STEPHANIE BURGIS grew up in East Lansing, Michigan, but now lives in Wales with her husband and two sons, surrounded by mountains, castles, and coffee shops. She writes wildly romantic adult historical fantasies (including the Harwood Spellbook series, with more than twenty thousand self-published copies sold) and has had more than forty short stories for adults and teens published in magazines and anthologies. Find out more at stephanieburgis.com.